'The
Shadowlink

Mages of Sterling Ridge

By

Stefanie Schatzman

COPYRIGHT

Name: Schatzman, Stefanie author.
Title: The Shadowlink Mages of Sterling Ridge
Description: Florida: Stefanie Schatzman, (2022, 2023, 2024)
Series: The Shadowlink

Identifiers: ISBN: 9781960353061 (Paperback, 4th Edition)

Library of Congress Cataloging-in-Publication Data
Registration Number
TXu 2-459-507

Acknowledgments

For Robert. Who encouraged me to write the story.

For Sarah. Who has a contagious belief in all things magical.

For Peter. Who offered valuable fantasy world information.

For Jaeden: Who offered, with humor, his support.

For Frank: Who offered his input on the story.

For Lilian. Who enthusiastically volunteered to draw Coal.

Table of Contents

PROLOGUE

Deep, rumbling thunder shook the two-story antique store as Nessa stood before a dim, musty-smelling room. A single flickering ceiling light beamed down on an old fortune teller booth, casting shadows on the black-haired gypsy, dressed in a high-collared dark dress. Her cold, hollow blue eyes stared blankly ahead.

Intrigued, Nessa stepped closer. As she did, the sounds of an old motor sputtering to life surprised her. With whiny spinning and clicking noises, the gypsy turned towards her. Her chest moved up and down as if breathing. Nessa wanted to run, but she stayed frozen in place.

The gypsy's eyes lowered to the dusty fortune teller cards in front of her. Her hands jerked back and forth over the cards until she picked one. Her blue eyes flashed. A heavily accented voice that didn't line up with the movement of her mouth said, "Your future has been read. Take your card."

Nessa hesitated for a second before snatching the card from the slot. She read the words, *"It's now or never."* The signature said Oracle.

The flickering ceiling light went out. The room went dark and eerily quiet as the gypsy stopped moving. Nessa backed away, watching the gypsy intently staring out as if she could see the future.

Chapter 1
You're So Stubborn

Nessa studied the fortune teller's card in her hand. The simple message that *it's now or never*, signed by the Oracle, had to be an omen. While she had failed to change his mind before, she had never had a fortune teller give her a sign. She raised her hand and kissed the card.

"Bring me good luck. I'm going to need it."

Conflicting emotions swirled around her mind as she made her way to her bedroom. She wanted more people to join the list of those who knew her secret. That part excited her. The other part frightened her because she needed to change his mind.

Nessa took a deep breath to calm her nerves. After all, she now had validation. She just needed to make him see it from her point of view.

She retrieved the enchanted key from her antique desk. Within moments, she stood before the room that was off-limits to everyone but her. She pushed the key into the lock, twisted the doorknob, and swung the door open. It escaped her hands. With a loud bang, the door slammed hard against the doorstop.

Startled, Nessa froze and wiped her sweaty palms down her jeans. *Why do I always get this way when dealing with him on this subject? It's because I'm weak. Look at me. Sweaty palms, nervous.*

"Get a grip or try another day. No, I can do this. I just need to be calm and forceful."

Taking another deep breath, Nessa tried to relax by focusing on the beauty of her favorite room. Her bare feet sank into the plush, white carpet while she paused, admiring the massive white furniture and fixtures. She watched as light radiated off the large crystal candelabra on the white coffee table and off the massive crystal chandelier in the center of the room. Even with the lacey white curtains and blinds closed, the entire room sparkled with a brilliance that vibrated with positive energy. Nessa soaked it in as she stared across the room at the large portraits of her daughter on the back wall.

Feeling better, she crossed the room and faced the closet door. Her three-dimensional achievement portrait, centered on the closet door, smiled back at her. Usually, the picture fascinated her, but not today. The portrait, transforming into a serious pose, showing elemental colors of red, blue, green, and white swirling in the background, would need to be appreciated another day. Today, while energized by the room's positive energy and the Oracle's prophecy, she needed to focus on the mission.

Nessa shut the closet door and ignored the dark as she had done hundreds of times. Besides, she could feel the energy of the floor-to-ceiling, massive mirror pulling her over to the back wall. Moving closer to the mirror, she came to a standstill within inches of it.

Nessa's left hand traced the ancient inscription and symbols carved into the mirror. She could only read the words Mirror of Durin, which Draon had taught her. No big deal. It wasn't the language that fascinated her; it was what the carvings did. Draon called them runes. Nessa called them spell ingredients. Whatever they were called, she really didn't care. Truth be told, she was elated that the mirror, which had been in her family for generations and linked to Draon, now belonged to her.

Just by touching the enchanted symbols in the required pattern, the mirror responded by emitting a faint gray glow. She stepped several feet back and sat down.

"Draon, I want to talk!"

In anticipation, she sat up straighter as some of the carved runes glowed and a thick fog spread across the inside of the entire mirror. Nessa leaned forward and searched through the dark fog for a tall figure in a long, crow-feathered cloak that should emerge at any moment.

Finally, after what felt like an eternity, a tall man with shoulder-length, thick black hair and pitch-black eyes stared down at her from inside the mirror. Without hesitation, she got to the reason for calling him.

"Draon, I was wondering if we could renegotiate our deal."

Nessa watched Draon raise his thick eyebrows, cross his arms, and, with a look of annoyance, stare down at her. She didn't care; she was going to push for more mages.

"They're all here, but we should have even more. Shouldn't the entire community be witches and wizards?" Nessa visualized every property within their rural community with a Shadowlink mage.

Draon responded in a calm but stern tone. "We have been through this so many times. The answer is still no."

Seeing Nessa was about to interrupt him, Draon held his right hand up to stop her so he could continue his one remaining thought. "We have a deal. I have fulfilled my part of it."

Nessa jumped up and marched the short distance to the mirror. Stopping within mere inches, she crossed her arms and stared up into Draon's black eyes. Draon stared back at her.

His irritation with her rebellious behavior didn't show on his face, but there was no mistaking his displeasure with her attitude. His crow-feathered cloak moved from a breeze swirling around him.

Nessa watched his cloak's movement and stepped back from the mirror. She didn't want to give up, but she knew that sign all too well. Rethinking her plan of action, she decided on a different approach.

Nessa dropped the defiant stance and implored Draon to reconsider his part of the deal. "We're spread all over the world. We need to come together, and this is the ideal place. I just know it! They need to know they have magical abilities! Please reconsider this!"

"It might be better for them not to know they are witches or wizards."

Even though he had voiced that thought before, Nessa didn't believe it. She totally embraced her magical abilities. She shook her head, unable to comprehend how anyone wouldn't want to know they were a mage. They were unique and powerful. It was like night and day.

"Why do you not see this from my point of view?" Draon asked.

"Because I love being a mage." Nessa gestured with her hands to add impact to her words.

"You do, and I am happy you discovered you are a mage. However, not all individuals with magical capabilities are inherently good. It is better for humanity if they are not aware of their powers. It is better for the magical world, too. It would also be unsafe for one small community to have just witches and wizards."

"You could test them and decide who would make a good mage in our community."

"Nessa, you are missing the point. We have an agreement. I have fulfilled my part of the agreement. The answer is no."

"You're so stubborn," Nessa grumbled as she returned to her original spot, sat down, crossed her arms, and stared up at Draon.

"Is that the pot calling the kettle black?" Draon smirked.

"You know, I'm not giving up."

"You never have since day one. I still remember that day. Kothar shot a red flare into the air to let me know someone stood before the Mirror of Durin. I flew to the fortress, raced up the stairs, and flung the door open to the room that holds our Mirror of Durin; there you were, demanding I come out and show myself. Somehow, you knew how to open the Mirror of Durin and saw me. You lasted a few minutes before you took off running."

"That was a terrifying encounter. You wore a crow-feathered cloak, towering with big black eyes. I might add that you were not smiling. I had no idea what I had just opened."

"Obviously, you got over it as you continually contacted me, and each time, after a few minutes, you would bolt from the room."

"You still weren't smiling."

"Your intrusion into my world irritated me. Nothing came to mind on how to stop you from contacting me. Most of all, I hoped you would not learn that you were a Shadowlink."

"Being stubborn is how I survived my childhood. I had no father, and my mother viewed me as an obstacle to her dream lifestyle. So, as scary as you were, you represented an escape from my world."

"I am glad you persisted, and I trained you through the mirror until you were old enough to travel through the portal."

"Where I gave you a new kind of headache." Nessa smiled at Draon and relaxed.

"Yes, your birthday gift of metamorphosis spells was horrifying. I witnessed those creatures in the direct line of your spell casting morph into different sizes, shapes, colors, and weird beasts. The fairylike creatures scattered as I activated a shield spell for my own protection."

"I remember." Nessa laughed, recalling Draon's look of horror at her wayward spells.

"However, that is not my favorite Nessa disaster. My favorite is when you built your first broom. Of course, you did not listen to the directions. Why would you pay attention to instructions when you had never paid attention on any other project? So, you did it your way. It barely looked like a broom. It definitely did not look like it could hold you and fly."

"I remember. I hopped on and rode that wobbly, pathetic broom. Then the pixies and fairies made it worse by spotting me on the broom and making it a race. I wasn't playing in their race, but you wouldn't have known it as the fairies conjured obstacles along the path, and the pixies kept nipping my legs. Not to mention, they also fought each other for the lead. So much chaos that I rode the broom upside down more often than right side up."

Draon roared with laughter. "Your early broom flying adventures were hilarious. They remain my favorite disasters."

"You know the real disaster happened when you teamed me up with Kothar doing potion inventory at the Stormfield medieval fortress. That gnome can take a perfect dream and turn it into a nightmare."

"He was shorter than you, and yet you met your match. If I remember correctly, you complained that Kothar was nothing but an ancient, cantankerous, annoying sourpuss that seemed to relish being miserable."

"That pretty much sums him up." Natalie laughed.

"Oh, you had other things to say about him. I had to remain serious when you claimed that if negative energy could produce gold coins, we would all be rich. To this day, when Kothar is speaking to me, I visualize gold coins popping out of his mouth."

"And, yet, we aren't rich."

"Not in gold or money, but we are rich in the ways that are important."

"True. Draon, you were a father figure throughout those years. You guided me and were there as I graduated from magic school and high school. You gave me the beautiful experience of Stormfield. There isn't a place in the mageless world that compares to the intoxicating fragrant flowers, the colorful plants and birds, the mythical creatures, the playful fairies, and the mischievous pixies. I had the rare opportunity to go on flying adventures, cast spells throughout Stormfield, ride Pegasus, and train with Samoon. What would have been a sad and lonely childhood turned into an amazing experience. Thank you, Draon."

"I am glad it was a wonderful experience for both of us. In the beginning, I was positive I had made a horrible mistake taking you on as an apprentice."

"Believe me, in the early days, I remember thinking of you as this rigid, scary, strange, towering man. I never thought we would get along, much less have a close relationship."

"We both took a leap of faith." Draon looked fondly at Nessa.

"We did. Speaking of a leap, yesterday I received a fortune teller message saying *it's now or never,* and that said to me you would soften and allow more mages."

Draon turned serious. "It's now or never could mean many things, but the one thing I know it did not mean is me bringing in more mages. You must bring Madison, Skylar, Joel, and Connor together and include Pru in the group."

"If I get that done, will you consider my request for more mages?"

"Let me see what happens with these mages."

"Okay, I'll give it a rest."

"Thank you," Draon replied with relief.

"Don't feel relieved yet. In a couple of weeks, I'm telling my daughter she's a witch."

"Are you warning me that Natalie is a mini-you?"

"She's shy and stays to herself, but she has my spirit."

"At my age, I am unsure I can handle another stubborn child."

"Oh, please, you're hundreds of years old. My childhood was a drop in the bucket as far as years when compared to your age."

"You did not make it seem that way."

Nessa laughed and stood up. Stretching, she stepped closer to the mirror. "Draon, I want to visit Stormfield one more time before Natalie discovers she's a mage."

"That would be nice."

"I'll try to get there next week when Karl is at work. Natalie stays up reading and sleeps late during summer break, so I'll make it an early morning visit. I'd love to spend time with you and see Samoon, Dikko, and the others."

"I look forward to your visit."

After the mirror returned to its ordinary look, Nessa stood in the dark, facing it. Solemnly, she recalled their conversation. She treasured their time together and their special bond.

"Draon, while you have left your Mirror of Durin, I want to tell you something. You are no longer a father figure to me; you are my father. I love you."

Still standing there, Nessa smiled into the mirror. She remembered how long it had taken him to get accustomed to her hugs.

"Next time I see you, you get a big hug."

On the way to Natalie's room, Nessa said, "Thanks for nothing," while tossing the fortune teller card into the kitchen trash can.

Natalie slept soundly on her side. Nessa brushed her long, black hair from her shoulder and lightly shook her.

Softly, Nessa said, "Nat."

Natalie rolled onto her back and sleepily looked up at her mother with half-open eyelids exposing dark eyes.

"I have a few errands to run this morning. Would you like to come with me, and we'll stop for lunch?"

"Can I get a rain check, Mom? I stayed up too late reading."

"Sure, kiddo. Go back to sleep. I'll get us something special from the deli for lunch."

"Thanks, Mom. Love you."

Natalie rolled over on her side while pulling up the covers.

"Love you, too," Nessa said as she walked towards the door and then quietly shut it behind her.

At 11:46, the fortune teller's card floated out of the trash can. Leveling at six feet, it burst into a shimmering blue orb before disappearing.

Chapter 2

A Nightmare

Draon exited the Stormfield fortress and spotted a bird flying in his direction. Even from far away, he recognized Beaker.

"No, it cannot be! This has to be a mistake!" Draon screamed as he froze in place.

Heartbroken, he watched the large beaked crow slow and approach him. He did not extend his arm out for Beaker to land. He did nothing except watch Beaker change course and fly higher. Still unable to move, he observed Beaker make another wide circle around the towering fortress. He watched as Beaker slowed his speed and readied to land on him.

Draon commanded his arm to stretch out to receive Beaker. Nothing happened. His arm remained frozen by his side as the full weight of what was happening registered.

In utter despair, Draon cried out, "Oh, my God! How do I get through this?"

His body shook as he crumbled; his heart shattered into a million pieces. Covering his face with both hands, a flood of tears streamed down his cheeks.

Draon struggled to regain his composure as Beaker continued to circle overhead. He knew he needed to get it together and lead, but he did not know if he could. Draon did not even know if he cared anymore. Overwhelmed with grief, he could not think straight. Minutes ticked into an hour before he mustered the strength to do what needed to be done.

As tears streamed down his face, Draon wiped what he could from his eyes, stood up straight, and raised his left arm. He tried to focus on his breathing and his outstretched arm. Desperate to maintain what little composure he had, Draon avoided looking at Beaker.

He closed his eyes and kept telling himself that this had to be a nightmare. It could not be true. No matter how hard Draon tried to avoid the truth, deep down in his soul, he knew it was true. Nessa was gone.

Draon's eyes remained shut as Beaker glided down and landed on his outstretched, trembling arm. As the bird's loud, mournful caws told the devastating news, Nessa's ring and crystal dropped into Draon's hand. Beaker lifted off Draon's hand and headed for Hogboon.

Clutching her ring and crystal, Draon tried to make sense of this nightmare in the quiet forest. He looked up and listened. It had become uncommonly quiet. He visualized the Stormfield magical creatures seeing Beaker as he flew across the land. Every magical creature knew that a bird and a mage were bound until the death of one of them. Upon a mage's death, the bird returns to Stormfield.

Draon should have sympathized with Beaker for returning to Hogboon, where he would revert to his hobgoblin form, but he didn't. He couldn't focus on Beaker's inability to leave Stormfield because he couldn't get his mind off Nessa. He sank into a dark mood.

Without warning, an ear-piercing scream erupted with such force that it caused the entire forest to shake as if there had been an earthquake. Trees swayed, branches dropped, flowers fell, and creatures stumbled and cried out in alarm. But the scream that reverberated throughout the land did nothing for Draon. Right then, he knew screaming a hundred times would change nothing.

He wanted relief, but there was none to be found. Instead, the torture increased as he acknowledged that Nessa was gone. He would never see her again. He would never talk to her again. As Draon grappled with this realization, it was the first time in his life that he wished the Alchemy

River did not exist. In this unrelenting pain, he would have been satisfied to live an ordinary life span.

Gripping Nessa's ring and crystal in his hand so tightly that they left deep marks, Draon faced confusion. He spoke with Nessa just a few hours ago. How could this be? She should have been able to save herself. The last thought was the one that he kept asking himself.

There were no answers or relief. He could not handle it. He needed to do something. Now. Draon summoned his feathered cloak. With the cloak roughly whipping around him, he transformed into a large, shimmering crow and took flight.

Chapter 3
Turbulent Storm

Draon materialized amidst trees in a small, isolated residential community high on a ridge. Standing in the center of the rural subdivision, he did not stop to consider why he had picked this place. He was not thinking at all. His sole mission was to release his pain.

Rising well above the ground, he raised his left hand towards the sky and activated the earth, wind, and air elements on his ring. Just before he lashed out with everything he had, he uttered a shield protection spell.

Without warning, the early evening sky turned dark as midnight. In that strange darkness, a ferocious storm of blinding lightning and bellowing thunder emerged. Rapid-fired lightning furiously raced across the night sky in fiery bolts of pure energy. Every few minutes, those electrical charges of blinding brilliance collided from opposite directions, resulting in high-flying, multi-colored sparks that lit up the entire night sky and surroundings like 4th of July fireworks.

The thunder that endlessly rumbled coincided with the terrifying lightning. As the lightning and thunder wreaked havoc throughout the community, the hurricane-like winds caused their own mayhem. The howling gale of the rainless storm was as constant and unrelenting as the lightning and thunder. Draon, shield-protected, was the eye of the storm, directing its rage.

With hands raised high into the air, the wind swirled around Draon as he directed the hurricane winds to lash out at the small community. He commanded the lightning to streak across the sky and down to the ground. Where he could not yell enough to end the pain, he had the thunder rumble on and on without a break. He faced the southeast and aimed most of his fury in that direction.

The storm took on a life of its own. It howled and whipped around Draon, mimicking the turmoil within his soul. He closed his eyes, experiencing the raw fury that swirled around him. Time passed, but the pain persisted.

Continuing to be one with the storm, Draon felt an unnatural increase in the winds. Annoyed, he flew high above the storm, searching for the magical creature overtaking the winds. Leaves, branches, and yard items swirled in the air, making the search difficult. After several minutes, Draon located Samoon, a Stormfield Sylph, forlornly drifting in the winds.

Draon watched her from a distance. He understood her pain, but Samoon had broken a cardinal rule. All about adherence, Draon internally debated whether he should confront her for breaking the 'no interaction with the mageless' rule.

Before he could decide, Samoon burst above the winds and leveled with the lightning bolts streaking across the dark sky. Draon saw her enraged expression just before she lashed out with everything she had on the community below.

Shocked by her fury, Draon decided not to acknowledge Samoon or stop her. He dropped back down into the heart of the storm. Returning his focus to the lightning and thunder, the air element on his ring dulled as he left the winds to Samoon.

Where Samoon was invisible to the mageless, Pegasus was not. An extraordinarily large white, winged stallion, he thundered in a few minutes after Draon had spotted Samoon.

"Is this for real?" Draon muttered to himself as he again rose above the storm to consider this new threatening dilemma.

Flustered, Draon wondered how Pegasus would think this was okay. Someone, and probably many, would see him. Ridiculous. Even in this raging storm, how could anyone miss a gigantic, winged, shimmering white horse flying within the dark storm? None. It would be front page news.

Draon got it. He really did, but it was a dangerous choice for Pegasus because of his sorrow for losing Nessa. Then again, how could Draon fault Pegasus for loving Nessa and wanting to release some of that pain? After all, she had spoiled him with Granny Smith apples to the point that he had allowed her to ride him. No one rode Pegasus…ever. She was the exception. Pegasus and Nessa had an exceptional bond.

That got Draon thinking about how Nessa had wiggled her way into the hearts of many of the Stormfield magical creatures. He started with the obvious: Samoon and Pegasus. Then, his mind raced to Kothar and others. He lost count of all the light magical creatures that had a special bond with Nessa.

Conflicted, Draon wanted to continue with the storm, but he knew there was going to be a world-changing disaster if the magical world spilled over into the mageless world. He rationalized that he could handle Samoon and Pegasus, but then he thought of Dikko. What if Dikko sought relief by using dragon fire? He could make Dikko invisible, but he could not stop his ability. Fire raining down from the skies was unexplainable in the mageless world. The two worlds would collide. Mythology, folklore, or whatever they labeled it would be validated.

Shuddering at that thought, Draon turned his attention to Stormfield. He needed to act now. While pulling his wand from a deep pocket inside his cloak, his ring connected to his wand to combine both to make it an unbreakable spell. Raising his left hand high into the air, Draon chanted a containment spell over the sounds of the howling winds.

"It is what it is, but it is no more. What once was two-way, now's a one-way door. A way to get in, but not a way free; Will be how it is; til removed by me."

After blocking the magical creatures from leaving Stormfield, Draon turned his focus on Pegasus. He knew Pegasus would add to the current thunder as his wings resounded like thunder throughout Stormfield. He just hoped Pegasus would stay in the sky and not create any springs and cause undue flooding by stomping on the ground. Again, Draon focused on his ring, and he chanted a melding spell for Pegasus over the boisterous thunder.

"One-of-a-kind Pegasus of brilliant white; transform to midnight black to meld with this night."

As Pegasus blended in with the dark sky, the water element on Draon's ring dulled. Now Draon could return his focus to the storm. Just as he resumed command of the lightning, the winds died down. Draon searched for Samoon, but she had abruptly returned to Stormfield.

Chapter 4
Natalie

Natalie, teary-eyed, watched the horrific storm from her bedroom window. So many thoughts swirled around her mind as she tried to come to terms with the horror of losing her mother.

If only someone would be with her, but Natalie knew it wasn't possible. Her father had walked in grief-stricken, hugged her, and left for his bedroom. The violent storm kept others away.

"Focus on the storm," Natalie told herself. She knew it was impossible, but she had to do something if she was going to survive.

As the minutes slowly ticked by, she watched the vicious storm continue to unleash its pent-up anger. Thunder rumbled, lightning flashed, and swirling winds howled around the house. Without warning, a gust of wind ripped the screen from her bedroom window. Natalie shrieked.

Tears stopped, eyes grew wide, and her heart hammered against her chest as she stared at a face pressed up against her window. There was a shocked expression as if the person knew her. Petrified, Natalie screamed again and instinctively jumped back.

Recovering, Natalie shook her head in disbelief. It had to be her wild imagination. No one would be out in this monstrous storm. They would be swept away or injured by flying objects.

As she questioned what she saw, Natalie forced herself to return to the window. She nervously looked for someone. No one was there. *Of course not.* Relieved, Natalie focused on the storm.

As strange as it seemed to her, other than the ghostly face, the frenzied storm brought her some comfort. Natalie felt a kinship with the fury of the unrelenting storm. The whipping winds howled in unison with the rumbling thunder. The lightning continually streaked across the sky. From the horrific chaos, it seemed as if the storm was lashing out from unbearable pain. Even the house shared in the pain as it shook and groaned from the outside turmoil.

Standing perfectly still, Natalie closed her eyes, took a deep breath, and tried to connect to the anger and fury of the storm. Maybe if she could become one with the storm, the urge to scream at the top of her lungs would go away. She knew she couldn't run away and never face this new reality, but maybe, just maybe, she could disconnect from everything for a short period of time. Desperate, Natalie was willing to do anything to escape this agony.

It was easier said than done. It was a constant struggle not to explode. *Stay calm. Focus on the storm.* She told herself those words, but it wasn't working.

"I can't do this," she admitted to herself.

Natalie cupped her hands over her eyes, and this time, she let the tears stream down her face until her sobbing caused her body to tremble.

Overwhelmed, Natalie screamed at the top of her lungs, "Mom! Mom, don't leave me!"

Natalie jumped on her bed, rolled onto her right side, and clutched one of her pillows. In a fetal position, she pleaded for her mother to come back until she wore herself out. Exhausted, Natalie crawled under the blankets and hid her face in the pillows.

More than once, she thought about stepping out into the storm and being swept away. She didn't, but it felt as if she would never get over this horrific pain. She burst into another round of uncontrollable tears.

Hidden in the blankets and pillows, Natalie asked the questions she had been afraid to ask herself.

"Would it have been any different if I had gone with my mother this morning? Would that have changed things? Was this my fault?"

Natalie knew the answer. She blamed herself. This was her nightmare. Distraught and consumed in pain, she lay there feeling guilty.

"Please bring my mother back."

At first, just the rumbling thunder and the howling winds battering the house answered her plea. Then came the faint cherry almond fragrance swirling around her bed.

Buried under many layers of bedding, Natalie was unaware of the familiar scent. Instead, she focused on her loss and her inability to cope with the pain.

Without her being aware, the fragrance continued to spread and fill the room. The strongest aroma stayed just above Natalie, waiting. Time passed. With sheer exhaustion amidst the raging storm, she fell asleep.

Natalie woke up overheated and dripping in sweat. She pushed the blankets away, smelled the fragrance, and jumped out of bed.

"Mom!"

The fragrance increased around Natalie while she frantically scanned the room for her mother.

"Mom, where are you?"

Natalie did a 360-degree circle before dropping to her knees and looking under her bed. She jumped up and ran to her closet.

"Mom, I can't find you!"

Natalie turned and leaned against the closet door.

"You're not really here, are you?"

The comforting cherry almond fragrance surrounded Natalie. She inhaled it, never wanting to forget the scent her mother wore every day.

Eyes closed, silent tears fell as the fragrance slowly dissipated and the storm diminished in power. Just as the finality of her mom's presence and the storm were happening, there was one last protest. A powerful lightning bolt struck nearby, knocking the electricity out in the entire community. The fragrance vanished in a sea of blackness. Everything had changed.

Natalie knew it would never be the same again.

Chapter 5
The Wizard in the Crow-Feathered Cloak

Ground energy rose and met the final powerful bolt of lightning descending from the sky. With the last circuit complete, explosive booms rattled windows as a brilliant flash of lightning struck the ground. Sterling Ridge plunged into pitch-black darkness.

The rumbling and booming sounds faded as Draon materialized at the Sterling Ridge front entrance. Even in the dark, the wizard in the crow-feathered cloak seemed surreal. His head, with shoulder-length thick black hair, made quick movements as he surveyed the area with unblinking black eyes.

For a few hours, he had lashed out in pain, but all that fury had provided no comfort. Now Draon felt drained and defeated. No spell or magical object would bring Nessa back. In the dark quiet, time seemed to stand still.

Without a word, Samoon had returned home during the height of the storm. Draon had wondered why, but he returned his focus to his anguish and resumed the winds and the lightning. Pegasus had stopped when Draon had stopped. Pegasus was now home.

"You take a piece of my heart with you, daughter," Draon cried, standing alone in the blackness, letting the storm of his pain die out. He had never felt more alone in his entire life.

Draon hoped Nessa knew how much she meant to him. He cherished their relationship and thought of her as his own daughter. He paused. Daughter. In that instant, Draon knew why he was there. He was lashing out at his loss, but he was also there for Nessa's daughter. In his pain, he could not see what had brought him there. Now he understood.

Draon sighed with relief. Some of the emptiness lifted as he realized a part of Nessa remained. He understood he had work to do. And, with that thought, Draon commanded the crows to station themselves.

Giving the crows time to fly to their posts, he stood still in the dark as the Sterling Ridge subdivision and the community below remained without power. It would stay that way until he completed his mission.

Draon listened to the crows that had stationed themselves at the four corners of the subdivision. Each crow delivered the same message three times before quiet again engulfed the community. After listening to their messages, Draon was satisfied that no one was outside.

Reaching for his wand tucked inside his cloak pocket, Draon brought it out and raised the wand high towards the starless night sky. No ring to use for the shield spells tonight. Draon wanted only the familiar feel of his faithful wand. He chanted the protection spell slowly and forcefully.

"Swirling, blending, and combining in strength, earth, wind, fire, and air unite.

Spreading, covering, and reaching in height, east, west, north, and south alight.

Doubling, tripling, and maxing in power, spread over these grounds this night.

Guarding, hiding, and shielding in defense, cloak the Shadowlink from sight."

As he chanted and stretched his wand higher into the air, a gentle breeze swirled around him. Elemental colors of green, blue, red, and white intertwined as the colors flowed out of the tip of his wand. Now vividly glowing against the dark, the breeze caught the elemental colors and spread them high and thin into the night sky and out along the perimeter of the community.

When Draon finished the eastern spell, he transformed into a crow and flew to the northern side of the subdivision. A growing number of crows followed him.

At the northern boundary, Draon repeated the enchanted words. The breeze caught the glowing colors, spreading the spell again into the night sky and out along the perimeter of the community. The wizard did this until he had chanted the spellbinding words at the eastern, northern, western, and southern boundaries.

Only visible to the wizard, the dome of protection was complete. The protection spell would safeguard and cloak the Shadowlink witches and wizards while they were inside the Sterling Ridge subdivision, except during full moons. Full moons had their own magical powers. Frowning at that thought, Draon was all too familiar with strange happenings occurring under regular full moons. He dreaded what might happen under the upcoming rare full moons.

Acknowledging it was a perplexing time and not sure of the next step, Draon continued to stand there. For the first time in his life, distraction and confusion ruled his mind. What was he going to do? Did he really care what happened in the mortal world? In the enchanted forest, Draon never faced these problems or pain. He wished he could go back to the forest and have everything the way it was, but that was not realistic.

He told himself to focus on Natalie and the mages that he had brought here. Omens warned of an approaching evil in the mageless world. They needed to be ready, but that was not possible until they accepted that they were mages. He did not know how he was going to do that.

Refocusing back to the task at hand, Draon had one more spell of protection to complete. In the blink of an eye, Draon disappeared and reappeared at the front entrance to the Shadowlink's home. Immediately raising his wand high into the night air, he began chanting a protection spell.

"Combining in raw power, elemental powers unite.

Encompassing this parcel, elemental powers alight.

Protecting the old homestead, elemental powers ignite.

Guarding the young Shadowlink, elemental powers full might."

The spell, like the ones before it, seemed to come alive as the elemental colors glowed and floated upward. This protection spell was specific to the Shadowlink and her property. While the spell spread over her home and entire property, a rather large black cat slowly and carefully walked around all the debris and out to the wizard.

"Hello, Lorcan." Draon forced a smile on his face as he looked down at the oversized, ruffled black cat. The cat acknowledged him by slightly nodding his head.

"I apologize for the devastating fury of the storm." Draon paused before continuing to explain himself. "The aftermath is what I still feel like inside. It seems so surreal. I cannot get my mind around it."

Draon watched as the cat hung his head low and cast his eyes to the ground. Knowing Lorcan mentored Nessa, Draon knew he had felt the connection break when Nessa had died. Draon stared at the cat for a moment, wondering if he had dealt with the pain. He couldn't tell, but he hoped Lorcan had found some way to deal with the loss.

Draon returned his focus to his new mission. This mission included a vow not to get close to Natalie. He never wanted to experience this pain again. Just the same, he hoped Natalie did not look too much like Nessa. That might be more than he could handle right now. On the other hand, he sympathized with Natalie. Knowing his pain, Draon could not imagine what she was going through right now.

Draon focused back on the mages and how he could approach them. He looked down at Lorcan and raised his eyebrows at the cat's ridiculous stance. Lorcan's body faced towards the back of the property, but his head was strangely twisted to keep an eye on the wand in Draon's hand. The cat looked as if it were poised to run.

"Sorry. I promise there is no chance of me unleashing another storm." Draon loosened his grip and slipped the wand into the inner cloak pocket.

He watched the cat unwind. It took a long stretch, shook, sat, and focused on the wizard.

"Did you ever see Natalie do anything that would show she was aware of her powers?"

The cat shook his head no.

"This is not right," Draon said, thinking back to his first encounter with Nessa. "Nessa never said how she figured out she was a witch. However, at a young age, Nessa was already casting spells and learning about the magical world. Her daughter is clueless. Where do we even begin without scaring her?"

Lorcan shook his head no, and then yes, and then no.

Draon smiled at the confused response from the cat.

"It appears you have no idea, and I cannot think of anything. I guess the best we can hope for is that she has powers equal to her mother's powers and abilities. When she finds out she is a witch, it will be a start. She will not have training, but survival instincts can cause her to react and defend herself."

The cat lifted his head and nodded in agreement.

"Strange times are heading her way. I do not like the ominous signs we are seeing. How do we warn her? I feel Natalie would be alarmed if I approached her. I am afraid, old friend, that you are going to be the one responsible for getting her to understand she is a mage. I have no idea how you are going to pull that off while in cat form, but it needs to happen."

The cat again nodded in agreement.

"I have placed a protection spell over the entire subdivision and another protection spell over Nessa's property. It works while Natalie is here, but only temporarily, and it will not function under a full moon. Let us hope this spell will aid her until she becomes of age and is familiar with her powers."

Draon shook his head at what a frustrating mess this whole thing was becoming. *Was there any hope? Was there enough time?* He would feel better if he could test her, but he knew that was not an option. At least, at the moment, he could not test her.

Lorcan meowed back in agreement and then shook his head in annoyance with his lack of ability to talk.

The long, crow-feathered cloak swayed in the breeze. Draon stared up into the night sky, trying to think of some other way to help. Suddenly, he remembered the crystal necklace Nessa always wore. The necklace Beaker had dropped in his hand.

The colorful gemstones atop his metal ring lit up as the green gemstones within the barrel glowed. Draon chanted a short summoning spell.

"Within the fortress of potions and charms, a crystal necklace waits to serve from harm,

Answer my summoning from outside lands, have Kothar deliver it to my hand."

Within seconds, Draon held the crystal attached to a silver necklace. He held his hand up and simply said, *"indivo Natalie."*

He quickly wrapped it with paper he retrieved from the right inside pocket of his cloak.

"If it ever reacts and warns her, it will get her attention to seek answers. You just need to place the crystal where she can find it."

The wizard leaned down and placed the poorly wrapped necklace before the cat. Lorcan lowered his head to get a closer look at the wrapping. He glanced up at Draon and then back down at the package. He gave it a swat.

"Lorcan, don't worry. When she finds it, she will want it."

Already annoyed, the cat jerked his head up, put his ears back, narrowed his eyes, and growled.

"I apologize. I did not mean to insult you. I know you understand the spell." Draon slightly bowed to the fuming cat.

He hoped his words would lighten Lorcan's mood, but the words did nothing to appease the frustrated cat. He watched Lorcan cast his eyes downward and glare at the unfolding package. Weary, Draon ignored the cat's bad mood and changed the subject.

"It is a long shot because I will look like a monster caught inside a mirror, but if she can find the Mirror of Durin, I may be able to provide guidance. She has a lot to learn. I can help if she accepts me and the power of the mirror."

Draon paused and stared up at the black sky for several minutes. Nothing came to mind. He turned his attention back to Lorcan.

"I am afraid even with all the witches and wizards here, it is going to be a challenge to get them trained in time."

Draon watched as Lorcan nodded his head in agreement.

"When will they learn to grow together, instead of always trying to control or enrich themselves at someone else's expense? We have lived for centuries, and it never seems to change. It is why magical beings and creatures have an unwritten code to let ordinary people make their own choices. They either appreciate the results or suffer the consequences. It has always been that way, but this time something dark is coming."

Draon looked down at his friend. He had been friends with Lorcan for centuries. He smiled at the green-eyed cat, who in his natural form was a green-eyed, three-foot-tall Ruiri gnome with a long white braid. In his gnome form, Lorcan always wore wild colors and chains of trinkets on his belt. Draon smiled, picturing the flamboyant outfits of the Ruiri mentors, who wore chunky necklaces to signify the elemental mage they guided. He thought of the third form and was glad Lorcan rarely morphed into that form.

Draon shook his head, wondering why that thought came to mind. He needed to focus, but then his thoughts drifted back to the first Shadowlink.

"It is a shame the Irish families forming the Shadowlink mages of long ago decided against the use of magic. They forgot their heritage. They used to be equals in our world, having received training and knowledge in our ways. All that was lost to the Shadowlink clan when they shunned magic. Hopefully, we can revive the Shadowlink clan with Natalie, Madison, Skylar, Joel, and Connor."

Draon heard the meows and looked down to see Lorcan shaking his head yes.

"Starting now, Lorcan, we need to persuade Natalie and the others that they are witches and wizards. We need to reconnect them to their heritage and have them accept that they are not mere mortals but powerful witches and wizards."

Draon hoped Nessa's firm belief that everyone who had powers would want to know they were mages was true.

With that thought, he remembered Pru, a weaver of charmed bracelets.

Unexpectedly, Draon announced, "I am going to visit Pru before restoring the power. Through Nessa, Pru is aware of me. While there, I will ask Pru to help guide Natalie toward accepting that she is a mage. However, that guidance might put Pru in danger, so two sentries will be stationed at her home to protect her."

Draon watched as Lorcan perked up. Looking like a bobblehead, Lorcan vigorously nodded his head up and down. He stopped midway through one nod as he remembered Draon was all about rules. Creativity wasn't his strong suit. Unimaginative was his strong suit, which meant he would create plain and boring sentries. Lorcan made a face like a regular cat sniffing a smelly sneaker.

Draon interrupted Lorcan's open-mouthed, smelly sneaker expression by stating, "I have one more spell to cast. Do not worry, as this spell is to repair much of the damage caused by the storm."

Draon concentrated on his ring. The green crystal tip of the ring lit up.

While the spell may have been only a few words, things began to happen around them. Trees and plants were mended, large outside objects were moved back to their original places, and repairs were made to damaged homes and buildings.

"I am repairing all homes and structures, but only about 50 percent for the properties. I want it to look like a violent storm happened, but I do not want to leave the community as a disaster." Draon said this as the glow from his ring disappeared. He looked around. This would be much easier to handle.

Lorcan glanced around and then nodded his head in agreement.

"We did not come up with a course of action. It will probably take both you and Pru to convince Natalie that she is a witch. Once she accepts she is a witch, it will be much easier to get the rest of them to accept they are mages."

Lorcan nodded in agreement.

Draon began surveying his surroundings and double-checking that no one was watching. It was time for him to leave before someone spotted him. Even in the dark, there was nothing normal about his appearance or the number of crows gathered in the trees above him.

"Take care of her," the wizard said while swirling the crow-feathered cloak around him. Instantly, the wizard disappeared, and in his place, a large, shimmering black crow appeared. Lorcan tilted his head up and watched as the glistening crow took flight, with all but one of the crows flying after it. Higher and higher the flock of crows flew until they were out of sight.

Chapter 6
Bouncy Green Warts

Lorcan watched until Draon melded into the black sky. Before he had a chance to focus on his mission, he spotted an oversized crow feather floating towards the ground. He trotted over to where it drifted downward. With his mouth wide open, he jumped high into the air and lightly bit down on the new treasure for his already enormous feather collection.

Grumbling, Lorcan stuffed his mouth with the large feather and the crystal-wrapped wad of paper. He trudged up the long driveway, tilting his head this way and that way. It didn't help. Halfway up the driveway, the gob in his mouth shifted. Lorcan stopped and dumped the load to the ground.

While he rested, he fumed that if Draon had done a better job of wrapping the crystal, it would have made his life easier. Hissing, he picked up the feather and the wad of paper and headed for the garage.

When he reached the garage, he opened his mouth wide and dropped everything on the driveway. He couldn't resist swatting the paper a couple of times until it landed in the dirt. He meowed in satisfaction before picking up the feather.

Lorcan headed for the gravel road that would take him to the back of the property. As he reached the road, the community's electricity was restored. He didn't notice, as the solar lights on each fence post lit his path to the old homestead.

Lorcan focused on the end of Draon's visit. He hadn't acknowledged Draon's last comment, nor did he pay attention to the crow that had remained behind. Existing long before the Shadowlink, he knew the entire story. Lorcan would mentor Natalie, but he couldn't do anything until she came to him. Tomorrow, he would introduce himself to her and only her. He was in no mood to deal with the mageless.

It needed to happen soon, but it wouldn't be easy getting her to enter the decrepit-looking homestead. Maybe Pru would help get Natalie in there. He just knew he had to get her inside the homestead, and then things would happen.

Lorcan began to think of various ways to entice her inside the old building. While he was rather proud of himself for coming up with one good possibility of getting her inside there, Lorcan wished Natalie would do it on her own. He was certain the place wasn't anything like she had envisioned.

When her family moved to this property, he reconnected to the Shadowlink and moved into the old homestead. Since that very first day, he had been feasting on the big, juicy roaches. He loved the sound of snap and gush. A sound he had repeatedly heard as he devoured thousands of tangy-tasting roaches.

Sadly, now only a few hundred were left, and they avoided him. It didn't matter. He knew their hiding spots. They weren't safe unless they hid near spiders. He shuddered, thinking of the terrifying spiders and their treacherous webs underneath the house. The image in his mind petrified him; he shifted his focus to the juicy roaches.

His mouth began to water, thinking about the delicious, crunchy shells. If he hurried, he would soon enjoy a nighttime snack.

Lorcan then remembered the angry pixies and fairies. Maybe being away from the old homestead had given them time to cool down. Maybe they now understood he had tried to ease their pain.

Slowing his walk on the gravel road to the old homestead, he focused on the fairies and pixies who should thank him, as his plan to help ease the pain of losing Nessa had been excellent. Justifying his behavior, he knew they certainly couldn't have been as clever and would still be crying. He gave himself five stars for creativity while he replayed the disaster in his mind.

Colorfully dressed in mismatched clothes in his true form of a three-foot-tall Ruiri gnome, he stood stunned, realizing Nessa had passed. It took several minutes to figure out how to handle the loss. Instead of lashing out in pain, his immense collection of mageless Halloween candles came to mind. With their carved faces, they could do the wailing and mourning. That was his brilliant plan.

Lorcan cast a spell over the entire collection. A hundred candles opened their mouths wide and burst into ghostly-like wails as their newly sprouted wings flapped and flew them out of the room.

Aimlessly bouncing off each other, walls, pixies, fairies, and anything else in the way, the wailing candles spread throughout the old homestead. As the wailing candles penetrated every single room and their long, mourning cries ghoulishly reverberated throughout the house, they morphed into floating nightmares.

Horrified, Lorcan watched as the candles developed flaring nostrils emitting thick, black smoke. Their wide eyes glowed red. A raging flame atop their heads caused hot wax to run down their faces, ghoulishly distorting their features.

Hot wax dripped everywhere they went. Within minutes, a dense fog of smoke filled every room. All that could be seen were the glowing red eyes and flames of the hundred wailing, demented candles floating throughout the two-story building. Pure pandemonium erupted.

The pixies and fairies endlessly screamed and threw fairy dust at the candles. The fairy dust transformed the flames into zapping sparklers. In full panic mode, the pixies and fairies rushed to find safety in cupboards, drawers, or anything else. They hid where those roaming, wailing, evil-eyed candles could not enter or zap them with their sparklers or drip hot wax on them.

The floating wailing candles knocked into each other, dropping hot wax on the wings. Candles crashed onto the old wooden floor. Alarmed, Lorcan shoved the floating candles out of the way and ran to a candle that was smashed on the ground. He stomped on the flame, trying to put it out before the house caught on fire. The furious, wailing candle squinted its eyes in anger and flushed red as its flame increased.

"Well, this has got to be at the top of the list of my most hare-brained ideas," Lorcan muttered as he turned and ran to their storage area. Upon entering, he slammed the door shut before any candles could enter. He leaned against the door to ensure it stayed shut and quickly uttered a reverse spell. Instantly, the candles returned to their original form, and all were safely back on the shelves.

Lorcan thought about the pixies and fairies and how they blamed him for the candles morphing into mini demons. It wasn't his fault. He thought they should have treated him better. His mind went back to the part where he had to face them after the candle escapade.

He leaned against the door, not wanting to face what was on the other side. The high-pitched, angry voices and banging on the door were scarier than the wailing, demon-eyed, smoke-emitting candles.

Continuing to lean against the door, Lorcan transformed into his black Maine Coon, heavily boned, muscular body. He perked up his ears and fluffed his lion's mane to increase his intimidating look. Still, he wasn't sure changing form would confuse them or soften their anger.

Lorcan half-opened the door. Peering out, the wrath of swarming pixies and fairies besieged him. They yanked him out. The door slammed behind him; total mayhem erupted. He had no power to block the avalanche of fairy spells. One fairy spell after another grotesquely metamorphosized his appearance while the pixies fluttered around, nipping his legs.

To protect himself, Lorcan reverted to his Ruiri gnome form and activated a protection bubble around himself. The pixies and fairies responded by kicking and spinning his bubble self around the room like a beach ball. It didn't matter how many times he apologized and tried to explain that it had helped with the shock of losing Nessa; they didn't want to hear it. As the fairies bounced Lorcan towards the front door, the pixies opened it and kicked him for a field goal out past the scarecrows at the fence. The door slammed shut as he easily sailed over their heads and halfway turned into a cat.

Overwhelmingly relieved that he had survived their fury, he used the monstrous fangs the fairies had given him to pop the bubble. He found a place to hide amongst the Azalea bushes. He hissed in annoyance at having to revert back and forth, but the laws of magic required him to be a powerless black cat in the mageless world.

Hidden, he reverted to his three-foot-tall Ruiri gnome form, where he cast numerous spells, getting rid of fangs, rabbit ears, purple eyes, pink fur, an elongated pigtail, and bouncy green warts. Restored to his normal appearance, he changed back into a black cat.

Lorcan sighed with relief that Draon didn't know what had happened in the old homestead. He hoped it remained that way.

Making the turn and getting closer to home, Lorcan wondered if the fairies still wanted revenge. In case they hovered at the door, he needed a plan to get back inside. Several plans came to mind, but he discarded each idea.

Just when he thought he had run out of solutions, he found the perfect answer. He would leave his feather on the front porch while he searched under the porch for the biggest, juiciest roach. Once he caught it, he would open the front door with it oozing and half hanging out of his mouth. The image of the grossed-out pixies and fairies screaming and flying from the room had him opening his mouth and letting out a yowl of amusement.

Chapter 7
You Little Brat

Natalie climbed out of bed, pulled the curtains wide open, and peered out of her bedroom window. It wasn't the devastation from the storm that got her attention; it was an enormous black cat sitting on top of a pile of rubble, gazing up at her window.

The cat spotted Natalie. Its emerald-colored eyes locked on her as he painfully lifted his left paw. Opening his mouth wide and tilting his head towards the sky, he wailed. One long, mournful wail after another shattered the otherwise quiet morning.

Dropping his head down and glancing at her, he saw he had her attention. He tilted his head skyward and wailed louder. He rocked from side to side, ready to topple over.

Shocked, Natalie stared at the injured cat as he continued to yowl. Several minutes went by before she couldn't handle it anymore and yanked the curtains closed. The wailing stopped.

This can't be happening! It just can't be happening.

Usually, she would rush out there, but she couldn't handle one more thing. Overwhelmed, Natalie didn't even have herself under control. However, closing the curtains made her feel as if she had abandoned the poor, pitiful cat.

Crawling into bed, Natalie completely hid herself under the blankets, trying to block the stray cat out of her mind. She didn't want to care; she didn't want to think, and she didn't want any part of this new reality.

She wanted to escape this nightmare and spend the whole day in bed asleep. *Darn it! What if the cat was afraid after being out in the violent storm all night? What if the cat was injured? What if the cat was hungry? He sounded like it was all three of those things.* She couldn't get those thoughts out of her mind.

Feeling guilty, Natalie knew she couldn't sleep worrying about the cat. Grudgingly, she tossed the covers aside and returned to the window. As soon as the cat spotted her peeking through the curtains, he lifted his paw and yowled.

Flustered about getting up and the distressed cat, Natalie hurried towards the kitchen in search of her father. He would feed the cat, and she would turn right around and go back into hibernation. That was the plan until she entered the kitchen and found her father at the kitchen table. Slumped in his chair, elbows on the table, and hands over his eyes, he seemed defeated.

Natalie wasn't sure what to do. Hug him or leave him alone. Her father wasn't a touchy-feely type of guy, so she decided to handle the cat. It was obvious her father was in no condition to deal with a stray cat or anything else.

Natalie rummaged through the pantry until she found a can of tuna. As the can opener whirled the can around and popped the lid, her father never moved. She grabbed two small bowls, one of which she filled with tuna, and a bottle of water. It would only take her a couple of minutes to feed the cat and make sure the cat wasn't injured.

Once outside, the incredible amount of destruction shocked Natalie. As far as she could see, the ground was covered in branches and leaves. It amazed her that the trees still had leaves on them. Then there were the things left outside. The storm scattered them throughout the property. Apparently, nothing escaped last night's storm unless it was heavy or bolted down. She knew what that meant, which was another reason to hibernate in her room.

As Natalie worked her way around all the downed branches, the black cat watched her every move. Until that moment, Natalie hadn't even considered the cat might be feral or unfriendly. *He sure is big and plump. Somebody has been feeding him.* However, as a precaution, she slowed her pace as she moved closer. Natalie didn't want to scare the cat away or have it hiss and snarl.

Within a few feet of the cat, Natalie pushed aside the debris, set down both bowls, and filled the empty one with water. The cat never stopped staring at her. She brushed some more debris away and pushed the food and water bowls closer to the cat.

If cats could give the look of snubbing, this cat had it down. Perplexed by the change of attitude, Natalie decided this was a spoiled rotten cat.

"So sorry it's not good enough for you."

The cat continued to ignore the food.

Out of patience, Natalie was done. She wanted to go back to bed. "Well, when you're hungry, you'll eat."

After saying that, Natalie turned and headed back towards the house. Instead of eating, the cat waited until she was halfway back to the house before getting up and sneaking behind her. When she opened the garage door, the cat scooted between her legs and moved ahead of her.

"Whoa, you're supposed to be outside eating!"

The cat ignored Natalie and pranced over to the door that would allow him inside the house. He sat down, faced the door, stared up at the handle, and waited for her to open it.

"Seriously, cat, you're supposed to be outside."

Natalie frowns at his behavior before gently pushing him aside with her foot. She opened the door.

"Ouch!" Natalie cried as the cat swatted her leg.

She bent down to pull up her pajama pants and look at her leg. The cat squeezed through the open door and strutted inside the house like he owned the place. He headed straight for her bedroom. Natalie limped behind him, mumbling not-too-kind things. It didn't stop the cat from jumping up on the bed, stretching, and then settling himself at the foot of her bed.

In disbelief, Natalie watched all this happen as if it happened every single day. Working his way into the house and marching directly to her room was a riddle. *How did he know?* she thought.

Shaking her head, she saw the little sneak pretend to be asleep, just like he had pretended to be hurt. She was on to his game. She saw the tiny slits and knew he was keeping an eye on her.

At a safe distance, Natalie leaned down level with his face and stared at him. He lifted his head and stared back at her.

"I knew it, you little brat!"

They had a stare-off for several minutes before Natalie realized she didn't have the energy to deal with the determined cat. Climbing into bed, she pulled the covers over her head and tried to blot out this new reality.

After a couple of days of no one claiming the cat, she named him Jericho. She couldn't understand how he could be so plump when he never seemed hungry or thirsty. He seemed content staying on her bed with her or traipsing to the kitchen behind her. He went wherever she went except for the bathroom. She told him there were limits, and he seemed to understand in a weird way.

Natalie stayed in her room until the day of the memorial service. Not expecting many people to show up, she told Jericho they wouldn't be long. She headed out with her father for the short drive to Stillwater, where the memorial service was being held.

Natalie and her father were surprised by the large number of people from his business and the neighborhood who showed up for the memorial service. They had expected a small response. Natalie would have preferred a small response. It was anything but that, as the service had every seat taken, and others were standing in the back.

After the service, Natalie stood with her father as a long line of people came through to offer their condolences. It was draining. Never comfortable in crowds, she awkwardly accepted the kind remarks and struggled to find the right responses. She fought to control her emotions.

When she had the chance, she escaped to a corner and stood alone. There, she observed people coming and going. Some of them nodded in her direction, but they gave her the space she needed.

Towards the end of the second and final hour, Natalie's interest peaked. A heavyset woman dressed in a long, flowing black dress entered the room. She wore a black hat with an elaborate black veil that hung below her nose. The attire seemed out of place for a low-key memorial service, but it wasn't just the ensemble that got Natalie's attention. The woman had several unusual bracelets dangling from her right wrist, and even from a distance, Natalie could detect the scent of sandalwood. Intrigued, she watched as the woman glanced around the room. Once she spotted Natalie, she made her way over.

"Natalie, I'm so sorry that I missed the service. I didn't intend to be late. Your mother was a dear friend of mine, and I wanted to be here for Nessa and you."

Natalie's shoulders slumped. She let out a sad sigh because the woman seemed to be upset and disappointed with herself. "It's okay. The service was full, with standing room only. I think Mom would have been shocked if she knew all these people would show up."

"No way. You have an exceptional mother."

Natalie shook her head yes. She blinked back tears, fighting to contain her composure.

"Where are my manners?" the woman exclaimed as she pulled her hat off. "I never introduced myself. I'm Pru, one of your neighbors. As I mentioned, your mother was a good friend, and I've been wanting to meet you for a long time. Unfortunately, these are not ideal circumstances. I am so very sorry for your loss. It's such a shock. Truly tragic."

Pru held out her hand with the bracelets. As Natalie shook her hand, she looked closer at them. She couldn't help but wonder what they were made of, as she had never seen anything like them. They were made of a gray material with gemstones interwoven into the weave.

Studying the bracelets helped Natalie manage her emotions. However, she wasn't prepared for what Pru said next.

"Natalie, your mother probably didn't mention me to you, but she often spoke of you to me. I'm going to say something that sounds strange now, but in time, it will make sense. If anything unusual or odd happens, please come see me."

Puzzled, Natalie jerked her head up and stared into Pru's blue eyes. She had no idea how to respond to what Pru said.

"I know," Pru laughed, "it sounds all dark and mysterious, but I promise, it will make sense in time. One more thing, if you don't mind."

Natalie shook her head yes. She stayed quiet, wondering if this would also be something strange.

"Your mother collected the spiderwebs in your barn for me. Your barn holds some rare spiders, and your mother was kind enough to collect the webs for me to use in making my bracelets. I know, I know," Pru said, laughing again as Natalie, shocked, looked down at the bracelets on Pru's wrist. "It isn't what people would consider a normal hobby, but it has its purpose."

Natalie nodded to acknowledge that she would continue to collect the spiderwebs for Pru. It was a strange request. Then, again, she remembered being out in the barn talking with her mother on several occasions while her mother swiped the spiderwebs off the walls and placed them in a black bucket.

She knew how to collect spiderwebs. She was just surprised her mother wasn't doing it to get rid of the spiders. A little disappointed, Natalie wondered why her mother had never told her the real reason for clearing the spiderwebs off the barn walls.

As Pru said goodbye, Wilfred and Jonathan, the owners of her favorite bookstore, spotted her and strode over to her. Both hugged her.

She couldn't remember a time when they weren't in trench coats. It didn't matter if it was summer, spring, fall, or winter. They always played opera music in their store, even though it was more of a country music community. Their eccentric behavior always entertained her, but tonight they were respectful.

"Natalie," Wilfred expressed for both, "the service was a nice tribute to your mother. We both wanted to get up and say something, but we were rather shy. I hope you'll forgive us."

Natalie nodded in agreement while Wilfred continued talking. "Please know we think your mother was indeed a very special person. In fact, she was one of our favorite customers. We considered her a good friend."

Natalie looked down, nodding to indicate that she understood.

Wilfred continued, "We are truly sorry for your loss. We tried to think of something to say to you that would help, but we couldn't think of anything. It's just so tragic; we can't begin to understand your loss."

Jonathan shook his head in agreement as each held one of Natalie's hands. She struggled to remain calm. If she heard much more, she would cry. She just knew it.

Before they said anything else, Natalie noticed a tall man standing alone near the entrance to the room. She hadn't seen him enter, and she didn't know how long he had been standing there. Dressed in a black suit with a fair complexion and black hair, he seemed to be observing the gathering more than wanting to be a part of it. Even so, it was what he was turning over and over in his left hand that had her attention. It was a round gemstone, a stone, or something else. She wasn't sure what it was. It had multiple colors slowly circulating within it. Mesmerized, Natalie found her emotional escape and tuned everything else out.

Wilfred and Jonathan turned around to see what had gotten Natalie's attention just as the stranger put the stone in his pocket. He made eye contact with all three before heading into a crowd of people.

"Do you know him?" Wilfred asked, still watching the stranger.

"No, I've never seen him before. Did you see what he had in his hand?"

Both Wilfred and Jonathan responded. "We didn't see anything in his hand."

Natalie frowned. *Am I the only one who saw it?* She wanted to approach him and ask to see the stone. What was it that made it seem alive? She had never seen anything like that before. What about him? She had never seen him before. Besides, he seemed odd. Why would he put it away just as others were going to see it?

"Natalie!"

Startled, Natalie focused and looked at Wilfred.

44

"Sorry, Natalie," Wilfred said with a slight smile, "we lost you again."

"I'm so sorry! My bad. He held an odd stone or something that had swirling, intertwining colors. I can't stop thinking about the colors separating and combining as they continually moved around the stone. He put it in his pocket just before you turned around. I wish you could have seen it. Somehow, I get the feeling he didn't want you to see it. The whole thing is weird. I'm sorry. I'm rambling."

Both Wilfred and Jonathan laughed before Wilfred became serious and spoke again. "You're not rambling, and don't worry about it, Natalie. It's fine. You're anxious right now. Unfortunately, you have a lot to work through, and most of it will have to be done alone. This tragic loss takes time to handle, and the length of time varies from person to person."

Jonathan said, "Time heals the deepest hurt. One day, you will handle this without pain. You'll find that your mother will always be a part of your life, and every day, you will think of her. You may even talk to her. That's normal. It'll get easier, we promise."

Jonathan's comments hit hard. No more pretense. Natalie covered her face with her hands and sobbed. Finally, releasing the repressed pain and emotional stress of the last two hours, the tears streamed down her face. As the tears flowed, it started to rain.

She felt the comfort of Jonathan's arms as he turned her and took her into a hug. She sobbed like a baby.

"Rain…you know what that means," Wilfred whispered.

"We now have the answer we wanted about Nessa. We were right," Jonathan whispered back, patting Natalie a little too fast and roughly on the back. Wilfred frowned; Jonathan slowed down to comforting taps.

Natalie kept her head down to soften the sound of her sobs. She didn't want her father to see her meltdown.

"Alchemist?" Wilfred whispered.

"Shadowlink?" Jonathan countered.

"Unlikely. They're rare."

"Seems strange Nessa never told her," Jonathan said loud enough that Natalie started to pull away.

"Take your time, Natalie. We're here for you." Jonathan relaxed as she stayed in his hug.

"Keep your voice low. We need to figure out how we're going to tell her." Wilfred then remembered Natalie's comment about the man with the strange stone.

"Jonathan, the man with the stone. I can't believe it. He's here." They turned their heads in unison, searching the groups of people for the man that Natalie said held a strange object. Now, it made sense.

"The Stormfield wizard and the oracular stone. It can only mean that Natalie is a Shadowlink. Oh, my stars, how did we get so lucky?" In his excitement, Jonathan rapidly patted her back again.

Natalie thought that Jonathan's rapid patting of her back meant he had changed his mind, and it was time for her to step back. She tried to push away as the tears continued to flow. He held steady, letting her know she was safe, causing her tears to turn into sobs.

"Let it out. This helps release some of the pain. We're here for you." Jonathan slowed the tapping as he looked for the man. His breath caught when he spotted him standing near Natalie's father.

"He's over there," Jonathan whispered, tilting his head and rolling his eyes toward where the man stood.

"The Stormfield wizard," Wilfred said in awe.

He gasped when the man stopped looking at the program in his hand and raised his solemn black eyes to theirs. He moved his head, indicating he wanted them to leave. They both nodded.

Natalie, comforted by the gentle hug, wished the tears would stop. *Time's up*, she told herself, but the tears flowed.

"He wants us to leave, but we can't abandon Natalie. Yet, we don't want to anger him; what do we do?" Wilfred whispered as adrenaline flowed and they started to sweat from the stress. Minutes seemed like hours. Just as they were at their wits' end, Natalie stopped crying.

"I'm sorry," Natalie said as she pulled away and wiped the tears from her face.

"No need to apologize," Wilfred said in relief as he pulled a handkerchief from his pocket and handed it to her. "It's clean."

That broke the sad mood; they all laughed.

"Thank you." Natalie wiped her eyes.

"You're welcome. Actually, we wanted to give you some good news: the next time you're in the store, feel free to pick out any book you want. It's on us."

"Oh, wow! I really appreciate that."

"It's our pleasure," Wilfred and Jonathan said as they looked at their watches.

"Oh, my," they said in unison, "we need to get back to the bookstore."

Before Natalie could even respond, they were out the door. She wondered for a moment why they had abruptly left. Had she made them uncomfortable with her crying? Probably. They were both old bachelors. Dealing with a girl in total meltdown was probably quite stressful for them. Even so, they were there for her, and she appreciated it. Now, she wanted to turn her attention to finding the stranger with the unusual stone.

Natalie glanced around the large room. She soon spotted the stranger a short distance from her father. Her father was speaking with a couple of friends from work, but she knew the stranger wasn't waiting for his turn to see him. So weird. *Why was this man even here?* she thought as she stared at him.

As Natalie tried to figure him out, he turned his dark eyes to hers. She should have looked away, but she continued to stare at him. He must have taken that as an invitation to come over because he started walking towards her. Alarmed, Natalie had mixed emotions about talking with him. Her heart began to race as she broke out in a cold sweat. She wanted to run, but she felt as though she was glued in place. She wanted to know more about that stone, but all these alarm bells were going off in her head. *What to do!* As if just thinking that brought the answer, her next-door neighbors, Mr. and Mrs. Jackson and their son, Joel, arriving late, hurried over to offer their condolences. By the time they left, the stranger was gone.

When they got home, Natalie went straight to her bedroom. Drained, she wanted to be alone. She didn't acknowledge Jericho but grabbed her pajamas and headed for the shower. Returning, she flopped down on her bed. Jericho sat waiting and took a stern look at her face. He seemed to take in the swollen area around her eyes.

Jericho stood up, walked over to her, and sat down facing her. His penetrating green eyes gave Natalie the strangest feeling that he wanted to hear her report. She really didn't want to talk, but as she told him all about the memorial service, she felt a sense of relief. When she got to the stranger with the unusual stone, Jericho's eyes widened, and his tail swung back and forth. Natalie wasn't sure she should keep going, but Jericho seemed riveted by what she said, so she continued.

Chapter 8
Defenseless Creature

Natalie walked into the kitchen with Jericho prancing beside her. Her shoulders slumped, and her heart accelerated when she saw her father. He should have already left for work. Instead, he sat sipping coffee, waiting for her.

"Hi, Dad." Her appetite disappeared as he motioned for her to sit down.

"Natalie, you've had a week to handle your grief in whatever way worked for you, but now it's time to get on with your life."

Natalie's father continued to speak about his expectations, but she wanted to hum or place her hands over her ears and tell him to stop. She kept her eyes down, bit her lower lip, and concentrated on not crying as he rambled about responsibility.

He stopped talking; Natalie looked up.

"Do you have any questions about what is expected?"

Afraid she would burst into tears if she spoke, Natalie nodded no. While nodding no, Jericho jumped on the table and faced Karl. He raised his head and let out a deafening, long hiss. His claws extended out. Natalie grasped Jericho just before he swung at her father, who jumped up and backed away from the table.

Jericho turned and growled at Natalie. She kept a tight grip on him. Her father grabbed his briefcase and made a hasty exit.

"Jericho, Dad's right. He just has a horrible way of saying it." Natalie opened her hands, releasing him. Ears down, tail swinging, Jericho hissed before jumping off the table.

She walked outside and stared in disbelief. How would she ever manage to clean up the property? It was too much. She wanted to turn around and hide beneath the covers in her bed, but her father had given her orders.

Overwhelmed by the enormous task, Natalie concluded the best place to start would be the large vegetable garden. Her father would want her to continue the work he had already started. He wanted the house and property to look nice from the front road. Natalie didn't care what other people thought. If she had to spend most of her waking hours during the hot summer working on the property, the garden would be her priority.

On the way there, she reached down and picked up long branches. Dragging the branches through the debris scattered along the narrow path between the house and the barn, she headed toward the burn pit.

The violent storm flashed in her mind. Her father hadn't mentioned any damage to the barn. She hoped it was okay. When she thought of the decrepit, original homestead next to the barn, she hoped it had been smashed to smithereens.

That ancient ramshackle place terrified Natalie. It was spookier than many of the haunted houses shown in old horror movies. She believed they could make a fortune renting it out to movie companies needing an old, gruesome building.

Like those demon-possessed haunted houses, this was a 100-year-old, two-story, paint-peeling, dilapidated homestead just left of the barn. The old wooden building never seemed to change, but Natalie's wild imagination had it infested with roaches, spiders, rats, and other creepy crawlers. The narrow, blackened windows with torn screens and unhinged shutters added to her vivid horror, creating a haunted-house atmosphere.

The terrifying scene intensified as six-foot-tall scarecrows stood behind a rusted, four-foot-tall black fence. They surrounded the building, starting at either side of the arbor over the entrance. Those ragged scarecrows looked as old as the century-old house. With yellow straw hair, black button eyes, red noses, and creepy, wide smiles, they always seemed to watch her.

They reminded Natalie of guards. As if she ever wanted to walk under the arbor, go through the rusted old gate guarded by the creepy scarecrows, go by the nightmarish three-headed tree stump, or enter that death trap haunted house. No worry, as that was never going to happen.

If the elevated wooden front porch floor didn't cave in under her, the zillion roaches lurking underneath in the dark would probably get her. Natalie knew she would die as soon as she saw an invasion of roaches. Of all the insects and pests out there, she feared roaches the most because they were large, nasty, and flew at their victims.

If the roaches didn't get her, there would be big, fat, hairy, starving red-eyed rats waiting for her. Natalie shuddered, thinking about the roaches and rats. She couldn't help but think there were probably blood-sucking bats hanging somewhere on that building, waiting to suck the life out of her.

It wasn't even just the roaches, rats, and bats. The building had a door on the outside of the second floor. If someone used it, they would fall straight to the ground. Natalie never understood why that door existed.

Her mother insisted on the haunted house with the door-to-nowhere and all the other creepy features remain. She had tried to reason with her mother, as the place terrified her, but her mother said it would stay, including the scarecrows.

Stepping out of the path, Natalie could see her father had cleared the debris along the gravel road leading up to the barn and all around the two buildings. She refused to look at the old homestead. Their red barn looming before her didn't appear to have any damage from the storm. With a sigh of relief, Natalie dragged the branches in her hands over to the overflowing burn pit.

Resuming her chicken chores, Natalie took care of the hens and chicks before returning to the front of the barn. There, she swung open one of the massive 10-foot-tall barn doors and secured it in place. The rakes, shovels, and other yard tools were just inside the door, hanging from long nails on the unpainted wooden wall. Natalie grabbed the nearest rake and headed straight for the vegetable garden.

As she walked to the garden, she wondered why she hadn't considered it before today. She hoped it had survived the storm. The grape vines had been at their peak, and it would be devastating if they hadn't survived the storm.

Just that thought brought an image of the grape vines before the storm to her mind. The front middle section of the garden held two varieties of grapes that had flourished, as they did every summer, along the double trellis. Overgrowing the massive trellis, the grapevines intertwined and completely covered the garden shed. Big, juicy green and purple grapes were abundant over the sprawling vines.

Reaching the four-foot-tall garden gate, Natalie stopped and peered over at the grapevines. Sticks were lodged throughout the vines, but the vines had survived. Plenty of grapes were on the ground, but many grapes remained on the vines. Relieved, she peered over at the row of pineapple plants that stretched the entire length of the garden. They, too, were fine and only needed the debris cleared away.

Natalie lingered at the gate, counting the pineapples ready to harvest within the next couple of weeks. A slight movement caught the edge of her vision. Turning, her eyes grew wide, and her mouth opened in surprise as she stared at a section of the grapevine. Half-covered in dense leaves, a dazzling, sun-reflecting, iridescent, purple and blue-winged, oversized butterfly balanced on a large green grape.

Calmly admiring the beautiful wings, Natalie jumped in shock as the butterfly lunged forward and took a huge bite from the nearest juicy grape. Confusion took over. How was that possible? Butterflies don't have teeth.

"That's not a butterfly head!" Natalie shrieked, dropping the rake and startling the butterfly. With its mouth full and juice running down its chin, it turned to look at Natalie.

Before either of them could react, Jericho jumped through the garden fence. He leaped into the vines, opened his mouth wide, and snapped his sharp teeth around the butterfly. Dropping and spinning around, Jericho darted towards the area of the fence he had used to enter the garden. Jumping back through, he made a mad dash towards the barn. As the cat fled with the creature hanging out of its mouth, the creature began emitting an ear-piercing, high-pitched wail.

It took a minute for Natalie to get over the initial shock of Jericho grabbing the butterfly. Once she recovered, she moved into action. "Stop!" Natalie screamed as she chased Jericho, but the cat never slowed down.

Even with the creature hanging from his mouth, Jericho jumped over the metal gate of the old homestead. He ran up the wooden steps. Stopping, Jericho kept his back to Natalie as he faced the dilapidated front door. His tail madly swung from side to side with his ears bent down.

Natalie breathlessly reached the fence. Wide-eyed, her heart thumped against her chest. Why would he pick this horrible place? Of all places, why this place? She feared touching the rusted fence or looking at the scarecrows.

"Please, Jericho, don't hurt it."

But Jericho continued to swing his tail and keep his ears down as if telling her he had ominous plans for the creature if she didn't rescue it.

Natalie slumped. She couldn't bring herself to do it. It didn't matter how gut-wrenching the wails were or how much time she stood there; she would never be brave enough to enter. The entire place terrified her. No courage existed to touch the fence, much less open the gate. Even if she could muster an ounce of bravery, she knew she would never have the nerve to be on the same side as the scarecrows.

"Please!" Natalie begged Jericho.

He kept his back to her.

"Jericho, please let it go."

The butterfly continued to wail as Jericho faced the dilapidated door. It was apparent he wasn't moved by the distressed cries or Natalie's pleas to let it go.

Feeling like a useless coward, Natalie burst into tears. She stood there sobbing until she glanced up and saw a scarecrow had bent his head down and stared at her. Inches from her face, it looked like a creepy clown to her. Her tears stopped.

She took a quick step back. Shifting her eyes away from the one closest to her, she glanced down the fence. Yikes! All the scarecrows faced her; all the scarecrows stared at her with their creepy, wide smiles.

Terrified, Natalie ran into the barn. She couldn't see the scarecrows, and they couldn't see her. She wiped her face and stood still until she calmed down. Stepping outside, she noticed the silence. The butterfly had stopped wailing.

Natalie hoped Jericho had let the creature go. She glanced in that direction but noticed the scarecrows instead. They were now looking over at Joel's second-story window. She couldn't see anyone in the window, but something must have gotten their attention. Natalie shook her head to clear the ridiculous thought.

How could any of these scruffy old scarecrows do anything but swing with the wind? They're scarecrows on sticks with hands stitched to each other. And yet they've survived for decades, and even during the deadly storm. How was that possible when the entire property looked like a massive attack had taken place? Why weren't these flimsy scarecrows ripped out of the ground and tossed to the winds?

Natalie didn't know. She backed away and returned her attention to yard work. They would be burning for weeks. Too bad she couldn't add the scarecrows to the burn pit.

She worked quietly, pulling sticks from the vines until a large crow broke the silence with its endless squawking. On and on, she listened to his shrill voice. "Shush," Natalie directed at the crow. However, it soon became apparent he had no intention of stopping.

She looked for something to toss at the bird, hoping it would find another place to screech. She couldn't find anything. Just as she thought about the garden hose at the other end of the garden, Natalie noticed Jericho sitting on the other side of the fence. The crow stopped squawking. She looked closer at the crow.

"You look like my mom's favorite crow, but I remember him as a quiet bird."

He tilted his head as he continued to stare at her.

Could this be the same bird? she thought while she studied him. The crow her mother had befriended was called

Beaker. That bird seemed to hang around her whenever she was outside, but that bird never made a horrible racket.

Crows typically were all the same to her, except Beaker got his name because of his big beak. This crow had the same large beak. While it was hard to tell, Natalie rationalized that this had to be a different crow. Obviously, this one had a bad trait of tattling.

Natalie turned her attention to Jericho. Upset with him, she leaned against the rake and said, "I'm mad at you. Now go away."

Jericho followed her from raking to dumping the wheelbarrow. He stayed with her even when she went to the house for a break. When Natalie came out, she had forgiven him and had brought him a treat. He snubbed it and walked away. The bird snatched the cracker from her hand, gobbled it down, and then stole Jericho's treat.

"I can't believe you ran off with that defenseless creature." Natalie shook her head at Jericho as the crow flitted from tree to tree to stay near her.

"Why are you following us? I don't have any more snacks for you." Natalie watched as the crow jumped to a lower branch, bringing it closer to them.

"Weird."

As evening approached, she realized she hadn't been alone all day. It may not have been the company she needed, but she appreciated their odd companionship.

On the last trip of the day, filthy and sweaty, Natalie decided to go through the small garage door instead of the door at the back of the house. As she came off the sidewalk, she spotted something near the garage gutter drain. It looked like a crumpled piece of paper, half-full of dirt. Natalie reached down and picked it up. Jericho stood next to her. He watched to see what she would do. The crow landed in one of the nearby trees and seemed interested in what she had picked up.

Carefully opening the paper at an angle to dump the dirt, Natalie found a clear crystal attached to a long silver necklace. She held it up into the sunlight and looked at it from all angles. The plain crystal looked beautiful to her.

It reminded her of the fancier version of a crystal necklace that her mother always wore. With that reasoning, Natalie knew it belonged to her. She slipped the chain over her head and placed the crystal inside her shirt. Smiling, she headed inside for a hot shower before preparing dinner.

As she finished putting the rinsed dinner dishes in the dishwasher, her arms and legs throbbed from all the outside work. She hobbled to the bathroom for another shower, but it didn't help with the pain. The pain intensified.

Natalie buried herself in her blankets and gathered her pillows around her. She tossed and turned, trying to get comfortable, but the muscles in her left leg tightened.

She jumped up and tried to put weight on her leg. Unbearable pain gripped her muscles, causing her to freeze in place. She didn't know what to do as the pain increased. Tears streamed down her face.

"Jericho, I hurt so much. I need sleep, but the pain is awful." Natalie crawled back into bed, wiping the tears off her face. It didn't help as they continued to flow.

"I'm sorry, Jericho." She watched Jericho jump off the bed and disappear.

She couldn't see Jericho standing in the dark at the back of her bed. He changed to his Ruiri form, uttered a spell, reverted to his cat form, and jumped back on the bed. Natalie fell asleep.

She spent the summer days working in the yard and loading the burn pit. Her father worked on the weekends, cutting up large limbs and damaged trees. The burn pit was lit every other day until it was time to extinguish the fire. Every day, the cat was there waiting for her. And, almost like clockwork, every other week, Jericho would make sure she watched as he caught some defenseless animal in his sharp teeth.

After the butterfly, Jericho caught a cardinal and raced to the front door of the old homestead; Natalie ran after him. There, Jericho sat, taunting her.

"Please," Natalie begged him, "let the bird go." It didn't matter how often she asked him; he continued to ignore her. She gave up and walked away.

The next time, it was a baby brown rabbit, and this time, Jericho pranced just ahead of her as he headed for the rickety old homestead. As he sat facing the front door, Natalie stood at the gate and yelled at him.

"You're a monster!"

He didn't respond. She tried a softer tone.

"Please let the rabbit go."

He turned and briefly faced her. Horrified, Natalie could see the legs dangling from his mouth.

"Stop it! Right now! Let the rabbit go!"

Natalie's face flushed with anger. She bit her bottom lip and tightened her hands into fists. Helpless, she watched Jericho hold onto the little rabbit. She couldn't take it. Fuming, she turned and stormed to the house. This time, she went inside and didn't come out until it was time to lock up the chickens.

Natalie ignored Jericho for several days. He behaved until she forgave him. The next day, he caught a long yellow snake. Jericho could have just sat there or crawled to the old homestead, and she would not have tried to rescue the snake.

"Seriously, a snake!?" She stood there watching him with that thick, long snake twisting and turning in an effort to bite him. Jericho ignored the agitated snake while he studied her. Deciding Natalie told the truth, Jericho released the snake and jumped out of the way as it lunged at him.

Natalie laughed at the scene before her.

"You're such a weird cat."

She meant it. Why did he taunt her with the animals he caught, even though he had no interest in them? She fed him, but he snubbed the cat food she put out for him. It always went in the garbage. Why did he hang around her when he didn't want to be touched? She couldn't understand why he stayed, but she had the strangest feeling he had adopted her.

Chapter 9
Something Bad is in the Works

Natalie hadn't had a break all summer. She went to bed sore and exhausted. She got up to repeat endless yard work. That went on until she started school. Now, she had one week of school behind her.

Tonight, she wanted to sit in the pavilion by the barn to enjoy the beautiful symphony of nightlife sounds. The fireflies might leisurely float along the pasture, each signaling for a mate. Deer would jump the fence and graze on the lush pasture grass. She would see nature at its best with a starry sky and moonbeams radiating down.

Before heading out to the back, Natalie stood in the driveway admiring the beautiful orange and pink colors spread across the sky by the setting sun. Jericho sat beside her and yawned. His tail flicked against her leg.

"All right, let's go. I can see the beautiful sunset is wasted on you."

They headed towards the gravel driveway.

"Natalie!" Joel yelled to get her attention as he approached the four-foot field fence that separated their properties.

"Hey, Joel."

"You got a minute?"

"Sure." Natalie headed over to the fence with Jericho by her side.

Jericho sat down, lowered his ears, and stared up at Joel.

Joel looked down at the annoyed cat. "Natalie, I wasn't going to talk about your cat, but doesn't it seem strange he wandered in, picked you, and no one else can get anywhere near him?"

Looking down, Natalie watched Jericho shake his head to fluff his lion's mane. She grew concerned as his fluffy black tail swung back and forth while he stared at Joel. She didn't know if Joel was the source of his bad mood or the delayed trip to the barn or something else. There was no telling with him.

Natalie looked up at Joel. "That storm was incredibly violent; Jericho may have traveled miles to escape it. When he couldn't escape it, he found a place to hide here. Sadly, no one claimed him."

While Joel hesitated to answer, Natalie wondered why Jericho had chosen her. Why did he show up when he did? Was it just a coincidence? Her mother had always told her there were no coincidences. She should always look for clues as to why something happened.

Natalie wondered why Jericho hadn't picked the house on the south side of her property. In that house were two sisters, probably Joel's age, who seemed to outdo themselves on bonfires and all things Halloween-related. That included buying the largest pumpkins and carving unique Jack-o'-lanterns for full display on their front porch. It was oddly funny since no one could see their house from the road.

They appeared to be obsessed with Halloween decorations throughout the year. Wouldn't it make sense that a short-tempered black Maine Coon cat would prefer their home? He would be a perfect familiar for the two want-to-be witches, but it didn't happen.

Since Joel didn't answer Natalie's comment about anyone claiming Jericho, she gave her opinion. "I never thought about it, but maybe the previous owner resembles me. However, if Jericho had been my cat, I would have plastered lost cat posters for miles. So, I'm thinking maybe someone who looks like me dumped him. I would never do that to a pet, not even this brat."

As soon as she made that comment, it reminded her of the incident with the strange butterfly, the cardinal, and the rabbit. She smiled at the snake incident because she believed the snake was seeking revenge.

"Maybe I should have named him Armageddon. He has a way of making people not want to have anything to do with him."

"Natalie, look at him. He's grumpy and looking like he wants to act on his grumpiness."

"He does seem grumpier than usual." Natalie glanced down at Jericho, who was watching Joel.

After a few minutes of awkward silence between them, while they watched Jericho, Joel looked up and said, "Armageddon…Maybe he is an omen, but I don't think so. Ever since that unnatural storm, I have had this odd feeling that something bad is in the works."

"Really?"

"Yes. That's why I wanted to talk with you. Are you sure you don't feel something is off?"

"Truthfully, Joel, all I've been doing is yard work, dinner, and household chores. Now it's school. I'm so tired at night that I open a book to read and can't keep my eyes open."

"Oh, wow. I'm sorry. Dad hired a company to clear our property."

"I noticed. I think Dad thought yard work would help us work through the passing of Mom."

"Did it?"

"Yes and no. I'm not up to talking about it."

"Okay. Sorry. Let's get back to the something is off subject."

"Okay."

"I started to research for future unusual signs or events. I came across an article about triominous signs. The article alluded to celestial signs, so I don't think your wicked cat is one of them."

"Who printed that article? Triominous signs? Whatever that means, it sounds like a stretch."

"It's a reputable magazine that mentioned a solar eclipse and an upcoming Full Cold Moon."

"That's only two signs. I believe tri still means three." Natalie noticed Jericho's ears perked up.

Frustrated, Joel responded, "I'm being serious, Natalie. A third sign was mentioned, but I can't recall it at the moment. All I'm saying is that after that violent storm, I have this weird feeling we're supposed to be preparing, but I don't know how or why."

Natalie thought it over and silently agreed with Joel. Something wasn't right. Her mother's passing, the storm, Jericho, and something else. What were they missing? She looked down at Jericho. He still stared at Joel.

"Well, when you figure it out, let me know." Natalie decided to leave before the cat inflicted an injury on Joel.

They sat at the pavilion, watching four deer grazing near the back of the pasture. Within minutes of darkness, frogs and other nocturnal creatures began serenading the night. Fireflies flitted across the pasture while a raccoon climbed down a nearby tree. Natalie looked up as a shooting star streaked across the sky.

"That's a good sign."

Several minutes later, Natalie heard buzzing and slapped a mosquito. More buzzing around her head and arms.

"Well, I guess we are one-for-one on good and bad signs." Natalie got up. Jericho walked beside her as they took the solar-lit gravel road.

Back at the house, Natalie picked up her father's plate and scraped the food into the garbage can. Since her mother's passing, he had lost his appetite.

She sighed as she rinsed the plate. Every night, he sat there looking as if he didn't have the energy to carry on a simple conversation. It broke her heart to see him so lost. She wasn't sure what would have become of her father if his job hadn't been so demanding. At least during office hours, he had somewhere else to focus. Here, it was just the two of them, and both were still mourning.

The dishes were in the dishwasher, and the kitchen was cleaned. Natalie retreated to her bedroom. She picked up a book, but her thoughts turned to Jericho, the nosy crow, the unnatural storm, and who had left her the necklace.

She had that uneasy feeling when you know something is off, but you can't figure it out. Until now, she had attributed it to the loss of her mother, but Joel felt it, too.

Now curious, Natalie got up and went over to her computer. Jericho hopped on her desk. She tried to brush him off the desk, but he lashed out at her.

She yanked her hand back and frowned.

"Jericho, you're a monster!"

Not attempting to push him off again, she focused on the search. A story popped up about a full blue moon and a solar eclipse on August 21. Trying to read around Jericho's head, Natalie discovered it was a rare occurrence because it hadn't happened in 99 years in the United States.

"That's interesting," Natalie said in a lackluster tone. She didn't think it was noteworthy because there were always new records or rare occurrences. Since school started, she had more pressing things on her mind. For one, she remained an outsider.

While it was nothing new, Natalie already knew that she didn't fit in with any of the popularity levels at school.

Just like all the prior years and all the other schools, she kept to herself and focused on her classes. Even during her lunch break, Natalie isolated herself by reading a book on one of the benches outside the auditorium. The thought of eating in the school cafeteria with a couple of hundred rowdy students filled her with fear. Besides, the lunch money her father gave her was used to buy books, except for the one she was currently reading. Wilfred and Jonathan had given her that book.

Turning her focus from school, Natalie smiled at the scene before her. Jericho still stared at the screen. She waited a couple of minutes before saying anything.

"Is it okay to turn the computer off?"

It was creepy how the cat turned and looked at Natalie as if he understood what was on the screen and what she had just said. She wasn't sure what to make of it other than she had one strange cat.

Chapter 10
Great American Eclipse

As far as Natalie could tell, there was nothing extraordinary about the upcoming total solar eclipse on August 21. Well, that would be true if she didn't count the growing number of black vultures perched on the wannabe witches' tall pine trees. Those pine trees overlooked her southern pasture.

Knowing the vultures were there, Natalie double-dreaded her early morning trips through the shadowy path to the barn for her morning chores. She especially dreaded it today, as tonight was going to be what the media dubbed the Great American Eclipse.

Her flashlight, illuminating the narrow path, shifted from the ground to the trees as Natalie made her way through the long trail. Her heart pounded as she worried about what hid in the dense palmettoes lining both sides of the path. Her eyes shifted upward as she looked at what perched on the crowded, skinny oak trees menacingly arched over her. Natalie focused on the movement from the trees, the rustling in the palmettos, the tree roots along the course, and any scary sounds. Nothing unusual happened. Exiting the path, she let out an enormous sigh of relief.

Then, she glanced at the pine trees. Her eyes widened in horror. She shuddered, seeing the numerous grotesque vulture silhouettes overwhelming the trees.

It plainly wasn't enough that Natalie had to deal with the confining path in the dark and the old, two-story, paint-peeling, ramshackle haunted homestead guarded by creepy, smiling, raggedy, six-foot-tall scarecrows. Now, there were ominous vultures. That added up to three terrible things. Natalie hoped that didn't mean three strikes and you're out.

Her eyes darted from the pine trees to the pasture to make sure it was safe to head to the tack room to scoop the chicken feed. Some vultures had their wings spread out wide, trying to gain warmth, while other vultures took flights over the pasture. With wingspans of five feet, Natalie watched in fear as they drifted closer and closer to her. Deciding to run, she bolted into the tack room and slammed the door shut.

Peeking out of the narrow rectangular window, she watched continuous black shadows drift over the pasture and near the barn. When vultures returned to the trees, other vultures took flight. Silently, the vultures drifted over the same area again and again, descending lower and lower. Natalie winced. Whatever they were hunting, the vultures continued their search.

Out of time, Natalie filled two scoops with chicken feed from the feed stored in metal garbage cans. She ran into the large enclosure to feed the older chickens. Between the drifting vultures, she ran back to the tack room for more feed and then ran to the young chickens locked in the enclosed back stalls.

Locking the stall doors open, she filled the two hanging feeders and then moved through the outside enclosure to secure that door. Whirling around to get out of there, Natalie gasped and dropped the empty scoops. A vulture stood close to her.

She backed against the door and stood frozen in fear. Two beady black eyes stared at her. The vulture hissed and hopped closer. Natalie tried to scream, but nothing came out. She wanted to turn and run into the enclosure, but she couldn't move. Powerless, Natalie, wide-eyed, stood there as the ugly vulture hopped closer. She could feel and smell its hot, putrid breath. *This is it. I'm done. Three strikes.*

Natalie squeezed her eyes closed and tearfully whispered, "Dad, I'm so sorry. Love you."

Right in the middle of the next hop closer, a powerful wind funnel appeared out of nowhere. The whirlwind dropped low to the ground, encircling the vulture.

Natalie's eyes snapped open. She watched the vulture's eyes bulge and a hiss catch in its throat as the furious, swirling winds pulled the vulture upward and away from her.

An eerie white glow allowed Natalie to witness the vulture struggling and hissing as its feathers were plucked one by one, and the bird, almost featherless, shrank in size. Within minutes, the funnel dropped low, the wind disappeared, and the vulture with just three tail feathers crashed to the ground on the other side of the fence.

A horrendous chorus of hissing filled the air as the other vultures took flight. Flying as one massive advancing shadow, the vultures flew over the pasture, making their way to the barn.

Terrified, Natalie ran for the tack room. She slammed the door shut as the first of the vultures flew right where she had been standing a few minutes before. Some landed on the woodpile. Some landed on the debris to be burned, and some landed out of sight. It seemed like the remaining vultures surrounded the barn. They had her trapped.

Natalie looked out at the nightmarish scene and nervously waited. Then, the same eerie glow that had allowed her to see inside the funnel spread over the barn and the entire backyard. She watched as the vultures grasped that they were in imminent danger. With a horrendous sound of beating wings, the vultures took off for the pine trees on the other side of the pasture. The glow remained as Natalie opened the door and stepped outside.

She had no idea what had just happened. It made no logical sense, but the glowing light remained. She looked around. Natalie couldn't see anyone, but she knew someone had protected her. Was it her mother? There wasn't her mother's signature fragrance, so she didn't think so. She looked up.

"Thank you for saving my life!" Her voice trembled and cracked as she spoke to her unseen hero.

The light blinked on and off. Natalie wasn't sure if her rescuer acknowledged her thanks, but after the blink, the light stayed on until she safely entered the house.

Once inside, her entire body shook uncontrollably. Feeling sick to her stomach, she headed to the bathroom. Natalie kept telling herself it was over and she was safe, but she was a nervous wreck. Splashing water on her face, she tried to calm down. The reflection in the mirror told her it wasn't working.

As ridiculous as it seemed that she had to choose whether to stay home or go to school, Natalie knew her father. Even though this happened and defied logic, her father would see it as more of her drama. He had no sense of humor about slacking in school or attendance.

She tried to sort it out because she didn't want to go outside or go to school. However, there wasn't enough time. As it was, she was cutting it close to getting to the bus stop on time. Still shaking, Natalie grabbed her bookbag and headed out the door.

Thinking that another vulture might get too close, Natalie jogged the half mile to the bus stop. When she caught her breath, she found it odd. The vultures appeared to be confined to the trees over by the southern pasture.

Joel was the first one to speak to Natalie at school.

"Hey, you interested in the solar eclipse tonight?"

"No, it's a school night. I want to talk to you about something else."

"Later. Right now, I'm wondering if you're a teenager. A total solar eclipse and you aren't interested?"

"Yes, I'm sure I'm 14, which makes me a teenager." Natalie frowned at Joel for pointing out that she didn't fit in with the other students. After this morning, she had no interest in the solar eclipse. She would hide under mounds of blankets and pillows in her bedroom.

"Remember what I said about the solar eclipse being a sign."

Throwing his backpack over his shoulder, Joel added, "Natalie, you look a wreck."

Without waiting for a reply, he disappeared into the moving mass of students.

Frustration soared as Natalie didn't have time to talk with Joel about the vultures. Nothing seemed to be going right today, including getting to her first class.

Spotting the smallest of openings, she shoved herself into the saturated stream of moving bodies and shuffled along with the rest of them. It was suffocating. Natalie wanted to kick herself for not using her usual method of exiting the building and walking around to the closest entry to her next class.

Finally, as the minutes ticked by, the mass thinned out. Another minute and she stood before the science classroom. She entered the room as the last bell rang. She ran to her chair and plopped down.

Science had a pop quiz, followed by a lecture from the teacher on tonight's celestial event. The teacher failed to mention that it would attract vultures. Before departing for the next class, the teacher assigned extra credit for a paragraph about the Great American Eclipse.

As Natalie walked out of that class heading for World History, she had already decided the extra credit wasn't worth it. Besides, she had an A in the class. Even if she didn't, she wanted no part of the eclipse.

Natalie again entered a sea of pushing and shoving teenage bodies as she tried to make her way over to the other side of the school.

World History was watching a boring old black-and-white war movie. As soon as the movie started, Natalie started getting pelted with rubber bands. It had to be someone directly behind her, with other students moving, so she took the direct hit.

She could hear the giggling from the girls witnessing the attack. Natalie's long, thick hair deflected most of the rubber bands. The teacher seemed oblivious to the annoying situation and the giggling. The last rubber band struck her right shoulder with force and caused a sharp pain.

Stifling a yell of pain, Natalie turned around and saw another thick rubber band aimed at her. Instinctively, she flung her right arm up over her face to protect her eyes while her left hand stretched out as if to say no. At the same time, the boy and his chair lifted and launched through the air. He crashed hard against the back wall. Screams erupted.

Shocked, Natalie turned around. She didn't want to look like she had anything to do with it. The teacher yelled detention at Gary as two students helped him get back into his chair.

Once seated, whispering among those at the back of the room grew loud enough that Natalie wanted to make sure they weren't pointing at her. Glancing back, she saw Lainey looking at her with a surprised expression. Natalie turned around and started packing her backpack. As soon as the bell rang, she bolted from the room.

Finally, school was over, and it was a long ride home on the school bus. As usual, Natalie sat behind the bus driver by herself. No one ever sat with her. Listening to the loud mixture of laughter and talking from the other students reminded her that she was an outcast. It usually bothered her, but today she happily sat alone. Opening her algebra book, she started working on today's assignment.

During the half-mile walk from the bus stop to her home, Natalie didn't see any vultures until she reached her property. Her heart pounded. All the vultures were still there.

After this morning's experience, she decided to do the outside chores in full afternoon sunlight. She refused to be outside tonight when numerous hideous vultures were flying or hopping about the property.

Before starting chores, Natalie dropped her bookbag in her bedroom. Then, she did a quick search for Jericho. She didn't find him and decided he was in one of his moods, where he disappeared for a few days. Calling him wouldn't help. He would return on his terms.

"He's definitely a strange one," Natalie said aloud, but she hoped the vultures hadn't gotten him.

She headed for the path between the house and the barn. As she did, her eyes widened in horror as a high, long pine branch holding three vultures cracked and slammed to the ground along with the vultures. At first, Natalie couldn't see them on the other side of the fence. Then, the vultures took flight and circled the pasture. She froze.

Standing still, she watched the hideous creatures circle the pasture. Carrion feasters. When there was a dead animal on the side of the road, it usually had several vultures gorging on it. This morning, she thought she would be just another statistic. She looked up and thanked whoever or whatever had rescued her.

After finishing the outside chores in record time, Natalie went inside and completed her homework.

She had just finished making spaghetti when her father walked into the house.

"Smells great," Karl said as he put his briefcase down. He walked over to wash his hands in the kitchen sink before settling down at the table.

Natalie brought two plates of spaghetti over and gave her father the one with the most food.

"Thanks. How was your day?"

"It was okay," Natalie replied, deciding not to trouble her father with the vultures. A logical person, she knew he could not process something so strange. Besides, he had enough on his mind without being alarmed about vultures.

There was a time when her dad used to laugh at Natalie's reports and tell her she had a vivid imagination. He would have rolled his eyes and deeply sighed if he had heard her vulture story of it going after her this morning. Natalie knew his reaction if he were himself. Sadly, he wasn't himself, and so she didn't want to bother him about the vultures. She hoped they would be gone by morning.

Her mind was on the vultures when she remembered what happened to Gary.

"Dad?"

"What's up?" Karl said in a worried tone. He put his fork down and waited for her answer.

"Today in class, someone shot rubber bands at me. The last one hit my shoulder and hurt. I turned around to see who shot them at me. I saw him with another thick band ready to launch. I raised my hand as if I could stop it, and he shot backward and hit the wall…"

Before she could finish, her father choked. She jumped up, but he waved her off as he tried to regain his composure. It took several minutes before he stopped coughing. Natalie sat back down and felt more comfortable when he took a sip of coffee. She gave him a minute and then asked him what was on her mind.

"Do you think I caused that?"

Her father went pale with a worried look, but tried to make light of it. "It was just a coincidence."

Natalie studied her father's eyes to see if he was being serious. She hoped that was true, but she knew her father knew as well as she did that her mother did not believe in coincidences. She had hammered that into both of them. There are no coincidences. Natalie made a mental note of it but didn't say anything else to her father about it. She nodded in agreement as she recalled Lainey's surprised expression right after it happened.

Natalie watched her father stare at his food, losing interest in eating. She knew it had to do with the incident involving the rubber band. Why had she said anything? He already looked exhausted and traumatized. She wanted to apologize for adding to his emotional turmoil. Before she could say anything, her father drank his coffee and abruptly left the table.

Her appetite disappeared. She cleared the table and cleaned up the kitchen.

Early in bed, Natalie lay there thinking back to some of the bedtime stories her mother used to tell her. Her mother insisted the stories were true, even though she only shared them with her. Natalie remembered little of what her mother said in the stories, except that they were full of magic and flying on brooms. She recalled often bursting into laughter and her mother's response. "You just wait and see; one day soon."

Natalie wondered what her mother would say about the incident involving the rubber band. She knew it would be a completely different answer from what her father had said.

That got her thinking about the vultures and the rubber band incident. Two unusual events on the same day. She got up and searched through her desk for a new notebook. Finding one, she jotted down the unnatural events of the day. Maybe these were coincidences, but she didn't think so.

Natalie wanted her mother there. This time, she wouldn't laugh at her stories of broomsticks and wands. She had a feeling that if she had been given the opportunity, she would have had her own wild stories to share with her mother.

Tears spilled down her cheeks. She missed her mother. Jericho wasn't even around to provide her with some distraction. As she wiped her face, she hoped he was okay. Natalie didn't want to lose him, too.

Desperately wanting to fall asleep early, she couldn't settle down with the day's events swirling around her mind. Before she knew it, it was late.

In dire need of sleep, Natalie decided to use the technique her mother had taught her long ago. She began building a story—a tale she had told herself hundreds of times over the years. The story started with the same elaborate descriptions of the place, the home, the animals, and the people. Even though it was repetitive, it took a while to fall into a restless sleep.

Midnight. The clocks were chiming. The chiming of the antique grandfather clock and the grandmother clock startled Natalie. Those clocks hadn't worked in years, and yet both chimed. Maybe her mother was reaching out. Jumping out of bed, Natalie ran out of her bedroom towards the chiming clocks.

"Mom!" Natalie screamed as she neared the large dining room where the clocks were located. Her father came around the corner at the same time.

Almost colliding, Karl demanded, "Natalie, what are you doing?"

"I think the chiming clocks have something to do with Mom!" Natalie exclaimed, watching her father glance around the room.

"The clocks haven't worked in years, Dad! Why would they work now?"

"I don't know," Karl faltered, "but Natalie, she's gone. We can't keep hoping that anything out of the ordinary is Mom trying to reach out to us. We can't keep wishing she were here."

He continued to stare at her with sad eyes. "Every day, I wish I could wake up and see her here with us, but she's not. Natalie, we need to move on if we are going to survive. Do you understand?" He turned away before she could see the tears.

Natalie stood with slumped shoulders and downcast eyes in the dining room, waiting and waiting—no more chimes.

So many unusual things happened today that it couldn't all be coincidences. The solar eclipse couldn't take full blame. There just had to be more to it.

As Natalie stood there, desperate for answers, she looked around the dining room. This room, with a massive grandfather clock and a wall-mounted grandmother clock, could easily have belonged to an earlier generation. Her mother decorated the entire house with old-fashioned, dark furniture and fixtures. She loved antiques.

It used to feel warm and safe. Without her mother, it now felt old and out of place for this century. She shook her head. Maybe a good night's sleep would help her escape her gloomy mood.

Natalie fell into a restless sleep. She found herself in an endless nightmare of her distraught mother trying to get her to understand something.

"Understand what, Mom!?" Natalie would ask.

Natalie couldn't understand her mother at all. Sometimes, when her mother spoke to her, a silver key would radiate and block the surrounding view.

"That's it," Natalie exclaimed, waking and sitting up. "Where's the key to Mom's private room?"

There must be something in the room that Mom wants me to see. Curiosity ignited; she needed to find the key. She knew her dad didn't know its location. Even if he did, he probably wouldn't tell her. That's fine. Tomorrow, she would begin the search for the key.

She lay back down and tried to keep her mind from guessing the hidden treasures. Wasn't her dad curious about that room? He never seemed to have any interest in it. He may not, but now Natalie's mind raced with questions of what could be so important in there. At this rate, she would never fall asleep.

Natalie forced herself to stop thinking about the room and concentrated on the boring story she had told herself over the years. She began by describing the home, the property, and the animals. She almost reached the people. Out of sheer boredom of repeating that story for the millionth time, she fell asleep and slept until the harsh beeping of her alarm clock.

In the morning, Natalie exited the path and discovered that only a couple of vultures were left in the trees. Even though she now carried a large can of wasp spray to spray any approaching vultures, she took a deep breath, released it, and relaxed.

Then, she spotted a shadow moving towards the pasture gate. Stepping back into the path to hide, she gripped the can of wasp spray. Seconds ticked by before she peeked around the palmettoes.

It was Jericho. In relief and amusement, Natalie put her free hand over her mouth to avoid breaking into loud laughter.

With a mouth stuffed full of long vulture feathers, Jericho struggled to get through the gap in the gate and the fence post and hold on to his treasure. He looked ridiculous. Keeping still, Natalie tried to count the many feathers hanging in every direction from his mouth.

Unaware of Natalie, Jericho pranced by with his abundant treasure. He left a trail of feathers like Hansel and Gretel left breadcrumbs marking a path. She imagined he would go back and forth throughout the day, collecting the feathers. There had to be plenty since that one vulture had lost all but three tail feathers.

Natalie continued to watch Jericho struggling to hold on to his treasure as he made his way to the old homestead. He seemed so comfortable with that haunted house. She wondered if he stayed there when he wasn't with her.

There were probably all kinds of holes in the building that were wide enough to let him enter. Shuddering, Natalie reasoned that it wasn't just him but roaches, rats, spiders, bats, and snakes. An endless list of creepy creatures. She didn't want to think about it.

After finishing her chores, she thought maybe a solar eclipse would draw vultures to certain areas. Maybe the wannabe witches had a bonfire late last night that drove most of them away. But that made little sense. Those vultures were aggressive.

And what about the whirlwind and glowing light that protected her? What about Gary slamming into the wall? What about the chiming clocks that hadn't worked in years? Add to all these unusual things a cat that collects vulture feathers.

Natalie could see a cat picking up one feather, but Jericho had stuffed his face full of vulture feathers. There was so much weirdness in two days. She wasn't sure what to believe anymore.

By mid-morning, not paying attention in any of her classes, Natalie convinced herself it had all been a lot of odd coincidences. She didn't count the whirlwind and the chiming clocks. Natalie didn't have an answer for those two things. Wanting to put this behind her, she went with the idea that there had to be a logical answer. She just didn't know what it was.

Natalie decided that when she got home from school, she would check the clocks before starting her mission to find the key to her mother's private room. She wanted to know what her mother kept so secret. Maybe an enormous cauldron sat in the middle of that room, or she had endless bookshelves full of books on potions and spells. Could there be a flying broom, a wand, or magic potions? Her imagination ran wild with all the stories her mother had told through the years. What was her mother hiding?

Half relieved and half feeling silly during her lunch break outside by the auditorium, Natalie let out a long laugh, thinking her mother was a witch. It was too much. Her father always called her the drama queen, and her mother the fantasy queen. They always did it in fun, but there was some truth to the titles. They had a title for him, too. They called him the general as he was always so serious. Everything revolved around rules and achievements.

Even with all these strange happenings, Natalie surmised that whatever the solar eclipse was supposed to bring, it must not have happened. That meant there wouldn't be any more signs. However, she would wait to see how Joel spun the solar eclipse story into some dire warning. Yesterday, she wanted to tell him about the vulture that almost ate her for breakfast, but now she didn't want to tell anyone about it. Instead, she decided she would keep a diary of strange happenings.

Joel sat in Natalie's algebra class. He had plenty of chances to see her about the solar eclipse. To her surprise, Joel didn't speak with her at school or at home. Natalie figured it must have been a big non-event for him. Probably embarrassed, he avoided talking to her.

After several days, Natalie forgot about the solar eclipse and continued her search for the key to her mother's private study. She had already tried to open the door with a skeleton key, but that key would shoot back out. It seemed the lock was charmed. Maybe there were wands, flying brooms, and potions in the study. She needed to find that key!

Chapter 11
The Hidden Key

The back wall of the family room had floor-to-ceiling custom bookcases mounted to the wall. The dark-stained wooden bookcases held an enormous collection of books. A custom-built cabinet displayed a collection of antique railroad lanterns. There was a large fireplace and four oversized plush recliners. This room's warm, welcoming feeling made it Natalie's favorite place in the whole house.

She stood there, looking at the various book titles, wondering if her mother had hidden a spare key in one of them. So often that happened in stories. Her mother, an avid reader, preferred books on gemstones, the power of a name or birthday, the power of numbers, and all things related to magic. It would be easy to spot her mother's books, especially against her father's books. She laughed. His books were boring, covering cars through the decades and do-it-yourself projects.

Carrying a chair over to the first set of bookshelves, Natalie climbed and looked at the books on the top shelf. Nothing there. She scanned the second row from the chair and pulled out a book about zodiac signs. Flipping through the pages, Natalie didn't see a key. She climbed down and looked through the other four bookshelves. Natalie repeated the motion of moving the chair and then standing on it to reach the highest bookshelves.

When Natalie reached the fourth section of the bookcase, she saw a strange book titled "The Evolution of Wands." "Really!" Natalie laughed. "Leave it to my mother to buy such a book."

She pulled the book from the shelf and marveled at its heavy weight. Awkward on the chair, she stepped down and sat in one of the recliners. To her surprise, the book had detailed drawings and lengthy descriptions of wands through the ages.

She read a few descriptions before she started flipping through the pages. In the middle of the book, Natalie found a photo of an antique desk marking a section entitled Shadowlink wands. She glanced at the etchings of wands before looking at the picture again. She looked closer and recognized the desk. Putting the photo back inside that page, she headed to her parents' bedroom.

Her heart rate increased, and sweat appeared on her brow as she entered their bedroom. There wasn't anything strange in the room except the unusual dreamcatcher with a colorful wooden hoop, red crystal beads, and black feathers on the wall behind their bed. It didn't matter. She invaded their privacy.

Natalie had already looked through the desk, but she must have missed a secret drawer. She dropped the front down and looked inside. It screamed antique, with old-fashioned slots and ornately carved pillars that seemed to conceal secret compartments. She had tried pulling on those pillars the last time she looked for the key, but the pillars hadn't budged.

She stuck her head inside the desk and looked at the front of the pillars. There, on the left, she could see very fine tracks. Grabbing it and yanking hard with both hands, it released and glided out. Sliding the side open, she found the key in bubble wrap.

With time running out before her father got home, Natalie took the key to her mother's room. There she stood, feeling a sense of intrusion on her mother's private life. This wasn't right. However, wasn't it her mother in the dream that directed her to the room?

"What if I don't like what I find out? Once I know, I won't be able to forget."

Saying aloud what she thought didn't help her. Uncomfortable, she stood facing the door while internally debating about entering the room. Minutes ticked by until curiosity and the dream prevailed. Taking a deep breath, Natalie put the key in the lock. The door swung open. She stood there wide-eyed and mouth open in shock.

Instead of dark furniture and brown tile floors, the room glistened in white. Lacey white curtains, white closed blinds, a plush white couch, a white writing desk, two white corner cabinets, and white carpet. A beautiful old-fashioned crystal chandelier hung in the center of the room. The white coffee table had a mirrored tray adorned with a beautiful crystal candelabra and some large, sparkling crystals. There were large, white, wooden-framed pictures hanging on the back wall. Each picture showed her as she had grown through the years. She bit her lower lip so she wouldn't cry. Her mother cherished her, and her love for Natalie was evident in the gallery of pictures.

She turned to inspect the objects in the far corner glass cabinet. She noticed it held a variety of silver candlesticks. Most of them were antique matching pairs. On the top shelf were four butterfly necklaces, each with different colored crystals. The necklaces surrounded a 4x6 photo in a simple white frame.

Natalie moved closer to look at the picture. She opened the cabinet and took out the photo. Her mother, at a much younger age, stood beside a tall man with black hair and dark eyes. The smiles told her they were close.

Who was this man? Could it be her grandfather? Her mother never talked about her parents. It made little sense, as she was obviously close to this man. Natalie continued to stare at the man. He seemed familiar, but that was impossible. This man would be in his late 60s. Running out of time, she put the picture back and shut the glass door.

Natalie didn't see any magical objects on display. She opened the desk drawers and looked around the room. Nothing. However, standing before the closet door, she came to eye level with a framed photo of her mother in her late teens.

Fascinated, Natalie studied the photo that had her mother switching from a mischievous teenage expression with a green background to a serious pose with colors of green, red, blue, and white sparking and making crackling sounds as they swirled behind her. Wow! Natalie had no idea such technology existed today, much less 20 years ago.

Focusing back on getting into the closet, Natalie opened the door and flipped the light switch. Nothing. She pulled it down and then up again. Nothing.

Peering inside the room, she discovered it didn't have a light fixture. Strange. She pulled the door wide open, allowing enough light to enter the closet. She could see that the walls were painted plain white. There were no shelves. Only a large, simple room with a massive mirror secured against the back wall.

For some unknown reason, Natalie had a strong desire to touch it. The strange feeling made her nervous. *Is that why Mom hid the mirror at the back of the unfinished closet?* Unsure, she hesitated before approaching the mirror. Standing before it, she stared at her petite figure reflected in it.

Natalie decided to stand there and see if something happened. As she stood there, the desire to touch it grew stronger. She couldn't resist any longer. Reaching out, she traced various symbols. As her hand touched the seventh symbol, the mirror clouded up.

Startled, Natalie jerked her hand away and stumbled backward. Recovering her balance and continuing to back up towards the door, she glimpsed a tall figure forming out of the mist. Now in full panic mode, she spun around to face the door. She bolted from the closet, slamming the door behind her.

Natalie continued running until she reached the door leading out of her mother's secret room. Swinging open the door, she ran through and slammed it shut. Tossing the key inside the desk, she fled her parents' bedroom and ran straight to her bedroom.

Chapter 12
Halloween

Natalie had nightmares about the thing forming in that mirror for several nights. *Why would Mom have such a strange mirror? It couldn't have been handed down through the family. It just couldn't have. Where did it come from? Did Mom know what it did?* She had to, or she wouldn't have had that mirror hidden away in the room's closet, which was off-limits to everyone else. Natalie didn't want to face the fact that she didn't know her mother very well.

Traumatized by the strange mirror, she continued with her regular routine. Joel hadn't mentioned any more omens. In fact, he stayed busy with debate competitions, so she hadn't spoken with him in weeks. That was fine with her, as his last warning had brought vultures; she didn't want to experience that again. As time passed, the days turned into weeks, and now Halloween was just a few days away.

Because of her mother, Halloween was one of Natalie's favorite holidays. Her mother had an enormous collection of Halloween decorations. Nothing too scary. Natalie's mother said Halloween was magical and not intended to scare people or be evil. Besides, her mother always said they should celebrate Halloween because they had magic coursing through their veins. They would giggle when her mother said, "But not a stitch of magic in your father!"

During one of the bedtime stories, she told Natalie they had some real magical items — wands, brooms, books, and potions — but she never mentioned an enchanted mirror. When Natalie asked to see them, her mother said she kept them in a safe place. She was waiting for Natalie to start high school. Since Natalie hadn't found any magical objects in her mother's secret room except for that strange mirror, she wondered where, if at all, her mother had hidden them.

Natalie lifted the lid off the first big box. She watched with amusement as Jericho placed his front paws on the edge of the box and peered in at all the Halloween decorations. Amusement turned to laughter as she watched him reach down and swat a few things around the box. He jumped down. His expression said it all. He looked at Natalie as if he had just sniffed dirty gym socks.

"Surely," Natalie said, laughing at the expression and reaching into the box, "you have missed some highly treasured magical tool."

Jericho sat there looking as if he needed a nap.

"Look, Jericho," Natalie exclaimed, pulling out a wand and holding it up as if she were going to cast a spell. "Even though I'm only 14, can I make a spell with this old wand?"

Natalie laughed as Jericho's eyes widened, and he appeared interested in the wand.

"You want me to try a spell on you?"

Jericho backed up as Natalie waved the wand in the air before pointing it at the box.

"Decorations plenty there be, with this spell, put them out for me!"

Jericho again had the smelly sock look on his face as his ears bent backward, listening to that horrible spell.

Natalie laughed. "That bad?"

Jericho meowed a few times, trying to tell her he was tempted to have something fly out of the box and chase her through the house.

Unaware of Jericho's struggle to contain himself, she swished the wand a few more times before giving up.

"Defective wand," Natalie muttered as she looked at the stamp that told her what country had made it. She threw it back into the box.

Jericho hissed, trying to let her know it was more the person with the defective spell.

"Guess it's up to me to get this place decorated."

Natalie focused on the decorations while Jericho took it as an excuse to sneak out of the house.

She spent the next few hours putting up Halloween decorations in her room, on the front porch, and in her music studio. Natalie didn't dare put any decorations where her father would see them. He never liked Halloween. With her mother gone, he surprised her by not telling her to throw the decorations out.

Then again, he hadn't disposed of anything that belonged to her mother. All her mother's clothes were still hanging in the closet, and everything stayed the same. It looked like her mother would walk through the door any day.

Natalie liked that her mother's things were still there, but maybe it made it harder to move on with life. She decided she didn't care. Her mother's things comforted her.

Thinking about it, only home comforted her. She remained an outsider at school unless a class project required a partner. There seemed to be a lot of class projects in science and usually Lainey picked her as her partner.

She frowned, thinking about the two of them sitting side-by-side, working on a project. She always kept her head down when they worked together so others wouldn't make snide remarks about beauty and the plain. They were two totally opposite people, and yet Lainey sought her out. She shook her head, not understanding the situation at all.

With decorations up, the days passed until Halloween. It fell on a school day. Natalie sat in her last class of the day and witnessed the same disruptive behavior in all the earlier classes: constant chatter, candy throwing, and tuning out the teacher. Why they didn't make Halloween a day off for students was beyond her. Somehow, she managed to avoid getting hit with flying candy.

As Natalie walked up to her garage, she noticed an orange and black-colored handmade invitation taped to the door. It was from the two girls next door. Weird. She didn't know them. In fact, she only saw them from a distance when they were having a bonfire or putting up outside decorations, which was almost daily. Natalie stared at the invitation as if it provided clues about these two peculiar girls.

She mulled it over for several minutes before she decided there were two options. The first option was to ignore the invitation. The second option was to go over to their home and get to know them. Natalie supposed that if she felt awkward, she would come home. Besides, it would be nice to have some friends. She decided to go. Since she wasn't sure how her father would react, she didn't mention the invitation at dinner.

After cleaning up the kitchen, Natalie dressed in black and ventured over to their house at 8:00 p.m. only to find them outside waiting for her. Natalie stared at them. They wore stunning royal blue floor-length dresses. Each held a magnificent broomstick. They looked like real witches to the point that she was sure they had wands hidden somewhere in those witch costumes.

"Hi, Natalie. I'm Madison," the taller sister with long black hair said while her dark eyes stared at Natalie. Natalie focused on the other sister.

"I'm Skylar. I'm glad we're finally getting to meet."

Natalie decided Skylar had a friendlier face with sparkling chocolate eyes. She avoided looking at Madison, who still stared at her.

After the introductions, Madison motioned for Natalie to start the walk down the haunted path. Ghoulishly carved pumpkins with flickering flames created dancing shadows along the trail to the bonfire. Mixed in with the flickering pumpkins were full-size plastic skeleton dogs, sheet ghosts, and oversized spiders hanging in trees. There were black cats with arched backs, gravestones, and a Haunted House sign pointing towards the bonfire area. At the end of the path was a full-size plastic skeleton horse with a skeleton on its back. Halloween music played from their front porch.

Natalie found this amusing and strange because the houses in their community were so spread out that they never had trick-or-treaters. Even the kids who lived in the neighborhood went to other neighborhoods. That didn't stop the wannabe witches from having elaborate Halloween decorations all year.

Halfway through the walk to the backyard, Skylar commented on Jericho. "Your black cat is beautiful."

"That's the first time I've ever heard anyone call Jericho beautiful, as he looks more like a miniature black lion. His personality is like a lion that hasn't eaten in weeks, meaning he is always grumpy."

"He is unpredictable. He sometimes visits us as he is doing right now."

Surprised, Natalie turned around to see Jericho following her. She went to scoop him up, but remembered he didn't like to be held.

"I thought he hated everyone except me."

"Oh, we don't touch him. Without a doubt, he's a one-owner cat. Sometimes, he visits our cat, which looks like he could be his brother."

Natalie thought about that for a moment. "When did your cat show up?"

"He showed up right after that strange storm."

"That's when Jericho showed up. It sounds like they could be brothers."

"I think so," Skylar commented, "because his behavior isn't any better than Jericho's."

Natalie sat near the fire, pondering the arrival of both cats on the same day, each destined for a different home. While she was mulling over the two cats, Madison and Skylar put their brooms by their chairs and focused on building up the small fire. She watched with interest to see if they would wave their wands and recite a dramatic spell. They didn't. She yawned as they placed more wood on the fire without wands.

The fire grew broader and higher. Now Natalie could feel the heat. She backed her chair up a couple of feet. As Madison and Skylar backed their chairs up and sat down, they leaned close to each other and started talking in low voices.

Natalie watched them and tried to determine if they had forgotten her. Madison looked up and stared at her. Finding that creepy, Natalie turned her head to focus on Jericho. He moved closer to the fire and seemed mesmerized by it. They had thrown some packets into the bonfire, producing a kaleidoscope of colored flames.

It wasn't long before another black cat appeared and approached Natalie. Madison and Skylar stopped talking long enough to say in unison, "That's Sharlow."

She put her hand down for Sharlow to sniff, but he wasn't having any of it.

"Geez," Natalie mumbled, "you are Jericho's twin."

Sharlow turned and walked over to Jericho. Soon, it appeared as if the two cats were communicating. One would give a couple of low meows, and the other would reply. This went on for several minutes. Watching the strange exchange between the cats, Natalie couldn't help but feel like both the witches and the cats were ignoring her.

"I guess there's always a first," Natalie said aloud, "because I would have never thought that Jericho would be fine with another cat. This can only mean that they are brothers."

"I agree," Madison replied and went right back to speaking with Skylar.

Natalie, slumped and bored, wondered why the two cats had separated. She remembered the star performance Jericho had given to get into the house. One could get away with the trick of wailing and holding up a fake injured paw, but it would be impossible for two huge cats to get away with that trick. She smiled, thinking they were pretty crafty cats.

Natalie glanced at the haunted path, listened to the eerie music, and then gazed at the fire. *Wow, this is boring. Seriously, boring. If this is what happens at parties, I should have brought a book. Better yet, I should have stayed home and read the book in my room. After all, I could have a drink and something to eat there.*

Glancing around, she didn't see any Halloween treats. No candy, cookies, or drinks. A big, fat nothing. She guessed this was a trick, not a treat. She stretched her legs out, slumped further down in her chair, and gave a strong clue of being utterly bored out of her mind except for watching the exchange between the cats.

Whatever Jericho and Sharlow were discussing seemed to involve Natalie. After completing their strange conversation, Sharlow marched over and plunked himself down in front of Natalie. Intrigued, Natalie stared down at him and waited. His eyes glowed as he tilted his head and studied her for several minutes. He seemed to be working through some problems. Whatever it was, just as quickly, he turned around and headed towards the old homestead near the back of their property.

"It's like an old Halloween movie. There's the mysterious black cat, weird witches, and a creepy old homestead. All we need is something evil to happen," Natalie said to no one in particular. Just then, she heard an owl hoot nearby. Jumping up, she started towards Jericho.

"Don't worry," Madison stated. "The owl won't go after the cats. He belongs to us."

That statement surprised Natalie. "How do you have an owl as a pet?"

"It's strange. We don't really see the owl, but every night since Sharlow showed up, it is nearby, talking up a storm."

"Stranger by the minute," Natalie muttered.

"We don't mean to be rude," Madison said, "but we're trying to figure out how much to say without you thinking we're totally insane. Most people already think that because we have Halloween all year round. Isolating ourselves by taking online classes doesn't help, either."

As Natalie sat back down, she asked, "How so?" She noticed Sharlow had disappeared.

"Incidences can mean something, or they can simply be a coincidence. Our instincts are telling us recent events have meaning."

"You aren't the first ones to say that," Natalie said, hoping to make them feel more at ease.

"Well," Madison started, "before I begin, do you have a bird that seems to hang around you?"

Natalie thought of the crow that stayed close when she was outside.

"Yes, it's a crow."

"That's what we mean," Madison exclaimed. "It's all piling up. There's the freak storm that started it. Then there are the black cats, the birds, and all those vultures that showed up for the solar eclipse. We wouldn't go outside while they were hanging out in our trees."

"That was smart on your part. I didn't have a choice. Those birds were bold. I had to feed the chickens, and one of those vultures came so close that I thought I would be its breakfast."

"That's a dreadful image playing in my head," Skylar said, shaking her head as if the image would disappear.

"When the vultures started gathering on the day of the eclipse, we discussed those hideous creatures that eat the dead as being an ominous sign," Madison said.

Skylar nodded her head in agreement and then changed the subject. "How did you get away?"

"It's a strange story. I've never told anyone about it. Of course, my father wouldn't believe me, so I'm still trying to figure it out myself."

"Maybe if you tell us, it will make sense," Madison said. She turned her complete focus on Natalie.

"I hesitate to say it. I don't want my first impression to be a bad impression."

"We won't think that about you," Skylar said. "I promise we can keep a secret."

Natalie studied them for a few minutes. Some people in the neighborhood made fun of their fascination with Halloween, calling them the nutty buddies. That didn't stop them from doing what felt right to them.

"Okay, this is the abbreviated version."

Both Skylar and Madison moved their chairs closer to Natalie.

"It was the morning of the total solar eclipse. Gloomy and dark outside, I reluctantly ventured out to the back to feed the chickens. I counted thirteen vultures."

Skylar interrupted. "Thirteen is a bad sign."

"Yes, it is. I already figured two strikes with the dilapidated homestead and the confining, shadowy path. The vultures made three strikes."

Madison interrupted. "If I thought three strikes, I would have turned around and gone back inside."

"Not with my father."

"I didn't think of a stern parent. Our parents let us get away with too much." Madison looked over at Skylar, who shook her head in agreement.

"That sounds nice."

"We didn't mean to interrupt your story. Go on," Madison said.

"Okay, here's the rest of the story. The vultures were restless and took continuous flights over my pasture. I fed the older chickens and ran to the tack room. I stayed there until I thought it was safe. Then, I ran and fed the younger chickens in the back stalls. As I locked the door to the young chickens' enclosure, I turned around to see a vulture near me. I froze. He hopped towards me. He was so close to me; I could feel and smell his putrid breath. I figured that was the end of me. Game over."

Natalie stopped, closed her eyes, and relived the moment.

"What happened next?" Skylar asked, anxious to hear the rest of the story.

Natalie stared at the ground, taking a deep breath. "A whirlwind came out of nowhere and engulfed the bird. It picked him up and pulled him high into the sky. As it went higher and over your property, the winds plucked the feathers off his body. With three feathers left, the vulture dropped on your side of the fence."

Madison and Skylar sat there stunned.

"I've played it hundreds of times in my head. No rational explanation can explain it. However, I'm sure I wouldn't be sitting here if it hadn't happened that way."

"Wow," Skylar said.

"While taking the bird away, there was a light with that wind that allowed me to see what was happening. After it dealt with the vultures, the light stayed with me until I got back to the house. I had the feeling something good protected me."

"Not meaning to upset you, but do you think it was your mother's spirit?" Skylar asked.

"No, Mom came to me the night of the storm. I knew it was Mom by her fragrance that surrounded me. The thing with the vulture was the wind and the light. There wasn't a fragrance."

"How incredible that your mother let you know she was okay. That's so amazingly special," Skylar said, tears glistening in her eyes.

"I agree with Skylar on your mom. On the vultures, that is weird. I can see why you didn't mention it to your father," Madison said, ignoring her sister's tears.

"He would yank me to counseling sessions. I don't blame him. I keep running it through my mind, trying to come up with a logical explanation."

"I don't think you're going to solve that one, Natalie," Skylar said, wiping tears off her face.

"I think you're right, Skylar. So, let me ask you a question." Madison and Skylar both nodded for Natalie to go ahead.

"Has one of your parents ever told you stories about your ancestors and magic?"

"We're adopted," Skylar said.

"No magic in our adopted parents, so it's strange we've always had a fascination with Halloween. Even more peculiar is that we have a natural talent for making brooms. We made the brooms we brought out tonight," Madison said.

With that, Madison went over and picked up both brooms. She brought them to Natalie.

Natalie studied each broom. They were beautiful, with intricate carvings along the handle. Each carving featured a large white, blue, red, or green gemstone at the center of the design.

"What do the carvings and the four gemstones mean?"

"After drawing the design, we researched the symbols and gem colors on the internet. They are the four elements…air, water, fire, earth," Skylar said.

"Your brooms are beautiful."

"What's odd is when we first considered making the brooms, we said we wanted to carve a design and add gemstones. We both sat down to draw up designs. When we showed each other the designs and the gemstones, the drawings and colors of the gemstones were identical," Skylar said.

Madison added, "It really freaked us out."

"Even stranger," Skylar said, "was an enormous pile of sticks and twigs on the porch of the old homestead. It's what we use to make the broomsticks."

Madison nodded her head as Skylar continued to speak. "The wood was already at the proper size needed. It isn't oak or pine. We're not sure what type of tree, but it's perfect for our brooms."

Natalie remained stuck on the part where they had said they went on the porch of the old homestead. "Did you go inside the old homestead?"

"No," Skylar said, shaking her head at the same time. "The scarecrows are creepy, the porch has broken boards, and that old homestead is probably full of spiders and roaches."

"It took a boatload of nerves just to run up there, grab a couple of big limbs, a load of twigs, and get out of there. We'll only do it on the sunniest days," Madison said.

Natalie visualized them, each encouraging the other to run up to the porch and grab the wood.

"You're brave. I'm terrified of the old homestead and the scarecrows. I swear those clownish scarecrows turn and look at me. I don't like clowns, and I don't like scarecrows that turn and stare at me."

"Us too!" both Madison and Skylar exclaimed at the same time.

Natalie relaxed and sighed with relief at being able to talk with someone about the strange occurrences and their cats.

She glanced over at Jericho. He sat close to the fire, seemingly watching the flames. Natalie felt Jericho focused more on their conversation than on the fire. She often had the impression that he understood her discussions and what was up on her computer.

As they sat there, Skylar jumped up and exclaimed, "I forgot to bring out the refreshments. I'll be right back."

When Skylar went into the house, Madison looked over at Natalie. "What do we do now?"

"Not sure," Natalie said, "but my mother used to tell me stories about our magical ancestors. I just don't remember the stories. Not even a little because I didn't think the stories were true."

Madison nodded her head in agreement. "It's strange for us because we come from different biological parents. Adopted at a young age, we don't know our history. Sometimes we get a flash memory about our early years in a pink and purple playroom, but nothing else we can piece together."

"Pink and purple playroom. That's unique," Natalie said, interrupting Madison.

"What makes it more unique is that we both dream that the walls are painted with various-sized purple balloons. Skylar likes pink, and I like purple, so that makes sense, but our dreams are identical. So strange."

"It could be a memory from a traumatic event in your childhood. No clue why you were placed for adoption?"

"None. We only have that weird dream, and then we're perplexed as to why we have the same talent and fascination for Halloween since we have different birth parents. We've asked our adopted parents, but they refuse to give us any information. They're very secretive and protective."

Skylar returned with the refreshments. Everyone took a drink and two cookies. As they munched on cookies, they watched the crackling, colorful flames. Sitting close to the fire, Jericho seemed focused on the fire and mesmerized by the unusual colors.

"Do you ever feel that your cat understands what you're saying?" Natalie asked the two as she took another bite.

"Definitely," Skylar answered.

As if Jericho confirmed the answer, he turned around and took his time looking at each girl. All of them froze and stopped eating.

It took a couple of minutes for the girls to relax.

"Thank you for inviting me over tonight," Natalie said to both Madison and Skylar. "I really appreciate getting the chance to meet both of you."

As Natalie stood up, she stretched, yawned, and then said, "Jericho, I need to get up early for school. I'm ready to head back."

Jericho turned around and pranced over to Natalie. The three girls watched him, and then they exchanged knowing looks. Natalie waved goodbye as they headed for the front road.

Walking back to her house, she mulled over how they had each spoken about strange occurrences. Something was happening, and they needed to learn more without having to wait for it to happen. She thought about getting some kind of protection.

Once the word protection popped into her head, Natalie looked down at Jericho. For some unknown reason, when Jericho was home, she felt protected. She laughed, thinking that with his personality, he was better than a guard dog. Jericho looked at her as if reading her mind and nodded. Spooky.

Once they walked into her bedroom, she grabbed her plain black pajamas and headed to the shower. The hot water relaxed her. Still toasty from the shower, she dressed, noisily sighed, and buried herself under a mound of blankets. Within seconds, she slept.

The blaring alarm clock woke her. "Why do mornings always have to come so quickly and be so dark?"

Natalie yawned as she trudged through the narrow path to the older chicken's enclosed coop. Standing before the large, enclosed cage, the beam from her flashlight showed mounds across the ground. Her heart raced as she clung to the fencing, pressed her face against the metal, and directed the beam to the ground.

Too traumatized to scream, she stared at the dead chickens strewn across the enclosed cage. The rooster must have defended his hens. His body was the only one scattered on the ground.

With a trembling hand, she moved the flashlight beam around the enclosure; she saw the spot where the raccoons had removed a large rock and dug into the cage. Horrified, Natalie backed away from the shelter. She continued backing away until she reached the path. On the path, she turned around and ran to the house.

Running into the house, she called her father at work.

"Dad!" Natalie cried, and then the rest of her sentence became a jumble of words in tears. She sat down at the kitchen table and leaned over the phone.

"Natalie, what's the matter!?" Karl asked, alarmed.

"Dad, the chickens!" Natalie wept, with the rest of her sentence more sobbing than words. Her tears fell on the table.

"Take it slow, Natalie. I can't understand you," Karl said, panicking but trying to sound calm.

"Raccoons with the chickens," Natalie cried.

Karl stayed quiet for a moment, listening to Natalie sob and trying to make sense of what she said.

"Did the raccoons get into the cage?" he asked, already knowing the answer.

"Yes," Natalie sobbed.

"I'm so sorry, Natalie. Don't go back there. We'll take care of them tonight."

That evening, they buried the chickens three feet deep within the enclosed cage and placed heavy stones over the massive grave. That wasn't enough to protect the buried chickens. Several days later, the raccoons dug up a leg of the rooster and left it lying on the ground inside the cage.

After crying for days, Natalie wondered why bad things continued to happen. There had to be a reason, but what?

Chapter 13
White Mist

With the end of the semester fast approaching, it had been weeks of endless studying and homework. Today was the rare day of no studying and no homework. Propped up by pillows, Natalie lounged on her bed and picked up the book she had started before dinner.

Riveting, she couldn't put it down. She tried. She kept telling herself just a few more pages, but the pages turned into reading the entire book. Now, irritated with herself for not locking the chickens into the inner shelter before dinner, she jumped up and rushed to the kitchen.

Natalie grabbed a flashlight and scurried out the back door. Jericho trotted behind her.

Entering the path to the barn, she groaned, seeing that the outside barn light hadn't come on tonight. If she had known, she would have brought a better flashlight. The large full moon produced more light than the weak light emitting from her flashlight. Not good.

They picked up their pace. Halfway through the narrow path between the house and the barn, a gentle breeze upgraded to wind. The numerous scrub oaks that arched over the path in their fight for sunlight were extra creepy. Many dead, brittle branches hanging low creaked and swung in the wind. Long strands of low-hanging Spanish moss swayed back and forth just above her head.

The yellowish light from the unusually large full moon cast dark, moving shadows on the ground from the arching scrub oaks and swaying moss. The thick, waist-high palmettos on either side of the path easily hid snakes and other deadly creepy crawlers. Those thoughts alarmed Natalie because she couldn't see the creatures in the dark or get off the confining path.

Natalie's imagination worked overtime. Her eyes darted from one side of the path to the other side of the path. Nervously glancing from side to side, she didn't see the looming spiderweb in the middle of the path.

Her face slammed into the web. Sticky webbing clung to her face and hair while the spider dangled just above her shoulder.

"Ahh, spider!" Her scream filled the air.

Before she could run her hands down her face and through her hair, Jericho's lion mane burst out, surrounding his panicked eyes. He jumped high into the air with his feet running before they hit the ground.

Focused on her own situation, she frantically wiped her sticky hands down her pants. What remained, she pulled off her hands and stuck those to her pants.

Breathing heavily, she leaned over and shook her hair. Something dark hit the ground and took off.

She stood up and saw Jericho running through the path. Calming down, she figured her scream had scared him, so whatever animal lurked in the palmettos also ran for cover.

That thought changed her focus from the ground to the trees. Now she worried about the hundreds of red bugs hidden in the overhanging, bug-infested moss waiting for a chance to jump on her. Even though Natalie knew it was the ground moss-infested, she itched.

By herself, Natalie focused on her surroundings and any unusual sounds. That's when she noticed the usual night sounds of crickets and frogs at the pasture lake weren't happening tonight. It was quiet. Too quiet. She only heard the palmettos hitting against her and the wind moving through the trees.

She picked up her pace as the temperature dropped and the wind strengthened. A warning chill ran straight up

Natalie's back, and the hair on her arms bristled as the cold penetrated her long-sleeved shirt.

She moved out of the path into the wide-open area before the barn. As she did, she told herself not to look over at the old and deserted two-story original homestead. She would die if that second-floor door swung open and something flew out of there. She didn't want to see any glowing red eyes peering out of the windows, either.

She wanted to kick herself for reading instead of locking up the chickens. She didn't like being at the barn in the dark.

Turning her thoughts to her father, she knew her no-nonsense father wouldn't understand her refusal to lock up the young hens. She couldn't do that to him, and she couldn't do that to the young chickens. The exposed, long, bare-boned rooster leg was a reminder of what could happen to the young hens if she didn't secure them in the back stalls.

"Why can't you leave the rooster leg buried? Let him be at peace." Natalie yelled out, breaking the eerie silence.

It upset her that she had already buried the leg three times. Three times, an animal dug it up. She hadn't moved the stones to bury the leg for the fourth time.

Standing there, she couldn't get the older chickens and rooster out of her mind. Reliving that discovery made her remember the vulture at the back stalls. She needed to go back there in the dark to lock up the chickens. What if she turned on the tack room light? She reasoned the light probably didn't reach back there making her dread going over there with her dim flashlight.

"Come on, Natalie. Get a backbone! The sooner you get this done, the sooner you return to the house!"

Still with his puffed-up lion mane, Jericho gave her a strange look.

Natalie looked at him and laughed.

"You look ridiculous. My scream wasn't that scary."

Jericho's rattled appearance gave Natalie the courage to head towards the side of the barn. Out of nowhere, she felt an icy push. Terrified yet maintaining her balance, Natalie spun around to see who it was, but no one was there. Her mood changed as her heart raced.

She couldn't decide whether to run for the house through the path or take the long gravel road. Which one? Before she thought it through, another ice-cold push hit her hard.

With Jericho in the lead, they both ran for the old chicken coup.

Natalie swung the wooden door open, stepped around the gravestones, and then yanked the narrow door to the inner cage open. She stayed away from the high-roosting boxes attached to the back of the cage. She stepped over the bottom of the thin ramp that the chickens used to climb up to the boxes. Trying not to disturb the wild vines that covered the sides of the inner cage, she sat down in the dirt and hoped the vines would hide them.

She grabbed Jericho and held him close to her. Biting her lower lip to stay quiet, Natalie panicked when she noticed a white mist rising from the ground around the gravestones. As it swirled and built in thickness, covering the entire outer and inner cages in its mist, it almost became solid white. The piercing moonlight could not seep through and expose them. Trying to calm down and remain still, she watched as small silhouettes took shape within the mist.

"What are those things!?" Natalie whispered to Jericho.

The forms became more defined. Staring at the ghosts of her deceased chickens, they watched as the apparitions left no space between each other. Growing in height, they encircled Natalie and Jericho. The supernatural forms turned and faced outward. A forceful wind swirled around the ghostly spirits, but the wind could not penetrate the apparitions. It howled and increased in force, but it still could not break through the spirits.

Just as it seemed this battle would last through the night, a stronger outside wind inserted itself between the spirits and the menacing wind. Building in strength, it pushed back the threatening wind and picked up the lone rooster's leg. With the spur facing forward, the rooster's leg flew with lightning speed into the heart of the coldness. Upon impact, the brutal cold shattered into hundreds of pieces, like glass. Instantly, the cold disappeared. Just as the white mist and the ghostly bodies had appeared, they began to sink back into the ground.

The barn light came on at the same time Jericho clawed his way out of her arms. Too shaken to yell at him, she stood up on wobbly legs that could hardly support her. Not moving nearly as fast as she had when they entered the coop, she stumbled outside the structure. Trying to calm down and not think about what happened, she brushed the dirt off her clothes.

Natalie could feel a lingering presence. A good presence. She looked up.

"I owe you again. Thank you!"

She headed over to the young hens. Stepping through the enclosure and into the back stalls, she saw the chickens safely settled in their nesting boxes. With relief, she shut the top and bottom stall doors and secured the clips. While locking the outside enclosure, strength returned to her legs. Natalie called Jericho. Together, they ran through the path to the house as fast as they could.

Crawling into bed, she closed her eyes and fell asleep. The bizarre night replayed in her mind, startling her awake. She grabbed a book off the nightstand. Half an hour later, she tried to sleep, but the strange night again took over her thoughts. She grasped the book and read it until exhaustion closed her eyes.

She fell into a nightmare. Howling winds circled and entrapped her in the center of the confining path. The arching branches with bony fingers reached down and grabbed her hair to keep her in place. The whipping moss attached to her hair and traveled down her face and shoulders. Hundreds of red-eyed bugs marched down the moss, covered her hair, and entered her nose. She screamed at the same time the grandfather and grandmother clocks chimed midnight.

Alarmed by the nightmare, she had a strange feeling she wasn't alone in her room. Someone stood near her closet. She tried to move her head so her eyes could turn enough to see over there. Was she seeing a thin shadow about three feet tall? She wasn't sure. Every time she tried to focus, there was nothing there. Turning on the table lamp verified nothing different, but it left her feeling as if something else hid in the room. With that feeling, she passed on checking the chiming clocks.

No way would she look in the closet or under her bed. Instead, she placed pillows on the edge of the bed and buried herself in the blankets. Safely wrapped with a pillow barrier, she made sure her feet and hands stayed away from the edge. There would be no hanging any parts of her body off the bed. She had heard enough of those awful stories to know what lurked in the dark. It didn't matter if they were silly stories to scare kids. It wasn't going to happen.

It seemed she only slept for a short period before a nightmare woke her. Tossing and turning after waking from each nightmare, she struggled longer and longer to get back to sleep.

No energy existed in her body as the alarm clock sounded, and she lay there replaying the horrific events of last night. The third of December would forever be etched in her brain as a living nightmare.

That recalled her other nightmare. School. Natalie wished she could stay home and take all virtual classes like Madison and Skylar. She dreaded school. She didn't fit in.

Gary came to mind as he frequently embarrassed her. She recalled his friends joining in until they needed her help. Too bad. Since they had no problem humiliating her, they could get help from one of their clueless friends.

Natalie shook Gary out of her mind and threw back the covers. To her surprise, she saw she still wore yesterday's clothes. She had forgotten she had rushed into the house and jumped into bed last night.

Buried under blankets and pillows, she had felt safe until the nightmares started. Then, it had turned into a long, weary night of waking from nightmares and thinking a creature was hiding in her room. Today, she would have less energy than a zombie. With that thought, she dragged herself out of bed and headed to the bathroom.

After showering and dressing, she appraised herself in the large bathroom mirror. She could see why she wasn't popular. She was as ordinary as ordinary can be.

Her long, wavy hair appeared black, but outside in the sun, it was auburn. Because it never behaved itself, it usually stayed in a ponytail. Her dark brown eyes and pale skin made her look perfectly average.

Her clothes were also average. She usually wore blue jeans and a black long-sleeved shirt. During the winter, she would wear a black jacket with a hoodie. Her ears were pierced. She always wore the same small onyx earrings that used to belong to her mother.

Except for straightening her bangs each day, she never put any effort into changing how she looked. She was just 1 of 800 students at the high school. And if she didn't get out to the barn and handle her chores right now, she would run out of time and miss the school bus.

Chapter 14
An Unlikely Ally

Anxious over last night's ordeal, Natalie dreaded the half-mile hike to the bus stop. Even under the best of circumstances, she didn't enjoy making the morning walk in the dark. She prolonged her departure until the last minute.

Hustling down the long driveway, she turned onto Cobblestone Drive. Out of nowhere, loud squawking shattered the quiet. Natalie jumped, looked up, and frowned. The pesky crow endlessly squawked at his arrival.

"Shh," she hissed at the bird. In response, the bird swooped down and flew close to her. Alarmed, she ducked out of its way.

Continuing to squawk, the crow flew higher while circling her. Angrily whispering, "Go away!" didn't stop the crow as he continued to screech and circle.

Natalie complained in a louder voice. "Stop! You'll wake the whole neighborhood and the Petersons' nasty dogs!"

The crow seemed to understand as he stopped squawking, but he continued to fly in wide circles over her head.

She wondered why the crow was now a nuisance. Whatever the reason, she didn't care. It needed to end. She picked up her pace; it didn't stop the crow. He continued to make wide circles around her. Slowing to her normal pace, she watched the bird continue to loop around her.

When she reached the last property on her street, she stopped and impatiently waited for the bird to land. Somehow, there had to be a way to get it to leave, as there was no way she wanted the kids on the bus to see a crow circling her. Within a couple of minutes, the bird stopped and perched on a nearby fence post.

"What are you doing?"

The bird stared at her as if it were evaluating her.

"Look, there's a full cat feeder out at the barn. Why don't you go get something to eat and leave me alone?"

Just as she finished speaking, the crow flew from the fence post and landed on her right shoulder.

"What! Get off me! Shoo!" Natalie yelled, spinning around as she swung her left arm up to knock the bird off her shoulder. The shifting of her backpack caused her to stumble. She took a few rough steps before regaining her balance.

The bird flew back over to the fence and stared at her.

"Whatever you're thinking, don't!" Natalie fumed as she repositioned her backpack and tucked in her shirt.

The crow took flight and started circling her.

"Look, I have enough problems right now. I don't need to have a bunch of kids see a crow circling me. It looks bad. Just stop!"

With that, Natalie stomped off and turned onto the entrance road. The crow didn't stop, but he flew higher over her as she made her way to the bus stop. When she reached her destination, the crow flew up to a high branch of a nearby pine tree. He stayed there until the bus arrived. As she stepped inside the bus, the crow flew off. "Good riddance," she muttered to herself.

She sat in the fourth row of algebra, her math book opened to the assigned page, and her notebook opened to the completed homework. Her thoughts were elsewhere. Nothing made sense. She knew her mother was right; there were no coincidences.

To prove that point, she decided this morning that she would run over to the old homestead. She needed answers, and she was sure the answers involved the haunted homestead. Flooding the area with all the outside lights on the barn, she mustered the courage to stand close to the rusted perimeter fence. First to catch her attention were the scarecrows. Hand-linked remnants of a bygone period, the tattered scarecrows circled the perimeter of the building, starting and ending at the arbor.

Natalie turned her flashlight to the wooden arbor over the rusted gate. Thick Jasmine vines covered the lattice. Still, she could see a fabric tube from the scarecrow standing against the arbor, winding up and around the arbor, and attaching to the scarecrow on the other side. She had no idea why there wasn't a break in the connection, but she had a feeling the scarecrows were the first line of defense. Guards. Her proof came last night. For the briefest moments before running for the chicken coop, she had witnessed a green glow from the scarecrows.

She looked past the scarecrows to the old, thick tree stump that stood close to the front of the homestead. It stood as tall as Natalie. After all the years they had lived there, it remained the same rough stump, with the top third sticking out more than the rest. She easily saw three distressed faces on it, but the one to the right with its mouth open wide in silent horror alarmed her the most. With her flashlight shining directly on it, deep holes where the eyes and mouth appeared were sunken pits that formed a pained expression. She half expected to see hundreds of long, slimy worms oozing from its mouth and eyes.

She came away with no answers. But, after last night, the homestead and the scarecrows seemed mild compared to all the strange happenings. Her notebook for unexplainable things now had many pages of strange events and odd behavior. It may have started out with the creepy homestead and scarecrows, but it went well beyond them. Now, there were occurrences that involved her.

Natalie replayed the various events in her mind. What was the connection? Homestead, scarecrow, storm, Jericho, butterfly, crow, vultures, rescued, ghostly white mist, annoying crow. Exhausted, she struggled to make a connection. Frustrated, she gave up and focused on the teacher.

Without pressure, the answer came to her. She jumped in her chair as she realized all these strange things started happening the day her mother died. It wasn't the storm. It had to do with her mother—even Jericho. He arrived the morning after her mother passed. She recalled her conversation with Madison and Skylar, who also had a cat and a bird show up the morning after her mother had died.

As she continued to process this revelation, the teacher called for Kelvin to go to the chalkboard and solve one of the homework problems. Getting up from his chair, Kelvin reached over and snatched Natalie's notebook. Shocked, she wasn't fast enough to grab her notebook back. She could only watch Kelvin stroll up to the front of the classroom with her notebook and face the chalkboard. He started writing the answer.

While Natalie fumed at him for stealing her work, she heard the screeching of Kelvin's chair being roughly occupied. She glanced over to see Joel sitting there. Joel looked at Mr. Xanders and gave him a thumbs-up sign. Mr. Xanders nodded yes, but he didn't seem pleased. As the teacher turned his attention to Kelvin and his work on the chalkboard, Joel handed her a note. She opened it and read, "Second Sign: Full Cold Super Moon." Her eyes widened with the realization that last night was a Full Cold Moon.

She had barely finished reading the words when the teacher's stern voice broke the silence.

"Joel, bring the note to me." Mr. Xanders extended his hand, waiting for the note.

Joel looked uncomfortable as he took the note back. He got up, shoved it in his left pocket, and headed towards the teacher. Lainey raised her hand.

"Mr. Xanders, Mr. Xanders," Lainey called out as she waved her hand in the air. For a moment, Mr. Xanders shifted his attention to Lainey. Even though Lainey was gorgeous with thick auburn hair and blue eyes and was one of the most popular girls in school, she never acted like she was better than anyone else. She also never made a scene that caused her to be the center of attention.

"What is it, Lainey?" Mr. Xanders asked as he motioned with his hand for Joel to give him the note.

"Is there an easier way to solve this problem? You know how much I struggle with algebra."

"No, that's the way it's done," Mr. Xanders said, focusing back on Joel and the note he now held in his hand.

She watched as the teacher read the note. He looked up at Joel. "Why didn't you just ask Natalie to join the debate team without disrupting the entire class?"

"I don't know," Joel said while shaking his head like he didn't know why he thought a note was the way to go.

Natalie didn't understand what had happened. How did he switch the note? How did he even know to have a different note? It didn't make any sense. She looked over at Lainey, who looked down at her math notes.

"Well, maybe you will come up with a better answer when I see you and Natalie after school."

Natalie's eyes went wide as she inhaled in shock at the teacher's comment. *This can't be happening. I'll have to stay after school because of that stupid note.*

She trembled at the thought of missing the school bus and having no way to get home. It was too far to walk, and it would be hours before her father could pick her up. Besides being exhausted from all that had happened last night, she would be stranded at school. For her remaining classes, she couldn't concentrate.

When the last bell rang at 1:55 p.m., Natalie shoved her books in her backpack and sprinted to Mr. Xanders' classroom. Maybe, if the meeting was short, she could still catch the bus. To her surprise, she rushed in and saw Joel and Lainey. Lainey looked over at her.

"I'm taking you home after the meeting."

"Thank you!" A crushing weight of dread lifted off her. She could breathe again.

The relief only lasted a few minutes as she wondered why Lainey would do this for her. No one at school had ever gone out of their way for her. So popular, Lainey was an unlikely ally. She questioned her motive because this probably wasn't good for Lainey's reputation.

Natalie's focus changed when Mr. Xanders held his hand out. "Produce the actual note, Joel."

Joel's eyes widened as he replied, "I gave you the note in class."

The teacher's frown, with his piercing blue eyes staring into Joel's, told him this wasn't a game. Joel pulled the crumpled note from his pocket and handed it to the teacher. Mr. Xanders looked at it. Then he looked at Natalie.

She uneasily glanced at him. The teacher continued to observe her. She felt like a bug under a microscope. Her face warmed, flushing deep red. She lowered her head and stared at her sneakers. She would do anything to avoid those ice-cold blue eyes.

With his blue eyes, snow-white hair, and appearance that was as ancient as time itself, it was hard to believe this was the same person many students nicknamed Santa Claus. Obviously, they hadn't been privy to this side of him or the uncomfortable stare that he was giving her.

"Natalie," Mr. Xanders began, "what do you know about the Second Sign and the Full Cold Moon?"

His question startled her. She glanced up. "Nothing."

He pondered her short answer for a couple of minutes. Then, he showed her the note. "Why would Joel give you this note?"

"Because several months back, Joel told me he was reading something about a triominous. He said it could be astrological signs such as a Full Cold Moon," She answered without taking her eyes off the note.

Curious, the teacher said, "Triominous. That's an interesting word. What would three omens have to do with you?"

She shrugged her shoulders; she didn't know. She didn't have an answer, and Joel wasn't saying anything. Lainey was listening, but she wasn't saying anything, either. Mr. Xanders stood there for several minutes looking back and forth at the two of them as if that would get them to admit to some evil Full Cold Moon influence.

The teacher turned his full attention back to her. "Did anything unusual happen last night during the Full Cold Moon, Natalie?"

The question surprised her. While her body slightly shook, she refused to look up and just shook her head no. She wasn't a good liar, even with white lies. She knew her eyes would give her away.

As it was, she could feel her face continue to burn from the blush. Hoping that with her head down, her bangs would cover her red face, her annoyance with Joel grew for putting her in this situation.

Continuing to study Natalie, the teacher sat down on the edge of his desk. "I won't ask any more questions about last night, but I noticed you were distracted in class today. You also look like you didn't get any sleep last night."

Joel and Lainey both turned to look at her. She kept her flaming red face down. To her, this was just another extension of the nightmares, except she was awake.

The teacher changed the subject. "Have any of you heard of a new club forming at school?"

All three of them answered with a no.

"I will deny it if you say you heard it from me, but I am warning you not to get involved."

Joel and Lainey stared at the teacher. Natalie, still blushing, glanced up before focusing back on the floor. What an odd thing to say.

"Many teachers helped when it was first introduced, but now it is a handful of people developing the program. Character...or character flaw...played a part in who took part. Money is going to make it happen. I am getting an ugly vibe from the person forming this pilot program. Don't get involved."

"Why are you telling us?" Joel asked.

"I've been teaching for over 25 years; I can read my students quite well. Instead of being part of the problem, I think you will be part of the solution."

Surprised, they glanced at each other and then looked back at the teacher. Although the answer made them feel that he highly regarded them, it didn't actually answer the question. What was it about the person forming the club and the program itself that was so insidious?

Instead of answering that question, the teacher added to the mystery. "This is the last time it can be addressed at school. School is no longer a safe place to ask questions or make comments about unusual activities or signs. Don't trust anyone. If you need answers, see Wilfred or Jonathan at the bookstore. They know what to do. Again, keep this to yourselves. Do you understand?"

His face and his tone of voice were all it took for them to know he was serious. They each nodded yes and stood there in awkward silence. Mr. Xanders changed the subject as he dismissed them.

"You should research what the Full Cold Moon means. Learn about the last sign. I believe you will find the answers at the bookstore. However, besides not joining the club, keep this to yourselves. Seriously, I mean it; do not draw attention to yourselves."

Exhausted from last night and dragging as they made their way to Lainey's purple sports car, Natalie's mind churned with what the teacher had said. Could it get any worse? She didn't see how.

Once they settled in the car, Lainey turned to her. "Do you have any idea what that was about?"

"I don't know. It sounds ominous. Truthfully, I didn't get much sleep last night, so I'm having difficulty making any sense of what he said. I got the part about not joining the club. I wonder what kind of club it's going to be that he is so against it."

Putting the car into drive, Lainey replied, "I'm not so sure it's the club. I think it's more about who is putting it together."

Natalie relaxed and leaned back in the seat. It was easy to pull out of the school and onto the main highway, as the only students left at school were those taking part in after-school activities. She sighed and closed her eyes. The last thing she remembered was being thankful she had a ride home. She was so tired.

"Natalie." Lainey shook her shoulder.

Startled, Natalie opened her eyes and stared at Lainey. Why was Lainey with her? Then she remembered that Lainey had given her a ride home. They were now sitting in her driveway. Puzzled, she wondered how they got there. She didn't give out her address unless she talked in her sleep.

Struggling to piece things together and wake up, she looked at Lainey's amused expression. Understandable. She had no idea what happened between school and home. She decided it didn't matter and stretched.

"I'm sorry; I had no idea I was going to crash."

"Don't worry about it. You looked exhausted. It didn't help that Mr. Xanders focused on you instead of Joel. Joel was the one who started the whole thing. However, there seems to be a lot more to Mr. Xanders than just algebra."

"I agree with you on Mr. Xanders. His Santa Claus reputation is misleading."

Lainey understood the reference and laughed.

"I really appreciate the ride, Lainey." Natalie opened the door and got out of the car.

"When Mr. Xanders said we had to stay after school, I panicked. My father works in another county and doesn't get home until after six. I have no cash on me. I guess I could have called my father; he would have arranged a ride for me. Obviously, I'm not thinking clearly, as last night was beyond awful. I wouldn't tell Mr. Xanders that, but it took a toll on me."

"Do you want to talk about it?"

Natalie thought about it. *Definitely, but I'll talk with Pru about last night.* She recalled Pru telling her at the memorial service that when strange things happen, she should see her. Today was that day. With an appreciative smile at the offer, she said "no" and closed the door.

She waved goodbye. Instead of leaving, Lainey hopped out of the car and faced Natalie. "If you ever need a ride, let me know. I hope we become good friends."

Before she could say anything, Lainey got back into her car and drove off. Natalie stood there confused. She didn't understand why Lainey wanted to be friends with her.

The brief nap on the way home from school had restored some of her energy. After completing her chores, she grabbed the bucket of spiderwebs and headed over to the northwestern section of the subdivision. Walking onto Pru's property, she observed all the ancient oaks that filled the front yard. What a beautiful piece of property. She knew it would be impossible for Pru to maintain ten acres, so she wondered who took care of the property for her.

From a distance, she spotted enormous candles on either side of Pru's front door. Seeing the carved faces, she burst into laughter. Wow! There is yet another person in the neighborhood who has Halloween decorations up all year. She marveled at the size of them with their large blue eyes, big noses, wide mouths, and thick bodies. But, as she got closer, she stopped and shrieked. "You have got to be kidding me!"

The eyes on both candles blinked and shifted towards her.

"I'm absolutely going to lose it," Natalie exclaimed. She tried to figure out if this was the latest in automated security systems or just one more strange phenomenon. Wanting answers from Pru but not knowing if she could handle one more creepy thing, she turned around to leave. Just as abruptly, she turned back around and faced the candles. Still in disbelief, she again turned and took a few steps to leave before she turned back around and then stood there. In doubt, she stared at the candles and tried to figure out what to do.

Growing impatient at her indecisive mood, the candle to the left of the door yelled, "Good golly, Miss Molly, would you make up your mind! It's a simple decision.

Either you leave, or you come closer. That's it. Now, make your choice."

Natalie remained stuck in place. *Do they really sell these in stores?* She had her doubts.

"We don't have teeth, so we won't bite," the one to the left said as they both opened their mouths wide and showed her they didn't have any teeth.

They might not have teeth, but they had a good set of lungs as they broke out into rowdy laughter.

"Is this for real?"

"Maybe not, but again, we can't bite, and we don't have feet to chase you."

"Even so, I'm not sure I want to get any closer to the front door. How about if I go around to the back door?"

"Nope. There's only one way to enter."

"Why should I believe a candle?" She couldn't believe she was having a conversation with two wise guy candles.

"Simple. When our wicks light, the door will unlock, and you can step inside."

By saying that, both candlewicks burst into flames, and she heard a dramatic click of the front door unlocking.

She stood there long enough that Pru came to the front door. Pru laughed when she saw the expression on her face.

"They do tend to talk a lot, but they are harmless. Come on in, Natalie."

Obnoxious laughter filled the air as she walked up to the front porch. Pru stepped back. She walked by just as they yelled, "Boo!"

Natalie nearly dove through the doorway into the foyer, adding to their amusement as they started bellowing as if they had heard a hilarious joke.

"That wasn't funny, boys!" Pru scolded them and shut the door.

Fortunately, Natalie had placed a cover over the spiderwebs. She handed the bucket to Pru.

"Thanks. I wasn't sure if you would want to collect the webs for me."

"I watched my mom collect them on many occasions. I always thought she was getting rid of them."

"No, she gave them to me. Let me put these up, and I'll give the bucket back to you."

They made their way to the back of Pru's house. There, Pru had a custom bookcase along the whole back wall of her living room. Natalie marveled at all the books. Then she watched with fascination as Pru selected a book that opened a secret passageway into a hidden room. Peering inside the room, she saw that there were seven long rows of shelves on each of the three walls. Every shelf had large glass containers full of Variegated Orb Weaver webs. In the dark, the gold and white flecks in the webs glittered off and on. When Natalie got too close, the webs increased the glitter activity, and the room took on a faint glow.

"Well, look at that," Pru murmured, "definitely a sign."

"What sign?" Natalie moved closer to a section of the shelving. She enjoyed seeing the webs glitter intermittently.

"Too early to tell."

They moved out of the secret room and into the living room. It appeared to Natalie that Pru didn't want to say the reason. Maybe she enjoyed playing the mystery part. It would go with the long, flowing dark dress she was wearing and the numerous white candles of assorted sizes that were lit throughout the room. She could smell a slight aroma from the candles, but it was the smell of sandalwood incense that dominated the room.

Looking around the room, it was warm and inviting. It had a massive bookcase and a large number of white candles placed throughout the room. There was a cozy burgundy chair with a large glass container placed down by its foot. Next to the chair was a small table that had five glass jars. Each jar was full of crystal beads in red, blue, white, green, and black. A simple bracelet stand stood on the table. It overflowed with completed bracelets hanging on it. The massive bookcase was a focal point; the other focal point was the spacious fireplace. Over the fireplace mantle was a displayed broomstick encased in a clear trophy case. Engraved on the case was Aerial MMXVIII.

"Wow, Pru, where did you get the broom displayed over the fireplace?"

"Not now," Pru countered as she repositioned some of the white candles on the other side of the room. Stunned by the short answer, Natalie wondered why Pru didn't want to talk about the broom. It was in a special case, which meant she highly valued the broomstick. Now, she was curious to have the story behind it.

The finished bracelets seemed to be valued as much as the broom. When Natalie visited the secret room, she noticed an entire row of glass jars filled with finished bracelets. There had to be at least 500 bracelets. She had the feeling Pru liked her bracelets too much to part with one of them. She didn't know anyone who had one, and she was sure Pru didn't sell them in an online store.

Besides, Pru was the only one who called them a charm. Even though they looked nice on Pru's wrist, it didn't exactly sound appealing to be wearing a woven spiderweb for a bracelet. Natalie smiled at the vision of a gray, fuzzy bracelet on her wrist that could glitter in the dark when Pru announced she had one for her.

Startled, she looked up to see Pru holding a Variegated Orb Weaver bracelet for her.

"Are you serious!?" Natalie asked, surprised that Pru was giving her one of her prized spiderweb bracelets. While unique, she was sure it would be extremely itchy.

"Yes," Pru replied, "after last night's Full Cold Moon, you need the protection."

Exasperated, Natalie exclaimed, "What is it with the Full Cold Moon!? I'm tired of hearing those ominous words with no knowledge of the meaning."

"It's the second sign, and you need to be prepared." Pru reached for Natalie's hand.

"The second sign to what? How do you know that I had a strange encounter last night at the barn?"

"The Full Cold Moon is the second sign that things are changing. You need to be prepared."

She looked up at Pru. It was obvious from her expression that she didn't know what had taken place last night. Pru also didn't know about the long night of seeing shadows in her room.

"I can't prepare for something I don't know about."

"The first step is to wear the charmed Variegated Orb Weaver bracelet. The second step is to keep your crystal close to you. And, last, but not least, is to make friends with the crow."

"How do you know about the crystal and that pesky bird?"

"I'm sure you heard the story from your mother many times about crystals." Pru fitted the Variegated Orb Weaver bracelet on Natalie's wrist.

"Yes, when I was much younger, I heard the story dozens of times, but until recently, I never wore a crystal. Besides, with all the weird things happening, the crystal hasn't done anything." Natalie shook her head in frustration.

Pru may know the tools, but she didn't know what was happening.

"Unfortunately, this time it will. Your assignment today is to make friends with the bird. Give him a strong name, and I promise you he won't be as annoying. Also, it's time for you to go into the old homestead."

"Well," Natalie strongly replied, thinking about the morning view of the homestead, "that isn't going to happen."

She shuddered thinking of that old, dark, and musty interior. The exterior was bad enough, but the interior was even worse. Roaches hiding and rats waiting. Even in a blinding light, there wouldn't be enough light to keep those creatures away. *Besides, what would be there that was so important that I had to risk my life? Nothing came to mind.*

"It's time for you to go in there. If you aren't comfortable, take it in stages. First, open the gate and stand inside. The scarecrows will not bite you or tie you up and burn you at the stake. They are guardians, not guards."

"How can you be so sure?"

"I'm absolutely sure that they will not harm you. I have candles; you have scarecrows."

"Well, I think the scarecrows were clowns in their previous lives. I don't like clowns. As far as your candles, I'm not so sure they aren't devious creatures."

"Granted, they have a warped sense of humor, which makes it hard to believe they are guardians. However, their sole purpose is to guard me and this place. They ensure only the right people get inside my house."

"I'll think it over. This is asking a lot."

"Get it done as soon as possible. We're running out of time."

Short-fused from a lack of sleep, Natalie couldn't tell if Pru was playing a cat-and-mouse game with her. "Why don't you just tell me what is happening and what I need to do?"

Pru shook her head no. "The answer is in the old homestead."

Natalie wasn't going to get any answers. *It didn't make any sense. We're running out of time, and yet there are no answers to my questions unless I go into the old homestead.* In frustration, she shook her head. She was already tired and overloaded with nightmares without going into the old homestead.

As Natalie opened Pru's door, a blackbird flew into her home.

"It's okay, he's mine." Pru stood still as the bird flew to her shoulder.

"You know, it's getting weirder by the minute." She shook her head as she closed the front door behind her.

The candles were waiting for her to exit. "Next time, bring some candy."

"What?"

"What do you mean what? What I said was simple to understand, but let me speak slower and repeat myself. Bring candy with you next time."

"Or what?"

"We're Halloween decorations year-round. Trick or treat. No treat, we trick." They both roared with laughter at their own cleverness.

"Do you have a favorite candy?" Natalie walked down the steps.

"We're sweet, so we like candies that are tart." More obnoxious laughter.

"Highly debatable, but I'm not in the mood. So, do I need to feed you your treats?"

"Nope."

With that, they opened their mouths wide and out shot their tongues that stretched over three feet from their mouths. When they saw Natalie's horrified expression, they burst into another round of roaring laughter.

As they laughed, she let out an enormous sigh of relief that she was beyond them and the steps when they stuck out their tongues. Still, she knew it would be another image to add to her nightmares. *How can I forget the abnormally long tongues and wide mouths? What strange characters. Of course, my scarecrows are just as strange.*

As she walked home, she spun the Variegated Orb Weaver bracelet around, admiring Pru's handiwork. Pru was a gifted weaver. The bracelet didn't resemble a spider web. It had a few black crystal beads intertwined in the weave, giving it a current, trendy look. She smiled while thinking, *As for it being a charm, that was questionable.*

During her walk home, realizing she had forgotten the bucket, it dawned on her that she hadn't told Pru what had happened last night. Pru knew something bad had happened, but maybe she was more concerned with Natalie getting the answers inside the haunted house. She had a feeling that if she mentioned the shadow in her room, Pru would give her the same answer. She needed to go into the haunted house. As she concluded that she really didn't get any answers, the crow circled over her head. She looked up and said, "Edgar."

Squawking erupted along with other weird bird sounds as he swooped down toward Natalie. Obviously, the crow was unhappy with the selected name. She laughed and said, "Malcolm," and got the same disapproving squawking and diving towards her as she continued her walk home.

"Okay, okay." Who would believe her that she had an assignment to name a crow?

"I guess a traditional name doesn't fit a crow. I could call you Nightstalker, but you're also a pest during the day."

While she made that statement, the crow landed on her left shoulder. She gently brushed it off. She watched the bird hover beside her. "Look, you can't be doing that because it isn't what normal crows do."

The crow circled her again. As Natalie walked by the depressing, dark gray two-story mystery house, she felt eyes staring out from behind the black curtains. The hair on the back of her neck rose. Everyone in the neighborhood had heard scary descriptions of the man who lived there.

"Not today." She began running.

It took a few minutes for her to concentrate again on a name for the crow. "I can't believe I'm doing this for you, crow."

Several names came to mind, and she dismissed each one without saying them aloud. Now back on her own street, she continued the search for the perfect name for the pesky bird. While Natalie thought about a name for the crow, the Petersons' dogs charged the fence and viciously barked at her. She jumped and warily glanced at their angry faces, their teeth exposed; she felt like running, but she knew better. She averted her eyes and kept walking.

Most neighbors had dogs, but these dogs were not friendly, and their size added to her fear of them. As she picked up her pace, the three large dogs moved along beside her. This was bad. One of her fears was that one day the owners would forget to close the gate when they left for work. Later, one of the kids would let the dogs out of their backyard pen. She didn't want to think about a face-to-face encounter with those vicious dogs. She noticed the crow didn't like all the barking and running up and down the fence either because he disappeared.

A huge sigh of relief escaped Natalie's lips when she moved beyond the Petersons' property, and the dogs retreated to the back of their property. While she calmed down, the crow reappeared and started circling her. Reaching the front of her property, the perfect name popped into her mind.

"I'm going to call you Coal. You're black as coal, and coal has the potential to become a diamond. So right now, you're this rough thing until both of us figure out what we do with each other."

Apparently, the crow approved of the name and settled in flying straight and at a much higher distance away from her.

Chapter 15
The Burning Crystal

Freezing temperatures, heavy rains, and blustery weather lashed out for days at a time. Warm days would follow only to have the temperature plunge again. Natalie dreaded the freezing temperatures, as the cold always seemed to seep deep into her bones. Even bundled up in a lined jacket, sweatshirt, blue jeans, thick gloves, and heavy socks, she suffered in the cold.

On the coldest days, Natalie rushed through her morning chores before catching the school bus. Bundled in layers of clothes and still freezing, she didn't pay attention to anything but getting out of the cold. However, on one particularly chilly morning, as she exited the path before the barn, her flashlight caught a glow coming from the old homestead steps. Natalie turned the flashlight to see Jericho observing her from the top step.

"Why don't you come in where it's warm?" Natalie yelled at him, but he continued to watch her. She ran to the gate and called Jericho to come to her, but he stayed. The brutally cold wind whipped through her clothing. Shivering, she called one last time.

"Jericho, come to the house!"

He didn't budge. Miserable and out of time, Natalie gave up. She remembered Jericho with his mouth stuffed with vulture feathers as he headed for the old homestead. She surmised that if it got too cold for him, he had a way to enter that haunted old building.

The continual wintry weather dragged Natalie down. A nasty head cold resulted in her being absent from school on Friday. On Monday, with a signed excuse, she dragged herself to the high school's front office. Pushing the glass door wide open, she gasped in pain. Her chest burned.

Dashing over to the students' submission counter, she leaned over it. The crystal pendant moved off her skin. She sighed in relief. Desperate to avoid more pain, Natalie reached into her shirt to yank the crystal out, but she froze instead. The Variegated Orb Weaver bracelet rapidly glittered.

At the same time, rolling waves of immense negative energy radiated off a tall, older man standing at the receptionist's counter at the far end of the room. Facing the receptionist, he hadn't seen Natalie's reaction. Now, he turned to look at her.

The hair on the back of her neck stood up. Alarm bells went off in her head as she shoved her hand with the glittering bracelet into her pocket to hide it. Forcing a coughing episode and then faking a weak smile, Natalie took in his hard-lined face and his unsmiling, cold, blue eyes.

He changed his expression to a friendlier look, but waves of negative energy washed over her as the burning sensation on her chest resumed. Her eyes watered from the pain. Her mouth opened to heavy, panicked breaths. It took all her willpower not to yank the pendant off.

Biting her lower lip to endure the burning, Natalie filled out the student form. Using only one hand, she awkwardly stapled the excuse paper to the form and dropped all of it into the basket. As she turned around and headed for the exit, she could feel his eyes return to a cold, hard glare.

Ouch, ouch, ouch, Natalie thought as she ran to the nearest girls' bathroom and locked herself into a stall. She pulled the burning crystal out and inhaled in shock. The clear crystal had turned black. Where the crystal had touched her, a bright red burn in the crystal's shape marked her skin.

"What does this mean?" Natalie asked herself as she continued to look at the burn mark on her chest and study what had become of her crystal.

What should I do? Should I go to class without my crystal? I never worried before, but what if the Full Cold Moon has released something bad? Why do people keep bringing up the Full Cold Moon? Can I trust Mr. Xanders and ask him? Probably not because he said not to ask questions at school. Besides, he wants me to go to the bookstore to get answers. I have a hard time believing the answers are there. She shook her head in frustration.

Her priority had to be protection. Her crystal black and dead wouldn't provide that protection. Glancing down at Pru's Variegated Orb Weaver bracelet, it had stopped glittering. She hoped it would protect her until she could get home and somehow replace the crystal.

As Natalie entered her science class, the front chalkboard displayed the day's assignment. She froze and stared at it. Someone yelled for her to sit down. Making her way to her chair, she kept glancing back at the chalkboard.

Things were going from bad to worse. She wouldn't need to worry about the Full Cold Moon anymore. A Super Blue Blood Moon would occur in the next few weeks. Somehow, Natalie knew that would be the last sign.

After the second bell rang, Mr. Parrish, sitting at his desk, asked if anyone could tell him what would happen on January 31. Only one hand went up, and it belonged to Lainey.

"Lainey," Mr. Parrish began, "tell me what you expect will happen on January 31."

"There are three events all happening on that date. It's been over 150 years since the last time it occurred, but we're going to see it on January 31. It's the Super Blue Blood Moon."

"Okay," Mr. Parrish said, "but what does that mean?"

"Well, it's a blue moon because it's the second full moon in the same month. It's also a supermoon because it will appear bigger and brighter than a usual full moon. But the most interesting part is that it will also have a lunar eclipse. The Earth's shadow will cover the moon, and it will look red."

Mr. Parrish had been nodding his head in approval as Lainey explained what would occur on January 31.

"Excellent, Lainey." He got up and walked around to the front of his desk.

"The last time this occurred was March 31, 1866."

Mr. Parrish stopped as someone shouted from the back of the room. "Are we all going to be possessed?"

Everyone laughed except for Natalie and Lainey.

Mr. Parrish waited for the laughter to end. Then he focused on Kelvin.

"Do you own a wolf skin belt?"

Kelvin stalled to add drama to his answer before simply replying 'no'.

"Well, then, you're no Peter Stubbe, so you should be fine."

As Mr. Parrish continued to talk about the Super Blue Blood Moon, Natalie focused on the experience with the man in the front office. *He looked like an old, angry guy radiating negative energy, but would that cause my crystal to burn and turn black? Could he be so toxic that he drained my crystal? He had turned and looked at me. Did he know something I don't know? It seems like many people are hinting at something, but not saying anything.*

Suddenly, Natalie noticed the teacher had stopped talking, and papers were being distributed. She hadn't been paying attention, but she took one and passed the last paper to the person next to her. A pop quiz on the Super Blue Blood Moon.

"This should be an easy test for you," Mr. Parrish said. "That includes you, Connor. By the many notes you were taking, you should have a 100."

Everyone knew Mr. Parrish was being sarcastic. Connor never paid attention. He had a goth look and was always writing in his notebook. It never had anything to do with science or any of his other classes. No one knew what he was writing, but he looked up and gave Mr. Parrish a thumbs-up sign.

After 15 minutes, the papers were collected and randomly redistributed to the students for them to grade. Natalie got Connor's paper. Shocked at what she saw, Natalie turned around and looked at Connor. He stared back at her. Natalie couldn't believe it. There were 12 questions, and for each answer, he had written a lyric on the Super Blue Blood Moon.

How can I mark his answers wrong? Amazed and impressed, she read each question and drew arrows from his answers to those that best matched the questions. It took her longer than the others to grade, but by the time she finished, Connor had an 80. She didn't want to turn in his assignment. She wanted to keep his song. Of course, she couldn't, and Connor would get his graded assignment back.

"Natalie," Mr. Parrish said to get her attention, "you need to turn that paper in for the student to get a grade."

As the teacher said that, he walked over and held out his hand. He looked down at what Natalie had done to Connor's paper.

"Interesting." Mr. Parrish looked over at Connor. Connor raised his eyebrows in question at the teacher's comment.

"Connor, it appears you have earned an 80 on the quiz."

Clapping, foot stomping, whistling, and obnoxiously loud cheers of congratulations erupted as students focused their full attention on Connor. Mr. Parrish tried to regain control of the class, but it was a lost battle. As the ruckus continued, Connor frowned and looked over at Natalie. Horrified, she knew his attire drew attention, but she also knew that Connor liked to isolate himself from others.

Turning away, she looked down at her notebook as if there was something that she needed to read. Head down, she hoped the class would soon come to order. It didn't happen. It seemed more like the dismissal bell would signal the end of the class.

While Mr. Parrish waited for the class to settle down, Natalie couldn't believe all this mayhem was simply for giving Connor some credit for his answers. She expected Connor would pack his backpack and storm out of the classroom. He didn't. In the meantime, the teacher reached his limit. Erasing the answer key on the chalkboard, he wrote in large print, YOU'RE ABOUT TO BE ASSIGNED A MAJOR ESSAY DUE TOMORROW. The class immediately quieted down.

"That's better!" Mr. Parrish walked around his desk and sat down. Looking long and hard at each student, he remained quiet for a few minutes. Just before the bell rang, he stated, "I hope there's an opportunity on January 31 for you to witness this rare event."

Natalie hurried out of the room for her next class. Connor caught up to her. "Hey, what did you do to my quiz?"

With only five minutes between classes, Natalie continued in the direction of her next class.

"You had the right answers, but not in the right places. I moved them around. It wasn't a big deal. The others made it a big deal."

She slowed down and glanced at Connor.

"Connor, I have a fully equipped music studio. If you're ever interested in practicing, you're welcome to use my place. My father said I could have anything but a swimming pool. I picked a music studio. Just let me know, and I can give you my address."

"Not interested, even though I already know where you live."

Surprised, Natalie stopped and stared at him. A boy almost crashed into her. Connor turned and headed in the opposite direction.

Wow, he is strange on so many different levels. Still, as she hurried to her next class, she decided to partner with him on a science project, so she might get a chance to know him.

For the rest of the day, Natalie didn't see the stranger. Even so, the day dragged on as she stayed on high alert. Time lagged as it seemed to take the school bus forever to drop her off at the front of her neighborhood. As soon as her feet touched the ground, she took off running and ran the entire half mile home.

Dropping her bookbag on the kitchen table, she turned around and headed out the door for Pru's house. She passed Joel's house when she remembered the candy. Turning around and running as fast as she could, she ran back inside the house, grabbed the two bags of candy she had in her bedroom, and took off again. Flying high above Natalie, Coal followed her.

As soon as she saw the two candles, they saw her. The left candle shouted, "I hope you remembered the candy. Otherwise, the trick we've been planning is about to happen."

Natalie lifted the two bags of candy up in the air for them to see.

"Well, hurry up! We haven't got all day!" With that, they burst into rowdy laughter. Since they were permanently stuck there, she laughed at the lame joke.

As she got closer, she saw their excitement about getting candy. Natalie told herself they were just animated candles, but it made her feel bad that they didn't get a lot of attention. She made a mental note to visit Pru more often and bring treats.

"Promise me I will be safely inside before you stick your tongues out."

Natalie watched them turn serious. "We will wait, but you'd better hurry." With that, their flames lit, and the lock released.

She opened each bag and put the candy in front of each candle. As she pulled on the front door, she heard the first big flicks of candy into their mouths. She ducked as Coal flew over her head and straight into the house.

When Pru saw Coal fly in, she laughed.

"So, what did you name him?"

"Coal. How do you know Coal is a male?"

"It has always been so."

"Okay, no more secrets."

Natalie watched Coal fly over to the kitchen counter, where Pru's blackbird ate crackers. Pru walked over and broke up some crackers for Coal. She placed the cracker pieces on a small paper plate in front of him.

"Those are your crackers, Merlin. These crackers are for Coal."

Pru finished with the birds and focused on Natalie's comment. "All the secrets are in the Grimoire."

"The what?"

"The Grimoire is a record of magic about your family. I believe you know where it's located."

Natalie's frustration increased. "I've never even heard of a Grimoire. Truthfully, I've never even heard of the word before now. How would I know where it's located?"

Natalie glanced in Coal's direction and grew even more annoyed as she watched him gobble up every little piece of cracker. Coal seemed to be starving, despite her daily feedings. Not only did she feed him, but he would steal cat food from the bowl near the back of the barn.

"It's in the old homestead."

"Oh, great. I need to go into the House of Horrors."

"That's not what it is, and sometimes things look bad to keep other things out."

"Okay, maybe another day. Too many things are happening all at once. Too many terrible things, and I can't take it all in yet."

Just as Natalie said that a ghost floated over them. Pru answered her, but she didn't pay attention.

"Did I just see a ghost? Did it just head towards the spiderweb room? If so, what the heck is that all about?"

"Mira." Pru didn't like to stand for long, so she headed for her oversized recliner and dropped into it. She pushed back and elevated her feet.

"Mira." Natalie, astounded at what she had witnessed, shook her head as if to wake up.

"Please bring a chair over and sit down while I give you a brief history, so this makes sense to you."

Pru waited for Natalie to get comfortable before she began speaking in a somber voice. "I was always different. While I wasn't accepted at school and in most social settings, my family also didn't accept me. I even have a different last name from my siblings. They like to mention the different last names to remind me that I'm not one of them."

Natalie sighed, feeling sorry for Pru. *How could her family be so cruel as to tell her she didn't belong?* She didn't want to hear any more of this story, but she knew Pru wanted to tell her.

"When I was twelve, I began to see unusual things. Twelve is early. Normally, sixteen is when mages discover their magical abilities. I learned that from your mother. However, my ability to see spirits came early. Most people can't see the ghosts that inhabit this place. I made the mistake of talking to ghosts and other spirits in front of my family. It didn't go well, resulting in many counseling appointments. It's hard to describe the devastation of no one believing me, but I learned not to talk about it. You're fortunate that you are just now coming into these gifts, knowing someone who believes in magic. While it normally happens on a sixteenth birthday, somehow the passing of your mother and the signs are causing you to get some of your abilities early."

"What do you mean by my abilities?"

Pru ignored her question and instead replied, "It isn't just the signs. Someone of great greed and desire for power has accepted evil in order to grow beyond natural ability."

Natalie gasped. "I think I met him today."

Pru dropped the footrest and sat forward as Natalie explained what had happened at school. At the end of the story, she handed Pru the blackened crystal. Pru studied it as Mira, and then the second ghost floated around her.

"I've been feeling a disturbance ever since the Full Cold Moon, but I was hoping it wasn't anything serious." Pru continued to stare at the dead crystal.

"I've never seen a black crystal, so it may be damaged beyond repair."

She held her hand up high over her head with the crystal dangling from the necklace held in her fingers. Both watched as Merlin swooped in, snatched it from her hand, and flew straight for the massive bookcase.

"Merlin, stop!" Natalie yelled.

Surely, he would hit the books and crash to the ground. Before she could move, Natalie watched in surprise as he flew through a small stained-glass door.

"Wow, a tiny door made for Merlin to access the hidden room. I never noticed it before."

Her eyes wide with amazement, she began to wonder about everything. Pru might fix her crystal. Merlin had his own tiny access door. Pru says she has abilities, but what are her abilities? Obviously, things were happening, but did she have what it would take to prepare for what was coming? While she focused on preparation, she noticed Pru speaking.

"Mira was the original owner of this house. Serena was the third owner of this house. Both of them died here alone. Sometimes loneliness is a terrible curse. Tragic."

Pausing, Pru sighed deeply before continuing her story.

"Anyway, back to my story. My family wanted me out of the house as soon as I turned 18. I couldn't support myself, so my rich, older brother searched for a place for me to live. Two deaths in this home and rumors that it was haunted made it ridiculously cheap. I guess the joke is that while he thought he had bought it at a cheap price and gotten rid of me, I ended up with two friends out of it. Friends that he and the rest of my family can't see. Not that they visit."

"That's sad." Natalie struggled to understand how Pru's family could be so mean.

"Well, the other part of the bad joke is that my brother's daughter often visits me and tells me things aren't going so well at home. Not that I have any bad wishes for them. After all, while he wants to pretend that I don't exist, he paid for the house, put it in my name, and gives me a monthly allowance."

Natalie perked up and instantly studied Pru's features. It seemed impossible. There's no resemblance at all. However, it was the only logical conclusion that Lainey knew where Natalie lived. In science class today, Lainey wore a bracelet that resembled Natalie's Variegated Orb Weaver bracelet.

As Pru watched her, she nodded her head up and down as if saying yes. She confirmed it. "Yes, Lainey is my niece."

"I would have never guessed." Natalie was stunned.

"Lainey isn't anything like her father…or her mother."

"That's a plus!"

"What's important is she knows the signs and what is happening. Unfortunately, Lainey doesn't have any powers."

"Isn't that a good thing? If she doesn't have any powers, it won't go after her. Right?"

"Unfortunately, no, but the Variegated Orb Weaver should provide Lainey some protection. It will act as a warning."

"You have powers. You said we don't get our powers until we're sixteen. Could Lainey get powers?"

"Not likely. Lainey is a little jealous of your potential powers."

With that, Natalie broke out into hearty laughter. To imagine Lainey being jealous of anything about her was hilarious. Lainey had the world at her beck and call just by her looks and brains. Natalie would remain ordinary her whole life, except for her powers. Powers that she knew she couldn't openly use. Pru's own family labeled her a freak for being able to see ghosts. Besides, without powers, she may have never encountered that man who caused her crystal to die. As she thought through this, she remembered needing another crystal.

"Pru, I need another crystal."

Pru's eyes widened. She looked shocked for a few seconds.

"I should have remembered your mother's pendant. On the bookshelves in your family room, look for the *Mystic Green Eternal Light Quest* book. It's dark green and thick. You'll need to rip the cover away from the pages. Your mother had a hole cut through the pages. She gave instructions for the amulet to be placed in the small box in there, and then the cover needed to be glued to the pages."

"My mother always wore that pendant. Why would she take it off and put it in that book?"

"Your mother was wearing the pendant when she passed. She had requested it to be hidden until you needed it. That's all I can say for now."

Natalie shook her head. "Why didn't the pendant protect her?"

"The pendant works in the magical world. It doesn't work in the regular world."

"I don't know why it had to be hidden. It makes no sense. I would have gotten the pendant right away, or Dad would have put it in Mom's jewelry box."

"Your mother had her reasons to hide the necklace. In time, you will receive the explanation from someone who has that knowledge."

Natalie frowned at that comment. "It seems like everything is going to be explained some other time. None of this makes any sense to me."

Pru ignored the comment. "If your crystal can recharge, it will take a few days for it to happen. In the meantime, you should wear your mother's pendant. Her pendant has more protective powers against evil magic."

"It's only been a few months since I've worn a crystal. I wasn't sure it was needed, but after what happened today, I don't want to be without one."

"Never take it off and always keep the pendant hidden. You can't talk to anyone about it. Also, let me give you a crystal to keep in your pocket."

Pru reached into the small table drawer and picked out a small crystal. She handed it to Natalie.

"Your mother's pendant won't react and burn like your crystal did today. The crystal I gave you will react just like the one you had on today if someone or something evil is near you."

Pru got up and stood before Natalie. "You need to go into the old homestead."

"Just one more thing, Pru." Natalie realized this had been on her mind for some time. "Are there others in this community that are like us, but they don't know it?"

"Yes. Your mother told me there are others in our community unaware of their magical abilities."

"Skylar and Madison must have magical abilities. They're adopted and have different biological parents, but they both have a fascination with Halloween. Joel has an interest, but I'm unsure about his magical abilities. If Joel has magical powers, maybe his entire family has powers."

"That's mostly true," Pru responded. "If one parent is from the Shadowlink clan, the children usually would be witches or wizards. Sometimes a child doesn't have any abilities. There are also the rare families where both parents have the Shadowlink clan bloodline. Some witches and wizards have more natural powers than others. That is because they would be a descendant of the Shadowlink or both parents have the Shadowlink clan bloodline."

"Why doesn't your brother or Lainey have abilities?"

"My brother and siblings are from a different father. Mother divorced and remarried. My father is a wizard. That said, I don't think he is aware he has magical abilities."

"Why didn't your father stop them from being so mean to you?"

"He didn't stay around. My mother made his life a living hell, so he dropped out of sight. I haven't seen him in years."

"Wow. It just keeps getting worse. I'm so sorry."

"Believe me, I lived in that hostile environment for years. I understand why he disappeared. I used to wish he would have taken me with him, but I have this house, Mira, and Serena. Lainey is like a daughter. I'm happy except for all these strange events."

"I'm glad it worked out for you."

"There was a time I would have believed it would never get better, but I have a good life."

"You deserve it, Pru. No one deserves the treatment you received because of your powers."

"Thanks."

"I have another question about magical abilities. Are you saying we are or aren't all from the same bloodline?"

"Your mother explained there were four mages from different families in the original Shadowlink clan. There was the Shadowlink, the Aerial of the air element, the Alchemist of the water element, and the Thaumaturge of the fire element. Each has a special talent, except the Shadowlink has all those talents, including the earth element."

"Wow, that is so cool. Skylar and Madison have an owl and have a natural talent for making brooms, which have the element symbols carved into the handles."

"It sounds like they're Aerial witches."

"I've never seen a bird by Joel." Natalie thought back to all the times they had talked over the fence.

"Ask him."

"I should. I wonder how many are in our subdivision. Knowing that would help. Do you know what element you belong to, Pru?"

"Yes, I know, but it isn't important right now. What is important is for you to go into the old homestead." Pru gave Natalie a no-excuse look.

Natalie ignored Pru's comment. "Pru, do you know what element I belong to?"

"Yes, I do, but I'm not answering the question. You will find the answer in the old homestead." Pru grew annoyed.

"Okay, okay, I believe you. I need answers. I want answers. The next time Jericho is sitting at the front door of the old homestead, I will go inside. I promise."

Pru sighed in relief that Natalie finally agreed to enter the homestead. "I promise you won't regret it. Your regret will be in not doing it before now."

Natalie highly doubted that would be true. She was already visualizing spiderwebs everywhere, dust so thick she couldn't breathe, rats in the walls, and roaches everywhere. Hordes of roaches would be running across the ceiling and dripping down to the floor. She shuddered at the scene playing out in her mind.

Pru interrupted Natalie's daydream. "It's time to allow Coal in your house."

"What? Coal's a bird. Isn't he used to being outdoors?"

"He's not a regular crow. He's your familiar."

Puzzled, Natalie responded, "I'm not sure what that means, but okay. If that's what he's supposed to do, I'll let him come and go."

"Let me know if you see that man again. Something's up, and it appears to involve your school."

Unfortunately, Natalie thought the same thing. Walking to the door, she thought of the teacher's warning. Perhaps that man is involved in the new program.

Natalie didn't even have the door fully open to leave before Coal zoomed through and was halfway across the front yard. She laughed, knowing he didn't trust the big-mouthed candles. She didn't trust them, either.

Before she made it to the steps, both candles lightly tapped her on her shoulders with their tongues. Natalie screamed, stumbled down the steps, and hit the ground. Safely out of range and unhurt, she stood up and glared at them.

Both candles looked contrite. "Sorry. We just wanted to show you our tongues." Sticking out their tongues, she saw that they were blotched with the colors of the candy.

"I like the red ones the best," the candle to the left stated.

"I like the green ones the best," the other candle volunteered.

"Those are Christmas colors, not Halloween colors," Natalie said, brushing the dirt off her jeans. "Besides, all those candies taste exactly the same. If you closed your eyes, I bet you couldn't tell me what color you were eating."

"Well, I guess you'll need to bring us a lot more candy to test."

Natalie didn't answer them but mumbled to herself as she walked away. "It's a good thing they don't have teeth. I don't think we could find a dentist that makes house calls to cavity-filled teeth on six-foot-tall talking candles." A visual of a dentist trying to fix their teeth while they yakked nonstop changed her mood for the better.

Coal waited in a tree at the edge of the property.

Walking the mile home, Natalie rehashed all the things Pru had said to her. The first thing she needed to do was find her mother's pendant. Now that Natalie had seen what a crystal could do, she wanted the double protection of one in her pocket and one as a necklace.

Walking into the house with Coal flying in with her, Natalie thought about the old homestead and her promise to Pru. Even though it looked like a haunted building in need of condemnation and demolition, she hoped Pru was correct that it was anything but dilapidated. There was only one way to find out. The next time she saw Jericho on the front porch, she would go inside.

Standing before the bookcase, she looked for the *Mystic Green Eternal Light Quest* book. She didn't see it the other day, so maybe it was in the fifth section of the bookcase. She started looking at the books within her range, but she didn't see the book.

She walked over to the kitchen table and grabbed a chair. After carrying it over to the last section of the bookcase, she climbed onto the chair and looked at the top two shelves. The book was on the top shelf. Natalie pulled it out and brought it down.

Plopping it on the kitchen table, she leaned over it and tugged at the front cover until it finally ripped open. All the pages had a small rectangle cut out in the middle of the book, making it perfect for hiding the pendant. Enclosed in a small cardboard box was her mother's pendant. Natalie took the pendant out and studied it. Pru had called it an amulet. Knowing that the amulet was a charm, Natalie looked at it more closely.

The pendant had a translucent blue shade. Otherwise, it was similar in size and shape to her pendant. Except this one had a silver crown with a link for the pendant to attach to a necklace. From the crown came four thin strands of silver running the length of the pendant. Within each of those sections was a different design for a bird. The designs were too small to determine the birds, except for the owl.

Natalie dangled the pendant from its necklace and started twisting it around and around. When she released it, she watched in fascination as the twirling pendant caused the different birds to flash before her. Recognizing the owl repeatedly, she made the connection to Madison and Skylar.

One of the birds had to be Pru's blackbird. One bird had to be her crow. Who had the fourth bird? Now, she was curious who else in the neighborhood had a bird? Joel had to be the fourth person. Somewhere, there must be a bird trying to connect with Joel. He was too interested in all these strange happenings not to be included. The next time she saw him, she would find out.

The birds got Natalie thinking that Joel, Madison, and Skylar hadn't lived there that long, and yet there seemed to be a connection. Was that the clue she needed to see if there were others who had recently moved into their subdivision and might have magical abilities? Startled, Natalie thought about Jericho and Sharlow. They both had odd black cats and old homesteads. Joel had never mentioned a black cat, and their family had taken down the old homestead when they built their home.

Pru also didn't appear to have a black cat, and as far as she could tell, there wasn't an old homestead on her property. The questions were piling up. Natalie needed to stop thinking about this and start hoping that the answers were in the old, haunted house. She couldn't believe her building excitement about entering that place. Last week, she would have run from the place; now, she wanted answers.

Chapter 16
The Old Homestead

Jericho pounced on the bed and marched over to Natalie. Even with a book blocking her view of him, she could feel his eyes boring holes into her. She lowered the book and grew alarmed at his behavior.

His tail flicked back and forth, his eyes narrowed, and his ears bent down as he stared at her. A low growl escaped his closed mouth.

Instinctively, Natalie pulled the bedspread up and slid her hands under it. She valued her fingers all in one piece.

"What?"

His tail continued to thump the bed as he glared at her. Natalie studied his fierce behavior for several nervous minutes. Nothing. She couldn't come up with any reason for the massive tantrum.

Jericho stretched out his claws.

"Jericho, why are you in a foul mood?"

He let out a long rumbling growl.

"Okay, okay. Give me a minute."

Closely watching him, she replayed the entire awful day in her mind, up to the point of opening the book that hid her mother's pendant. She remembered leaving the shredded book on the kitchen table. *That's it!* It had to be about her mother's pendant. As weird as it seemed, Natalie knew the pendant brought on the tantrum.

"Jericho, when I entered the school's front office today, I met a man reeking of negative energy. Within seconds of encountering him, my crystal burned against my skin. Pru's charm bracelet furiously flashed to the point it had to be hidden. I knew I couldn't react in the office, so I waited until I could go to a bathroom. Do you understand?"

Natalie saw the ears come up, but he continued swishing his tail back and forth and stared hard at her.

"Jericho, the pain was excruciating. I couldn't get to the bathroom fast enough. As soon as I hid in a stall, I pulled the crystal out and discovered it had turned black. Where it had touched my skin, it left a burn mark."

She watched Jericho calm down. The mad pounding of his tail against the bed stopped, but he stared and waited. She got the impression he wanted to hear the rest of the story.

"Before I say anything else, I just want you to know that we have had several feral cats, and none of them have been as weird as you."

Now feeling her fingers were safe, Natalie took the extra pillows and plopped them on top of her pillow. She leaned into them and rested her head against the headboard.

"Okay, here's the rest of the story. When I got home, I went to see Pru. Her bird took my crystal to the Variegated Orb Weaver room to try to restore it. However, it's going to be a few days, so Pru told me where I could find my mother's pendant. I still don't know why it had to be hidden, but that's why I'm wearing it."

Puzzled, she paused and studied Jericho's face.

"It's strange that you knew the book held my mother's pendant. I didn't even know it. The whole thing is weird, including why it would bother you to find me wearing Mom's necklace."

Jericho reached out and placed a paw on her hand. No claws, but his unpredictable mood had her pulling her hand away.

"If that's your apology for your tantrum, I accept it."

Jericho tilted his head and studied her.

"Are you sure you're a cat?" Natalie stared back.

Jericho turned around and got ready to hop off the bed.

"My horribly strange cat, it looks like you got the answer you wanted."

Jericho turned and glanced at Natalie. She sweetly smiled at the cat and waited. He briefly narrowed his eyes and studied her before turning back.

Natalie kept an innocent expression and bit her lip to avoid laughing. *Please jump now, or I'm going to burst out laughing*, she thought while struggling to remain calm. A small giggle escaped. She reached for a pillow in case she had to push her face into it. Jericho hesitated.

Come on, Jericho, jump off the bed, she silently pleaded. Finally, he jumped.

"Oh, and I promised Pru I would go into the old homestead the next time I saw you sitting on the front porch."

She roared with laughter as she watched Jericho frantically try to turn midair to land back on the bed. Too late. Her laughter increased when she heard a loud thump. Bent over, arms crossed and clutching her sides, she continued laughing as Jericho flew high above the bed before pouncing down on it. Wasting no time, he marched up to her and stopped within inches of her face.

"Please…" Natalie couldn't speak. Tears fell as she continued laughing. Her sides hurt. He wasn't helping with his wide-eyed expression.

"Jericho…" Her mind replayed the jump, the thump, and the bounce on the bed. She laughed harder.

Wiping the tears from her face, she tried to get herself under control. Nearly impossible to stop laughing, she pressed her face against a pillow. For several minutes, she took deep breaths, trying to calm down.

Finally, she had some control. She looked at the cat and decided he didn't believe what she had said. Strange reaction for a cat. Then, again, none of this made sense.

She studied him. It seemed he wanted her to repeat what she just said to him. She waited too long; his claws stretched out and began digging into the bedspread.

"Relax, Jericho. It's not a trick. I mean it."

She watched him back up a few steps. He paused and studied her.

"Don't get me laughing again. My sides are already killing me."

He backed up some more steps and paused.

"Stop it. You need to go, but before you do, know that I won't go in there on a school day. So if you want me to go into the homestead, it has to be Saturday. Got it?"

Natalie watched him walk to the edge of the bed and turn around to look at her again.

"Jericho, what is going on in that head of yours?" Natalie shook her head.

He took one last look before he jumped off the bed and trotted out of the room.

Torrential rain started in the wee hours of Saturday morning. As thunder rumbled, Natalie rolled over and looked at the alarm clock. It was only 4 a.m. Ugh. With luck, the storm would move on, and it would be a sunny day. She wasn't looking forward to going inside the haunted house in full sun. Stormy weather made it worse. It had to be a bad omen.

Throughout the next few hours, the heavy rain pounding against the house and the rumbling thunder kept waking Natalie. Looking at the alarm clock, she saw that only minutes had passed since the last time she had checked it. By 8 a.m., she gave up and got out of bed.

Without a doubt, she knew Jericho sat on the old homestead's front porch waiting for her. She decided not to keep him waiting. Dragging herself to the shower, she stayed in there to warm up and wake up.

After she dressed, she went in search of a big can of bug spray. If roaches were going to be coming out of the baseboards in this nasty weather, she would be ready. Natalie also grabbed the flashlight with the brightest light. In this gloomy weather, she did not know if she could even see in that decrepit old building. If only Jericho would let her change to Sunday.

Sloshing through the path to the barn, Natalie dropped the umbrella and the bag with the spray and flashlight at the tack room to get the feed for the chickens. Putting the two scoops under her shirt to keep the feed dry, she bolted out of the tack room, flung the small gate wide open, and ran over to the chickens. Without the umbrella, the rain pelted her as she struggled to keep the scoops under her shirt and unlock the door to the back stalls. By the time Natalie finished feeding and locking the chickens in for the day, her clothes were sopping wet. Shivering, she retrieved the umbrella and popped it open to stop the chilly rain from pelting her.

Rounding the corner of the barn and heading towards the old homestead, Natalie spotted Jericho sitting on the front porch. He perked up when he saw her. She slowed to a standstill before the rusty old gate. Taking a deep breath and eyeing the drenched scarecrows, Natalie reached for the handle and slowly opened the creaking metal gate. For once, the scarecrows looked straight ahead and not at her. With the creepy scarecrows out of the way, she faced the three-headed tree stump. Each step, slow and deliberate, brought Natalie closer to the haunted tree stump. She didn't care if she looked silly and dramatic. The stump was creepier than the scarecrows. Natalie glanced over at the agonized faces. Jericho studied her.

Natalie yelled over the downpour that bombarded the umbrella. "If you think I'm going to stick my hand in this haunted tree stump to retrieve a key, you're out of your mind!"

Jericho ignored the comment. Turning his back to her, the front door creaked halfway open. He looked back at her one last time before he stepped inside.

Walking as if her shoes were filled with cement, Natalie laboriously took one step at a time to the porch. She dreaded what waited for her on the other side of that door. She visualized layers of dust, spiderwebs, roaches, and rats. She hoped to be wrong, and Pru to be right.

No turning back now. Natalie took a deep breath and released it. She took another deep breath and slowly let it out before putting the umbrella down. She grabbed the flashlight and the bug spray. With the flashlight on and her left index finger positioned to press the bug spray button, she was ready.

Natalie stood outside and peered in through the half-opened door. She gasped! Looking back at her was a small, pale creature. The creature had short, pointed ears, a plump nose, large eyes the color of Jericho's eyes, white fur jutting up as eyebrows, and a long white ponytail. The creature, dressed in colorful, mismatched clothes, wore a multi-colored, chunky beaded necklace. Frozen in place, Natalie continued to gawk while realizing there was plenty of light behind the creature.

"Finally!"

Flabbergasted, Natalie stuttered, "You…you speak Eng…lish!"

"I speak many languages, including English! You call me Jericho. My name is Lorcan. At my pleasure, I mentor your family."

Recovering, she recognized his form.

"You're the creature I saw in my room!"

"I am indeed." Lorcan grinned.

"Wow," Natalie whispered, "I don't know what to say. I mean, why do you mentor my family? What are you?"

Natalie's fascination with Lorcan had her solely focusing on him. However, the pixies and fairies waiting on the other side of the door had been quiet for long enough.

"Let her in, let her in!" they all squealed in high-pitched voices while pushing Lorcan out of the way.

Two fairies snatched the flashlight and bug spray from her hands. Four pixies grabbed hold of her hands and dragged her inside. As the door slammed shut, a whirlwind of two dozen magical creatures engulfed Natalie. Swirling, whirling chaos overwhelmed her, making it only possible to get glimpses that the place wasn't hideous.

Relieved that she didn't have to deal with roaches in the dark, she tried to relax as pixies and fairies dragged her further into the room.

A red-dressed fairy yanked the hair of the blue-dressed fairy, pulling on Natalie's hand. A loud cry of outrage filled the room as fairy dust flew from the offended fairy to the red-dressed fairy. While they fought, a purple-dressed fairy and a green-dressed fairy grabbed Natalie's hands and yanked her forward. A yellow-dressed fairy sat on Natalie's right shoulder, giggling.

Soon, it was a whirlwind of color and fairy dust as the pixies and fairies fought for the privilege of escorting her inside. Natalie stumbled during the mayhem of pixies and fairies getting shoved or flung off to be replaced by others.

Shrieks of anger filled the air as they turned to pulling hair, biting, and throwing fairy dust balls at each other. The air, thick with multi-colored fairy dust, forced Natalie to shut her eyes. The constant din of shrill fighting voices gave her a headache.

Through the colorful haze, she squinted over at Lorcan, looking for help, but he ignored her and watched with fascination as the flurry intensified around her.

"A little help, Lorcan!" Natalie yelled as the fairies plopped a humongous, colorful wreath of flowers on her head.

"They're showing you how excited they are to have you with us." Lorcan laughed at the wild drama encircling Natalie.

Natalie shivered from her drenched clothes. She peered down at the sticky fairy dust clinging to her hair and her clothes. Ganging up on her, they spun her around, causing the flower wreath to tilt. She grabbed it and frowned at Lorcan.

Several fairies fluttered in front of Natalie, blocking her view of Lorcan. Two pixies straightened the flowers on her head. As they did, the yellow-dressed fairy added shimmering pink streamers to the wreath.

They squealed with delight and added rhinestones to the streamers. Then, they flew around her, trying to decide what to do next.

"Okay, I see they aren't going to settle down or leave you alone."

Lorcan pulled a small wand from his pocket. He held it up to get their attention. Too busy squabbling and trying to take Natalie's hands off her ears because they wanted to replace her small earrings with big, gaudy flower earrings, they didn't notice Lorcan.

Lorcan mumbled an amplification spell before he made three loud taps on the wall to get their attention.

Natalie sighed with relief as the pixies and fairies stopped and nervously glanced over at Lorcan. They stayed frozen, except for the flapping of wings, and watched as he dramatically pointed his wand at them. The gaudy earrings fell to the floor as shrieking erupted and filled the air. The pixies and fairies zoomed across the room in their rush to escape.

"Thanks, but next time, warn me before you have them screaming and trying to burst my eardrums." Natalie checked that she still had both of her earrings. She glanced down at the gaudy earrings on the floor. She couldn't believe they were attempting to put those two-pound ugly things on her.

"Sorry," Lorcan said, and then he bent over and roared with laughter. They were so predictable.

While he laughed, Natalie stood in a colorful pool of rainwater. Her clothes were soaked from the rain. Her face, hair, and clothes were a rainbow of fairy dust colors. Disheveled from all the jostling and wearing the lopsided, enormous crown of vibrant flowers, Natalie realized she looked a mess. The headache matched her look.

"They meant well," Lorcan choked out through his laughter. He needed to refocus to regain control of himself. He tried. Really, he did, but he couldn't avoid looking at her. He held his ribs as he roared with laughter.

"I guess this is payback for me laughing at you the other day." Natalie folded her arms across her chest and rubbed her arms to get warm as she waited for his answer.

Lorcan's laughter turned to snickers. One final outburst and then he had himself under control. He straightened up, pulled his wand from his pocket, and pointed it at Natalie. Before Natalie could react, he mumbled a few strange words. Instantly, she became dry and warm. The flower crown and colorful fairy dust vanished.

"Thanks." Natalie could clearly see again. No lingering fairy dust in the air. She sighed in relief, tucked her shirt in, and redid her ponytail.

Lorcan put his wand back in his pocket. "You're welcome. Now, take a minute to look around this room before we get started."

Natalie had no idea what that meant, but free from the swarm, she could finally see inside the building. She turned around and looked at everything in this large, open room.

A name for the room popped into her head. She would call it the Room of Mirrors. Mirrors of various sizes and shapes covered each wall. It seemed the mirrors spanned the ages. Some were modern, some were antiques, but all were beautiful. One huge crystal chandelier hung in the center of the room, reflecting sparks of light in the mirrors.

"Are some of these two-way mirrors?"

"What does that mean?"

"Can there be someone on the other side of the mirror that sees us, but we don't see them?"

"Nope."

"Anything special about the mirrors?"

"Maybe, but it could also be that I just like mirrors."

"Like you like feathers?" Natalie laughed.

Lorcan let out a hearty laugh and grabbed his still-hurting ribs. "So, you noticed I collect feathers?"

"I watched you march to the old homestead with a mouth stuffed with vulture feathers."

"Well, then, here is your first lesson. Feathers have magical power. The feathers of the bird you are associated with have even greater power for you. Your bird is a crow. Start collecting crow feathers you find…don't pluck your crow."

Natalie gave a disgusted look at the thought of plucking Coal or any other bird. Lorcan laughed and then grimaced. He rubbed his sore ribs.

"Let's go on a brief tour before our special visitor arrives."

"Who is it?" Natalie wasn't ready for more surprises.

"Someone who is going to test your powers."

"Can't you do it?"

"Nope. It's beyond my skill level."

Lorcan opened the door to his collection of Halloween candles. Natalie went inside the room and looked at the rows and rows of candles with various Halloween facial expressions.

"How did you manage to find so many different Halloween candles? I'm seriously jealous. I've only found a few, and that is through endless searches using my computer."

"But now you're in the world of magic. A Halloween store will carry a wide assortment of candles. And, if they don't have what you want, they will make it."

"Really? That's awesome. Do the candles from a magic shop have any special abilities?" Natalie picked one up and studied it before putting it back down.

"Not now, and I hope never again."

"Good to know, I thought that blue one in the corner moved its eyes."

"Where?"

"That one." Natalie pointed into the corner where two tall blue candles with wide eyes and open mouths stood.

"Give me a minute."

Lorcan ushered Natalie out and closed the door behind her. He stepped out a minute later.

"This time it worked."

"Want to tell me about it?" Natalie's curiosity spiked as they headed toward another room.

"No."

Lorcan opened the door to a room of gemstones. Natalie walked in and stared in amazement. Everywhere she looked were cauldrons of gemstones. It looked like a pirate's stolen treasure. She walked over to a large cauldron pushed against the north wall.

"What are these?" Natalie picked a red gemstone from the cauldron.

"It's a ruby." Lorcan took it from her hand and carefully put it back.

She walked up to the next cauldron and said, "Amethyst."

"Correct."

She took her time at each of the twenty overflowing cauldrons.

"This is amazing. Thanks for showing it to me."

Natalie opened the door and entered a room with several shelves on three walls. Those shelves were loaded with various-sized, colorful, liquid-filled bottles, some of which contained powders. Various-sized empty cauldrons were piled in the center of the room.

"Wow, a potions room. Do you have those strange things we read about, like the eye of a newt?"

"It's all here and more."

Natalie opened the door to another room that contained artifacts associated with animals. She didn't like seeing mounted heads and skeletons, so she didn't venture inside.

"This is going to be the last room associated with magic I show you right now. I'm going to save my favorite room for later."

Lorcan opened the door to a faint pleasant odor. Natalie peeked in and saw dried herbs and plants hanging. She saw other plants on the ground in various-sized pots.

This room didn't interest her, so she took a minute to scan the room. Then Lorcan closed the door.

They marched up the narrow wooden stairs to the living quarters.

Lorcan knocked on the door before entering the first room. Twelve fairies hovered near the back wall over by their beds. They watched Natalie.

Mesmerized by their beauty and their iridescent purple and blue wings, it took Natalie a few minutes to realize it was a tiny fairy she had seen in the garden. A clever, but failed scheme to get her into the old homestead. She regretted not falling for it. This was beyond her wildest dreams. Pru was right.

Lorcan knocked on the door to the next room before opening it. Twelve pixies hovered near the ceiling. They were just as excited as the fairies to see Natalie. Braver than the fairies, they came down and fluttered around her for several minutes.

She held her left hand out, and a pixie fluttered over and sat on her hand. The pixie stared up at her as she studied the small creature.

"Hey!" Natalie yelled as another pixie dragged that pixie off, and it promptly sat down on her hand.

Horrified, she watched as the rest joined in and fought for the privilege of sitting on her hand. She dropped her hand as Lorcan brought his wand out. The pixies scattered to the other side of the room. Wide-eyed and looking innocent, they watched Lorcan. Natalie tried to stay calm, but she couldn't. She burst into laughter at their devious personalities before shutting the door.

Heading towards the room on the opposite side of the hallway, Lorcan stopped her. "Nope. That room is off-limits."

"Is it your room?"

"It is," Lorcan remarked as they headed towards the staircase.

"A bachelor's pad." She smirked as she envisioned a total mess in his living quarters.

When Lorcan ignored her comment, she changed the subject. "I conjured up all sorts of horrifying images of this place. It's an ancient, wooden, and dilapidated structure. It had to be infested with roaches, spiders, and rats."

"At one time, that was true. Not anymore." Lorcan sighed in disappointment as he led her down the staircase.

"Well, I can truthfully say the scarecrows also scare me."

"They're just guardians to ensure only the right people enter the homestead."

"They kind of resemble clowns. Clowns scare me, which means the scarecrows are creepy. The creep level increases when they bend their heads down and their black button eyes stare at me."

Lorcan laughed. "I've seen how you act around them. However, they're not alive. There's an unbreakable protective spell intertwined throughout them and the entire perimeter to protect this place."

"So you say."

"Believe me, they're only creepy if you don't belong here." Lorcan hopped off the bottom step.

"Since we're speaking about guardians, what are those sarcastic candles guarding Pru's house?" Natalie stopped outside the Room of Mirrors and walked in front of Lorcan.

Lorcan lowered his voice. "Shh…I illegally added character to those two candles. They're also guardians, just with more personality and protective abilities than the old scarecrows."

Before she could ask another question, Lorcan stopped her. "Our visitor has arrived."

Natalie walked into the room, saw the man, and froze. Even in a strange cloak of black feathers, she recognized the mysterious man at her mother's memorial service. Her heart began to pound; she didn't take her eyes off of him.

As she stared at him, Natalie watched the man struggle to contain his composure. She wasn't sure why. She just met him, so it couldn't be something she did to annoy him. Confused by his reaction to her, she continued to stare at him.

His eyes seemed familiar to her. She didn't understand why, as he hadn't been that close to her at the memorial service. She wished he weren't that close now, as he made her uncomfortable. She turned her head and focused on Lorcan.

She couldn't get his attention. He seemed to be studying the man.

"Lorcan," Natalie said his name in a low, urgent voice.

Lorcan glanced at her and shook his head no before focusing back on the man.

"Draon, do you have the oracular stone with you?"

Draon glanced at Lorcan before looking down at his cloak. He pulled the stone out of an inside pocket.

Natalie recognized it. She stepped closer. As she did, the sparkling red, blue, green, and white liquid within the stone intertwined and separated, swiftly circling within it. Draon raised his eyebrows and, this time, in amazement, stared at her.

"Is it supposed to do that?" Lorcan asked, stepping over to Natalie.

Draon didn't answer. Natalie didn't hear the question. Fascination gripped her as the colors intertwined and separated while racing around the stone.

Time stood still until Natalie felt Lorcan tug on her hand. She glanced down before returning her attention to the stone. Lorcan tugged harder on her hand.

"What?"

He focused on Draon. "Draon, it's time to read her powers."

Draon nodded. "Hold out your hand."

She stepped forward and held her left hand out. Draon placed the stone in her palm. Instantly, bursts of multi-colored sparks flew out and repeatedly zapped all three of them. In surprise, Draon and Lorcan yelled and jumped back.

"Ouch! What the heck!" Natalie looked from the stone to them, wanting help.

She extended her arm away from her body, but the sparks still zapped her arm and hand.

"Ouch! Ouch! Ouch!" She wanted to drop it.

Draon recovered and lunged forward. He yanked the stone from her hand, shoved it into his pocket, and backed up.

"Is it supposed to do that?" Lorcan asked, still wide-eyed and surprised at what had happened.

"No," Draon curtly replied.

"I've never seen it do that before," Lorcan said, puzzled.

Natalie rubbed her arm and hand. She wanted to scratch the red spots where the sparks had hit her. Her focus changed when Draon called her name.

"Natalie, you are a Shadowlink. You have powers in the air, water, fire, and earth elements. You already have your full powers. It will be up to Lorcan and the Crossroads to train you."

Natalie glanced at Lorcan, looking for support, but he looked surprised as he studied Draon. She turned back to Draon. His deep frown made her uncomfortable, as did the tense atmosphere in the room. Everything about this situation made her uncomfortable.

She glanced down at her Variegated Orb Weaver bracelet. It wasn't going off. She guessed it didn't go off when someone intensely disliked someone. That's the vibe she was getting from him, as if he could hardly stand being in the room with her.

"Keep me informed on her training," Draon said as he started to leave.

Lorcan didn't even have time to answer before Draon walked out the front door.

"Wow, and double wow!" Natalie exclaimed after Draon left. Lorcan raised his eyebrows, questioning what she was thinking.

"Wow, on my powers and wow on how much that guy doesn't like me." She fought hard not to cry.

"It's complicated, but know that it really has nothing to do with you." Lorcan motioned for her to follow him.

"I don't know how you can say that after what I just experienced." She couldn't shake Draon's coldness towards her. Her eyes brimmed with tears as her heart pounded.

"Time will prove what I said is true. Now, focus on the tour. I saved my favorite room for last. Besides, it's the most comfortable room on this floor."

Her heart continued to break knowing she repulsed Draon. Her voice trembled as she identified the room. "It's the room with the feather collection."

"Good guess." Lorcan picked up the pace as they made their way over to a room on the north side of the house.

"I noticed you don't seem to have a lot of furniture," Natalie said, but she didn't care about the furniture, her reading, or anything else. Draon had pretty much ruined the day. *How was it possible to meet him and instantly know he didn't like me?* She struggled with that thought as Lorcan opened the door to the feather collection room.

"Most of the furniture is upstairs. The bottom floor is for my collections."

Half-heartedly walking into the room, Natalie noticed it had rows of shelves from floor to ceiling along the southern and western walls. The eastern wall had floor-to-ceiling shelves on the left and right sides of an antique fireplace. A large portrait of Jericho in an aristocratic pose hung above the mantle. Glancing over at the northern wall, she noticed that it had shelving covering the walls on each side of a window, as well as a smaller shelf underneath the window. Every shelf in the room was filled with large glass jars. Most of the jars were full of feathers. The only breaks in the endless rows of jars of feathers along the walls were the fireplace, the portrait, the door, and the window. It was a massive collection.

The middle of the room was the only space for furniture. On top of a large, braided rug existed the ugliest furniture in the entire world. Natalie couldn't get over the hideous couch and chairs. Plastered in horrendously gaudy and colorful large flowers, the outrageously dreadful pattern hurt her eyes to look in that direction.

It wasn't easy to avoid because the bulky couch and the wide chairs on either side of the couch consumed the entire middle section of the room. Repulsed, she scanned the room to find something to focus on instead of those awful pieces of furniture.

She found it by stepping closer to the portrait of Jericho. Surprised, she watched as the portrait changed to

Lorcan. Natalie took a step back, and it returned to a portrait of Jericho. She stepped forward and watched the regal black cat transform into Lorcan, wearing his colorfully mismatched clothes and beaded necklace.

In a better mood, she would have enjoyed watching it change between the two forms of Lorcan. She wasn't in a good mood.

"Um, Lorcan, aren't you running out of space for feathers?" Natalie turned away from the portrait and moved closer to the immense collection of feathers. There weren't many empty jars.

"Nope, one can never have too many feathers. Besides, this is just one of my rooms for feathers."

Since the rooms upstairs were living quarters, Natalie figured Lorcan stored feathers in his bedroom. What else was he storing up there?

Almost needing to climb into the regular-sized chair next to the couch, Lorcan sat down and motioned for Natalie to sit in the other chair. Her mood changed when she saw Lorcan's feet dangling in the air. He looked so small. Remembering Lorcan as the terrorizing Jericho, she smiled.

"I may not be able to read your mind, but I have a pretty good idea of what you are thinking. Knock it off," Lorcan said in a miffed tone.

"Sorry. It's just hard to see you and Jericho as one and the same."

"My attitude is the same regardless of the form. Remember that," Lorcan said as he mumbled the last word. Before she could ask him to repeat what he had said, the furniture shrank in size. Now, she was the one who looked ridiculous, stuffed in a small chair. Somehow, it was okay for Lorcan to laugh at Natalie looking silly.

"Okay! Lesson learned," Natalie said, stretching her legs out so she wasn't so cramped in the tiny chair.

Lorcan mumbled again, this time reversing the spell. Instantly, the furniture reverted to normal size. She made a mental note not to tease Lorcan about his size. Mentioning doing something about the gaudy flower pattern on the furniture was probably out of the question, too.

"I'm confused. You used your wand in the other room, not here. How do you know when or when not to use your wand?"

"Ruiries don't need wands. It's just a prop to get the attention of the pixies and fairies. They see the wand; they know I'm serious."

"So, do I need a wand?"

"Yes, and no. More on that later. And before you ask, I mumble because you aren't ready to learn or use spells."

Natalie hadn't even thought about his mumbling. Now that she knew the reason, she would pay close attention to see if she could understand what he said. But, for now, her attention was on how much Draon disliked her. She wanted to focus on him again.

"Jericho…I mean, Lorcan, why does Draon dislike me?"

"I won't talk about it. It isn't my place. Just give him time, and he'll come around."

"You really think so?"

"I will always speak the truth with you."

"Thank you. May I ask another question on a different topic?"

"Sure."

"Was my mother a powerful witch?"

"Very powerful."

"Why couldn't she save herself?"

"She didn't have time to react."

Natalie sat still for a couple of minutes, thinking about her mother's final minutes. She sighed and changed her focus. "Why didn't my mother tell me I was a witch? She told me stories, but I didn't really believe them. I mean, who believes they have magical powers?"

"Your mother wanted you to have a normal childhood. She knew firsthand that it's impossible if you get your powers early, as she did. Besides, she was concerned for your father."

"Does my father know?"

"Absolutely."

"He never said anything to me."

"He doesn't know anything about our world, and he really doesn't want to know. We had a brief talk the day your mother died. He's scared, and he fears losing you."

"That's absurd! Why would Dad ever think he would lose me?"

"You're a mage. You have incredible powers. In fact, I've never seen the oracular stone act like it did with you...something's different."

"Well, he's my dad, so nothing is changing there. Changing the subject, does Dad know you are also Jericho?"

"Yes, it was the reason you could keep me. He didn't always like my behavior, but he knew I was there to protect you."

"I appreciate that, especially during the full moons."

"If we had been in here, I could have protected you. But you wanted nothing to do with the homestead, so it wasn't me. As a cat, I only have the ability to turn into my true form. I have no powers as a cat. It's why you saw me in this form in your room that night. Even though I was breaking a rule, I wanted to make sure I could protect you."

"So, you can't be yourself in my house?"

"That is correct. I've broken the rule a few times lately because the mageless world limits where I can be myself."

"That's a bummer. So, if it wasn't you, who helped during the full moons?"

"It was Samoon the first rare full moon. The second rare full moon was Samoon, and the spirits of your chickens. I won't go into Samoon now, but I will tell you that your love and care for your chickens brought their spirits back to protect you."

"Wow, that's amazing! I can still see them circling us and the shattering of the cold. What is Samoon?"

"Nope…not saying. It's up to the mentors when and where they tell their mages. The first goal is that the mages need to meet their mentors. The second goal is training."

"I hope it starts soon. Who would have ever guessed?"

"That magic's real? You have had several things happen that should have told you that you aren't ordinary."

"I know. I have a whole notebook of strange or unexplainable things that have happened, and then there's you and Pru. Even so, magical powers? Come on."

"Well, there's a whole secret world out there, and it's time for you to discover it. To do that, we need to gather the witches and wizards in the neighborhood for a meeting."

Chapter 17
Gathering of the Trainees

Natalie wanted to be alone after the awful meeting with Draon. She couldn't shake his displeasure with her or his abrupt departure. Lorcan's words of giving him time seemed hollow compared to what she experienced.

A deep sigh escaped as she walked into the potions room. Stacks of various-sized empty cauldrons took up the center of the room. Shelves lined three walls and were loaded with various-sized bottles filled with potion ingredients. Walking along the walls, she glanced at all the different colored potion bottles before heading out.

Remembering what the next room held, she opened the door and peeked inside. She frowned. Mounted animal heads and skeletons weren't her thing, especially if it involved magic. If anything moved, she would scream loud enough to bring the ceiling down. Backing up, she closed the door.

Natalie headed towards the feather collection room, but she changed her mind. The eye-straining, gaudy flower pattern on the hideous furniture made that room unbearable. *No thanks. I'll be happy if I never need to spend a moment in there.*

She headed for the gemstone room. A smile spread across her face. Right then, she decided that it would be her favorite room. She walked in and spent a couple of hours picking up and studying gemstones from the huge cauldrons.

On Sunday, she knocked on the homestead's front door. It flew open, and six fairies yanked her inside. The door slammed shut. Grabbing her hands and flurrying around her head, they directed her to the kitchen.

Natalie sat down on a small white chair. Blue and red-dressed fairies flew over with a glass of green liquid.

Some of it sloshed on the table. An orange-dressed fairy complained as she brought a towel to wipe the mess.

Trying not to laugh, she watched the extreme drama of cleaning up the little mess. Then, she focused on the green drink. It looked disgusting, but she decided not to comment on it. Still, she didn't want to drink it, either.

Low voices became louder, high-pitched voices as the fairies demanded she drink their punch. She reached for it, but she didn't pick it up. More shrill complaining.

"Okay, give me a minute while I work up my courage." Natalie raised the glass to her nose and took a sniff. It smelled sickly sweet.

Lorcan walked into the room as Natalie took a tiny sip.

"They won't tell you, but some of their punch concoctions should carry warning labels. If unsure, take a tiny sip. Better yet, drip some in the sink and see if it starts eating the metal." Lorcan laughed at his comment as he sat down. The blue and red-dressed fairies brought him a drink.

Natalie watched Lorcan sniff the green punch before he took a sip. He smiled and took a gulp.

"One of their favorite activities is making punch. Another favorite activity is being overwhelmingly helpful."

Natalie stood up. She reached for her glass to return it to the sink. The orange-dressed fairy snatched it out of her hand. The glass flew from her hand and shattered on the floor. Immediately, five other fairies scolded the orange-dressed fairy.

Lorcan shook his head as Natalie held her hands over her ears and bolted for the gemstone room. Before she could close the door, six fairies flew in with her. She groaned, knowing it wasn't going to be an enjoyable experience.

It started off with one fairy handing her a small gemstone. Soon, each fairy held a gemstone, waiting for their turn. Natalie had no choice but to ooh and aah over each piece given to her. Between each ooh and aah was a heavy sigh.

It would have been amusing watching some of them struggle to stay in the air with a heavier gemstone, but they were demanding. Sometimes three fairies would have something to show her at the same time. They didn't want to wait for their turn.

She dreaded those moments. Being careful not to upset one of them, she would hesitate to select a piece. A wrong choice resulted in a dramatic meltdown. It wasn't easy on her ears, nor was it fun watching the others gather around the one offended and glare at her. She wished the fairies were more aloof like the pixies, but no such luck.

Natalie loved the gemstone collection. She enjoyed the positive vibe and the sheer beauty of the immense collection. A treasure ruined by the shrill, squealing, demanding fairies.

After two hours of fairy drama, she had had enough. She stood up and got ready to leave. Then, she thought about it. It would always be like this unless she fixed it now. With fairies floating around her, waiting to show her their favorite pick, she closed her eyes and tried to block them out.

Lorcan peeked his head in and burst out laughing.

"Trying to cope?"

"Yes, I am, and I'm failing miserably." Natalie looked to Lorcan for help.

"You're a novelty. They don't get out into the real world, so you are the new thing to entertain them."

"Ugh."

"Don't expect it to get any better." Lorcan shut the door.

Natalie closed her eyes and again concentrated on how to have this room to herself. Suddenly, Lorcan's words gave her the answer.

"Put the gemstones up and gather around me."

She waited for them to get back to her. Six fairies hovered in front of her.

"I appreciate how each of you assisted me today. I have a better appreciation of the gemstones and this room. That said…shh…that said…shh…I need alone time…"

High-pitched voices became loud with disapproval.

"Shh…I have a deal that benefits both of us." Natalie waited for them to calm down.

"I remember one fairy went outside, but it was for a very special purpose. Lorcan says you aren't allowed out of the house. Is that correct?"

High-pitched chattering confirmed it was true.

"Here's the deal. One day a week, I will bring you something from the outside. It will be something unique and, most of the time, entertaining. For this special surprise each week, all the fairies and pixies will not enter the gemstone room. The gemstone room will be my sanctuary. Do you agree?"

The elated fairies swarmed her before flying out of the room. She left right behind them to retrieve their first surprise.

Late Sunday afternoon, Natalie rested comfortably on the floor of the gemstone room. Propped up on two of her bedroom pillows, she held a large ruby up in a stream of incoming sunlight. Twisting and turning the sparkling ruby, its beauty mesmerized her. Positive energy enveloped the room. Time seemed to be at a standstill until Lorcan noisily entered the room and slammed the door shut behind him. Startled, she sprang up and tried to clear her head.

"How did you get the fairies to stay out of here?"

"Easy." Natalie shook her head, trying to shake off her daydreaming. "You don't let them outside. Fascination with the outside world keeps them in line. By leaving me alone in here, I bring them things from the outside world. That includes the pixies who leave me alone."

"So that's why their rooms have kaleidoscopes?"

"Yup, it seems kaleidoscopes are popular. Fortunately, they can mass-produce anything once they see it, unless it's food."

Lorcan shook his head before switching to a more serious topic. "Next weekend, we need to have a meeting with Skylar, Madison, Joel, Pru..."

Natalie interrupted Lorcan before he could finish. "Are you sure Joel is a wizard?"

"Definitely. Draon gave me the names."

"I've never seen his bird."

"Oh, it isn't the usual bird. His familiar wanted to talk, so he decided to be a Rose-Breasted Cockatoo."

"A cockatoo!" Natalie burst out laughing.

"It fits his familiar. He wanted to yak, and those birds are known for clown-like antics, which describes him perfectly." Lorcan fumed.

"Is there a rule that a bird matches a mage? Mine is a crow, Pru's is a blackbird, and Madison and Skylar have an owl."

"Those are the traditional birds for those elements. However, it's not written in stone, if that's what you mean," Lorcan huffed.

"How do these birds become our familiars?" Natalie wondered for the first time what possessed a bird to attach itself to a mage.

"That's for another time. We're off track. The last mage is someone called Connor."

Natalie looked at Lorcan in surprise. "Connor? I don't know a Connor except at school."

"Well, you need to find him. He lives somewhere in your community. The only additional information I can give you is that it would be a property with an old homestead on it."

"How can that be? Joel doesn't have an old homestead. We watched that building getting torn down before they built their new home."

"Yup, that was a big mistake. It's going to need to come back, and that takes Draon." Lorcan shook his head.

Natalie's heart began to pound, thinking of another visit by Draon. She frowned and decided she wanted nothing to do with him. If possible, she would make sure she wasn't around when he was here.

"Natalie, you can't avoid Draon, and he can't avoid you. Figure out how you can keep your composure around him. That'll help him get over his issue."

"I'll try, but if he's short with me and considerate with the others, it won't work."

"Please try. Now, where were we?"

"We were talking about old homesteads as a clue that a mage lives there. Joel doesn't have an old homestead, and I don't recall one on Pru's property. Plus, the creepiest house in the neighborhood has an old homestead, which I doubt has a mage. It doesn't seem old homesteads are reliable for figuring out if a witch or wizard lives there."

"True. Draon has his reasons for not having an old homestead on Pru's property, but that is about to change."

"Why are homesteads so important?"

"If you lived in Stormfield, another enchanted forest, or enchanted lands, you wouldn't need a homestead. However, out here with the mageless, no homestead, no Ruiri...which is someone just like me. There's another very important reason you won't learn until you start your training."

"Wow. Who would have known these old decrepit-looking buildings were so important?"

"As you have discovered, looks can be deceiving. Now, your job is to find Connor. Next Saturday at 10 a.m., I want all of them here."

Monday arrived too soon. Before Natalie knew it, she found herself back at her dreary high school. Focused on magic instead of school, she wondered if reciting a spell would complete her school assignments. As soon as she thought that, she reprimanded herself. Making bad choices at the start was not good, but she really, really wanted to start her training with Lorcan. She sighed. Before Lorcan could begin training, she needed to find Connor and inform him and the others about the meeting.

Knowing she had powers, Natalie felt bold enough to speak with Connor before the bell rang. She went outside and ran around to the door that brought her to the science wing. She walked as fast as she could to her classroom. Arriving a full two minutes before the bell, she headed straight for Connor. Standing before him, he glanced up before going back to his writing. She continued to stand there.

"What?" Connor said in a flat tone.

"What street do you live on?"

"Why?"

"Someone asked me if I knew a Connor who lives on Ashton Drive, and I said no. Ashton Drive is in my neighborhood."

"Yes, it is," Connor stated without looking up or answering the question. Awkward silence engulfed them. The bell rang. Disappointed, Natalie walked over to her chair and sat down.

She couldn't concentrate on anything Mr. Parrish said in class. Connor must live in her neighborhood. Why hadn't she ever seen him coming or going? How was she going to get him to come to her place? Maybe it would be better if Joel asked him. She sighed in relief, knowing it wouldn't be a problem to get the rest of them to meet at the old homestead.

Heading towards the barn, Natalie spotted Madison and Skylar near the fire pit at the back of their property. She wanted to speak with them, but first, she had to deal with the chickens. She ran to the back of the barn and chased the chickens into the back stalls. After locking them in, she ran through the pasture and up to the fence. Gasping for breath, she paused for a couple of minutes before yelling at them.

"Madison, Skylar!"

Both stopped adding wood to the fire and turned to face Natalie, pushing their black hoods back.

"Can I come over for a few minutes and talk to you about something super important?"

"Sure," they both yelled back.

Natalie jogged towards their property. Madison and Skylar headed towards the front entrance. They met Natalie in their driveway.

"You won't believe all that has happened since the last time I saw you. It's incredible!"

"You want to talk here or back at the fire?" Madison asked, watching Natalie continually move to stay warm.

"Let's go to the fire. It doesn't matter how much I bundle up; I'm always cold."

"I can make some hot chocolate," Skylar volunteered.

"I'm fine. I need to get to Pru's house this afternoon, but I wanted to speak with you first. I do have a favor to ask of you."

Natalie took a breath and continued without waiting for an answer. "Do you have any candy that I can borrow and pay you back later?"

"Halloween year-round here! Of course, we have candy," Madison said with a smirk.

"Thanks. Do you have any tart candy?"

Natalie laughed at their raised eyebrows, questioning the strange request.

"Pru has these two huge candles that guard her house, and they really like tart candy. I know it sounds weird. Actually, it is weird. You have got to see them to believe it. In fact, if you have the time, why don't you come with me and meet Pru? She makes charms...real charms like the bracelet I'm wearing. If you come, I can explain what is happening on the way over there."

"Oh, wow! That sounds incredible. Candles that eat candy and someone who makes charmed bracelets. We definitely want to see the candles and meet Pru," Skylar said.

"Give me a minute to go inside to let our parents know the fire is burning, and we're going over to a neighbor's house," Madison said.

"Do you want to grab the candy, or do you want me to get it?"

"I'll grab it, Skylar," Madison said as she headed towards the house.

On the way over to Pru's house, Natalie explained about the candles, their long tongues, and their warped sense of humor. She told them about her weekend with Lorcan in the old homestead and that they should go into their homestead and meet Sharlow in his Ruiri form. Natalie told them there was a meeting on Saturday in her old homestead at 10 a.m., and it would last most of the day. She finished up on what she knew about Pru's abilities as they entered Pru's property.

They walked by the ancient oak trees at the front of the property. Entering a clearing, Madison and Skylar spotted the candles.

"Oh my," Skylar exclaimed, "they are huge."

"It goes with their attitude." Natalie focused on the candles.

The candles spotted them and watched as they approached. They decided on demented behavior. They widened their eyes, cocked an eyebrow, smirked, narrowed their eyes, and made all kinds of weird facial expressions.

Watching the strange behavior, Skylar decided she wanted nothing to do with the candles. She shook her head no and handed the candy to Natalie.

"Hey, can you gals move a little faster? We're starving over here," the candle to the left shouted at them.

Madison and Skylar slowed and walked behind Natalie.

"Well, it's going to take a minute before you get these treats. All these candies are individually wrapped." Natalie raised the bags to show the sarcastic candles, the large bags of candy they had for them.

"We aren't picky."

"Good grief, you two are pigs!" Natalie exclaimed when they were close to the steps. Both candles started making pig noises. She rolled her eyes as she handed Skylar a bag while she opened the other bag. Skylar opened the second bag but never took her eyes off the candles.

"Same rules, guys," Natalie warned.

"We know, we know," both candles shouted. "We promise no tongues will appear until you three are safely inside. We got it. Now hurry up!"

"Fair warning…when you get near the door, they're going to yell boo. They can be total jerks," Natalie whispered.

Madison and Skylar, alarmed, were already standing close to each other. Walking to the spot to place the candy, Natalie waited.

"What??"

"You haven't unlocked the door."

Their flames lit, and then there was a loud sound of the door unlocking. "Is that better!?" both candles sarcastically replied.

Natalie put down a pile of candy in front of each candle. She motioned for Madison and Skylar to follow her. Just as they reached the door, the candles yelled, "Boo!" Even with the warning, Madison and Skylar screamed. Laughter erupted as all three crashed through the opening, almost falling over each other.

Regaining her composure, Natalie said, "Pru, I've brought some guests!"

"I'm in the family room."

Once in the family room, Madison and Skylar spotted the broom displayed over the fireplace and read the Aerial MMXVIII.

"It's an interesting design," Madison said.

"It looks nothing like our brooms," Skylar said.

"True." Madison turned her attention to the overwhelming number of white candles throughout the room.

Looking over at Skylar, she raised her eyebrows. "Wow! Simply wow!"

Natalie wasn't paying attention to Madison and Skylar's observations. She wanted to get the introductions out of the way so she could get to the real reason she was there.

"Pru, this is Madison and Skylar. They're the ones that make the brooms."

Pru smiled, leaned forward, and shook Madison's hand, and then Skylar's hand. "When Natalie mentioned she had neighbors who make authentic witches' brooms, I was looking forward to the day I would meet you. It's an honor to finally get this opportunity."

Flat-out changing the subject, Natalie exclaimed, "Pru, it happened! I did it! I spent the weekend at the homestead, and it's as you said it would be. The best part is the training starts this Saturday at 10. Lorcan wants you to train with us."

"Natalie, I'm so proud of you. You pushed through your fears, and you did it. These are amazing and exciting times. We're going to be trained."

Pru turned her focus to Madison and Skylar. "Mostly what I know is what Natalie's mother told me, except for making the Variegated Orb Weaver bracelets. That is a natural talent...probably like your natural talent for making brooms."

"That sounds like us. Skylar and I are not from the same biological parents, but we have the same passion for brooms. As we told Natalie before, when we decided to make them, we each drew up a design. When we looked at our designs, they were identical."

"Interesting. How Natalie's mother started to bring Variegated Orb Weaver webs to me is a mystery, but it is just what I needed to make the charm bracelets. And now that you are both here, let me fit each of you with a bracelet."

Pru reached over to the stand where several bracelets were hanging and removed two of them. Madison stood in front of her with her right hand extended.

"What do they do?"

"They will provide some protection against evil, but mostly they will warn you when evil is near you. When your bracelet flashes, it's a warning. The faster it flashes, the more you are in danger."

"This is so cool," Skylar said as she twirled her bracelet. While thrilled about the bracelets, the bracelets didn't glitter.

"Pru, do you mind if I open the Variegated Orb Weaver room to show them what the bracelets do?" Natalie already started walking over to the bookcase.

"Sure. Madison and Skylar, please follow Natalie." Pru remained in her chair as Natalie pulled the book that opened the secret room. Madison and Skylar followed her inside. They marveled at the endless apothecary jars of spiderweb material and completed bracelets. As Natalie moved close to one section of the spiderwebs, they glittered.

In awe, Madison and Skylar watched the whole room light up from the twinkling spiderweb material.

"That's what it will do when it's warning you. I'm not sure why they go crazy in here when I stand too close to them. I asked Pru before, but she would only say it's a sign and wouldn't say anything else."

"I didn't think I'd ever want to be anywhere near a spider or web, but I have to say the bracelets are amazing," Madison said.

"I agree, except roaches are my weakness."

"Roaches are right up there with spiders," Skylar said as they reached Pru.

"Thank you so much, Pru. We love the bracelets," Madison said, looking at Pru and then glancing down at her bracelet.

"Thank you, Pru. We're glad we met you. We can't wait for Saturday when we'll see you again," Skylar said.

"I'm looking forward to it, too."

"What we aren't looking forward to is dealing with your dreaded candles," Natalie stated as they headed for the front door. Pru laughed.

Standing at the door, Natalie had a plan. "Let's take off running."

Without saying another word, all three burst out the door, down the steps, and out of reach before they slowed down.

Taken by surprise, the candles took a minute to react, and then they yelled at the girls, "No fair!"

"Sorry, guys. Rude behavior begets rude behavior."

"Rude? We're not rude. We're entertaining and incredibly handsome," the one to the left of the door said while winking and giving a cheesy grin.

Heartily laughing, Natalie struggled to get the "in your dreams" words out.

They walked back and stopped in front of Joel's house.

"I hope he's home, so that will leave Connor as the last one to inform about Saturday." Natalie imagined Connor would think she was crazy.

"We hope so, too," Madison said.

"Wish us luck in calling our owl into the house. With our Halloween obsession, we don't think it will surprise our parents when the owl roosts in the house," Skylar laughed.

"You've been conditioning them all these years with your year-round Halloween decorations and broom-making."

"True, speaking of brooms, we'll wait until tomorrow when it is full sunlight to venture into the old homestead," Madison said.

"I don't blame you. It took me forever to muster the courage to go inside my homestead. I came prepared with a flashlight and bug spray, thinking it would be dark and bug-infested, but the infestation turned out to be fairies and pixies. Believe me, it's amazing."

"Thanks, Natalie. Giving you that Halloween invitation was the best thing we've ever done," Skylar said before the girls started walking towards their home.

"Mrs. Jackson, may I speak with Joel for a moment?"

"Come in, Natalie. I'll go get him."

Mrs. Jackson motioned for Natalie to follow her to the family room. A light evergreen scent filled the air as she headed for an overstuffed chair in the beautifully decorated room. She looked across at the red brick fireplace mantel, which was covered in family photos. She smiled at the elementary and middle school pictures.

Walking in, Joel stopped in front of her and cracked a joke. "Natalie, you never come over here. Are you desperate for help in algebra?"

"Ha, ha," Natalie said, fighting to contain her excitement. "I have something to tell you that goes way beyond algebra, but we need to be careful not to be overheard."

"Let's step into the backyard and hear this exciting news." Joel rolled his green flannel sleeves down to stay warm outside.

"That's perfect. In fact, can we go over to where the old homestead used to be?"

Giving her a strange look, Joel shrugged. "Sure."

Standing on the center ground of the former old homestead, Natalie told Joel everything. He listened, but midway through, he crossed his arms. His facial expression never changed.

I can't believe it; Joel doesn't believe me. Even though he had the warning signs and the feeling that they were supposed to be doing something, he didn't believe her. Awkwardly, they stared at one another. Natalie thought all was lost, but Jericho approached them just in time. She looked down and knew why he showed up.

"Joel, please come to the old homestead with me. Right now. If it isn't what I said it is, I will never talk to you about this again."

Seeing the desperation in Natalie's eyes, Joel only hesitated for a moment before nodding his head in agreement. They walked to the front road and then over to Natalie's property. They didn't speak until they reached the gravel driveway headed for the old homestead.

"That's a wild story you spun back there, Anderson. I know I'm the one who started it, but nothing happened. Maybe if you get new scarecrows and trash those old, battered ones, you won't let your imagination run wild. You really should change them out. In fact, they creep me out when I look out my bedroom window. Sometimes my imagination runs wild because it looks like they tilt their heads upward and stare at me."

"I'm sure they stare up at you. I often feel like they turn and stare at me when I'm near the barn. Believe me, it took all my nerve to get past them and the creepy stump. I'm absolutely never going to touch them."

Natalie wondered if Joel thought it strange that the gruff black cat led the way to the old homestead. He didn't comment on it.

They followed Jericho to the front door. Standing before the door, Jericho gave three ear-piercing, high-pitched meows. The door slowly creaked open. Amused at Jericho's dramatic behavior, Joel waved Natalie and Jericho inside.

Once Natalie entered, Joel peeked past the front room and saw the beautiful Room of Mirrors. Noticing nothing unusual, even though he was expecting a dusty, empty building, he stepped inside.

The door slammed shut. Spinning around in shock, Joel grabbed the doorknob and tried to turn it. The door was locked. Spinning back around, Joel screamed. Lorcan stood before him.

"Not a believer, Joel?" Lorcan said as Joel backed up against the door and stared at him in utter shock. Eyes wide with disbelief, Joel didn't move.

"It's awfully quiet in here," Natalie said.

"We can change that." Lorcan looked in the direction of the staircase. "Come out, come out, wherever you are!"

Like locusts, the high-pitched chattering fairies and pixies zoomed down the stairs and surrounded Joel. Erupting in a swarm of chaotic activity, they yanked, tugged, pushed, and pulled Joel into the center of the Room of Mirrors.

"Watch out for the flowers in the hair," Natalie laughed. She remembered over five pounds of flowers on her head the first time she met the pixies and fairies.

Lorcan allowed them ten minutes before he tapped the wall with his wand. They didn't go screeching off. They moved back, sprinkled fairy dust over Joel, piled him with Hawaiian leis that matched the flowers in his hair, and straightened up the crown of flowers. With bursts of giggles and fairy dust in the air, they flew off to their rooms.

Looking ridiculous, Joel stood there. Knowing it had happened, he struggled to accept it.

"Joel," Lorcan said in a serious tone, "training starts this Saturday at 10 a.m. You will be here all day. Got it?"

Joel, frozen in place, nodded his head yes.

"Thanks, Lorcan." Natalie grabbed Joel's hand, spun him around, opened the door, and pulled him outside.

Once outside, Joel took a deep breath. He slowly let it out. Removing the crown and placing it on the nearest scarecrow, he said nothing until they shut the gate behind them.

"I kept thinking the signs meant something, but nothing happened. You know how you get that uneasy feeling that you should do something, but you don't know what? Well, nothing happened, so I couldn't understand why I felt that way. That meeting with Mr. Xanders was the strangest thing that has happened in all these months. Then you come over with this wild story." Joel took the Hawaiian leis off and held them in his hands. A reminder of what had just happened.

"I should have been more forceful in speaking with you, Joel, before now. Many bad things have been happening to me. Instead of talking with you, I went over to Pru's house and talked with her. She's the one who pushed me to go into the old homestead. By the way, you need your old homestead."

"What!? It's gone. That I know for sure. I may wonder what happened in your old homestead a few minutes ago, but I'm sure mine is gone. Toast!"

"Lorcan says Draon will bring it back, and your parents will never know they had it demolished. You need the old homestead for your Ruiri to live in. Besides protecting you, your Ruiri will mentor you. Lorcan, my Ruiri, will hold the first meeting. After that, I don't know what happens."

"You know, this is a lot to take in at once." Joel studied the Hawaiian leis in his hands. They were now standing in his driveway.

"I agree. I spent the entire weekend in the old homestead getting comfortable with it. Ultimately, I may need help with algebra because I can only think of magic. It's so exciting! We start training on Saturday."

The last statement brought Natalie back to Connor. He was the last person to be informed about the Saturday training.

"Joel, do you know Connor O'Neill?"

"Yes, he's the goth kid."

"Connor lives in the neighborhood. He's the last mage that needs to be invited to the training. Do you think you could do it? I tried to get some information from him, but I think the incident in science has me on his jerk list."

Surprised, since Natalie was so predictable, Joel had to know what happened. "What did you do that was so bad?"

"I had everyone in class making a ruckus over him. Believe me, he didn't appreciate it."

"He wouldn't. He's a loner. Sometimes I hike on the vacant property at the end of the road where he lives. I'll ask him."

"Wow, so he does live in the neighborhood."

"He and his mother moved here about the same time we moved here. Is the training just for people from our neighborhood? Do you know how many are going to be at the training?"

"Just from our community. It will be Pru, Madison, Skylar, Connor, you, and me."

Joel relaxed. "How did we get this way?"

"That we find out at the Saturday training, but I will say that it tends to run in at least one side of the family."

Joel's eyes grew wide in surprise. Natalie laughed and started walking towards her property. If she didn't leave now, he would inundate her with questions for which she didn't have the answers.

Chapter 18
Do You Know Your Clan?

Anxious to get together with the other mages and start training, Natalie couldn't believe how the week seemed to drag on forever. She ignored Joel, so nothing in their behavior gave away their secret. Connor behaved as always. Aloof and writing in his notebook, no one could tell he guarded a world-changing secret.

She easily ignored them, but she couldn't ignore Lainey. Her despondent and distant behavior bothered her. Pru must have told her. She looked over at Lainey. Lainey ignored her. She sighed. *I'm sorry, Lainey. It must be pure torture to know but not be a part of it.*

Finally, after a long and restless night, Saturday morning arrived. Too excited to stay in bed after seven, Natalie got up, showered, and headed to feed the chickens and check on the feeder for the feral cat colony. Before eight, she stood at the old homestead door.

Lorcan opened the door and smirked. "Isn't it amazing what a difference a week makes? Two weeks ago, I couldn't get you in here; now you're early. Come in."

A long, wide table with eight chairs consumed a large part of the Room of Mirrors.

"How come eight seats?"

"Breccan will join us."

When Lorcan saw Natalie's confused expression, he simply stated, "Sharlow."

"Does he need to stay in cat form?"

"No, even though it will be hard to tell us apart." Lorcan added paper and pencils to the table.

"I'm sure we'll figure out who is who by the outfits." Natalie rolled her eyes as she visualized the outrageous color combination Breccan would be wearing.

Annoyed by her comment, Lorcan snapped, "True. Now go to another room. I have things to do."

Natalie headed to the gemstone room. Excited and unable to settle down, she knew the gemstones would keep her calm until the meeting started.

She studied an emerald gemstone near the window as Pru, Madison, and Skylar entered the room.

"Wow, it looks like a pirate's treasure," Madison said, walking over to Natalie.

"Our mentor has a small collection compared to Lorcan's gemstones," Skylar said, standing beside Madison.

"I don't have a mentor yet, so it'll be interesting to see what he brings to the old homestead yet to be created."

Pru, Madison, and Skylar walked around the room, looking at each cauldron overflowing with gemstones.

"Lorcan must be rich," Skylar said as the door opened.

"Who's rich?" Joel said, stepping in and shutting the door.

"Not us," Madison said.

Lorcan called everyone to the table precisely at ten. Connor entered the homestead and strolled towards the table. Unaware of Breccan prancing right behind him in cat form, Connor frowned at having everyone's attention. Irritated, he stared back at them. Then he noticed they weren't exactly looking at him. Turning around to see what had their attention, Connor screamed as he watched Breccan transform into his Ruiri form right before his eyes.

"What are you screaming about?" Lorcan said as he walked back into the room.

Connor turned around to see who was talking and saw Breccan's twin. Terrified for a moment, he wavered on whether he wanted to bolt for the door or sit down with this strange group.

"Sit down, Connor," Lorcan demanded. "The door is locked. You aren't going anywhere."

Connor scowled as he sat next to Natalie. She smiled over at him. He didn't return the smile.

"Connor, do you have a black cat?" Lorcan asked.

"Yeah. He showed up the day after the storm. I call him Oxley."

"Ever been in the old homestead?"

"Nope."

"Oxley is your Ruiri. Just like I chose to mentor Natalie, Oxley chose to mentor you. Your first assignment is to go into the old homestead. Oxley is to you what Girvin is to us. However, I have a feeling you'll continue to call him Oxley."

"Yeah, sure." Connor tried to visualize his fat, lazy cat morphing into something like Lorcan.

"Joel and Pru, within the week, you'll have homesteads. It's a complex process that Draon has already started. People won't even remember that those buildings weren't there. Joel, your Ruiri is Murphy. Pru, your Ruiri is Cashel. Next item, you each have a bird. Bring the bird inside."

Natalie laughed when Lorcan said each had a bird. She remembered Joel had a Rose-Breasted Cockatoo.

Lorcan looked over at Natalie. "Do you care to share what you think is so funny?"

Embarrassed, it took Natalie a moment to answer. "Joel has a Rose-Breasted Cockatoo."

Astonished, Joel looked over at Natalie. "How do you know? Can you hear him from your house? He's loud, obnoxious, and rarely shuts up."

Lorcan answered while the others laughed. "I told her. If you have him caged, let him out. He should be free to come and go."

Lorcan turned to Connor. "Do you know your bird?"

"Maybe. There's a red-winged blackbird that seems to follow me around the yard."

Startled, Natalie looked over at Connor. Pru has a red-winged blackbird. Does that mean Connor belongs to the same clan as Pru?

Lorcan continued. "That would be your bird. These are not ordinary birds, so give them worthy names. They are your familiars."

"What does that mean?" Madison asked.

"They understand you and can help you. Your Ruiri will work with you and your familiar. After today, you'll receive guidance from your mentor. The Crossroads will provide training." Lorcan waited to see if anyone would ask about the Crossroads. No raised hands. Interesting.

Lorcan continued. "Do you know your clan?" Lorcan looked around the room.

Natalie knew her clan, but she wasn't volunteering any information. Lorcan rested his eyes on her. She ignored him. Focused on the paper in front of her, she silently hoped he would not ask her.

"There are four clans. There is the Aerial of the air element, the Alchemist of the water element, the Thaumaturge of the fire element, and the Shadowlink linked to the ancient wizard and versed in earth and the other three elements. As I say your name, I will say your clan. Then you are to go into the room over to the left to have your powers tested."

Hearing those words, Natalie's heart raced. She knew who waited in that room.

"Madison...Aerial." Madison anxiously walked over and stepped into the room.

As soon as the door closed, Lorcan called Skylar. "Skylar...Aerial." Skylar got up and nervously waited outside the room.

"Joel...Thaumaturge." Joel jumped up, surprised and pleased that he was the clan of the fire element.

"Connor...Alchemist." Connor waited a couple of minutes before he stood up. It was obvious Connor had no interest in the water element. Lorcan saw the lack of excitement.

"Connor, Alchemist is also potions and charms. Charms can be things that people never think of being enchanted. You'll find Alchemist is a powerful element."

Connor slightly smiled and seemed to consider what Lorcan said.

Madison and Skylar returned to the table. Joel was still being tested. Lorcan looked over at Pru and said, "Alchemist." Pru stayed seated. She would wait until she didn't need to stand at the door.

Madison leaned over to Natalie. "We both have full powers in Aerial and some limited power in another element."

Lorcan overheard them. "It would be a surprise if someone sitting in this room didn't have their full powers in their primary element. Draon carefully selected strong mages."

Madison and Skylar beamed at hearing they were powerful mages.

Skylar also had some news. "Natalie, we forgot to tell you we have two owls. When we called our owl to come inside, two owls flew into the house. They're so cute. Little screech owls. It's a good thing they can tell us apart because we can't tell them apart."

Seated, everyone whispered about their readings except for Madison. Madison looked from Lorcan to Natalie and then back at Lorcan. "What about Natalie?"

The room grew quiet as they focused on her.

"Natalie is a Shadowlink."

"No way," Connor muttered as he and Joel raised their eyebrows in surprise.

Blushing, Natalie kept her head down.

Taking the attention off her, Pru asked, "I don't understand the element factor and the spells and potions factor for our group. I thought witches and wizards had magic as part of them, and they just learned how to use it and control it."

"Very good observation, Pru," Lorcan stated as he thought of how to answer the question.

"What would course through a mage to give them powers? Something in their blood? A special area in their brain? Why are some people born with magic and others aren't? In your case, it's because of the original Shadowlink and the Stormfield wizard, which is Draon."

"Draon being the man that tested us?" Joel asked.

"Yes, your powers originated from him, but what about the others that didn't come from the original Shadowlink clan?" Lorcan asked. "It's hard to say, but in your case, it's because you are always connected to at least one element, if not more elements, to a lesser degree. Your primary element flows 100 percent in and around you. You need to learn how to appreciate it and harness it. Use it always for good. Your elemental power is your dominant power. Because an element is within you and serves you, you have the connection to use the magic that most people associate with witches and wizards."

Lorcan looked around and saw all of them, except Connor, trying to process what he had just said. He laughed.

"The simple version. Energy, frequency, and vibration are a part of you. You just need to learn how to tap into it."

"Thanks," Pru responded, still puzzled by how this would work out.

"How old is Draon?" Joel asked.

"Not important," Lorcan responded.

"How long has the Shadowlink existed?"

"Joel, for centuries. However, that isn't relevant to your training."

"Wow, Draon must be hundreds of years old."

"Shh," Pru said, looking at Joel.

"Joel, focus on your training."

"Yes, sir." Joel shifted in his chair and focused on Lorcan.

"We're going to start out with a simple, mageless exercise. I want you to practice at least five minutes each day. Take a deck of cards and turn the cards over. Concentrate on making pairs with as few mistakes as possible. The actual mission is to learn to go with your instinct. In time, you will learn to let your instinct make the choice. A heightened instinct is vital in magic."

Lorcan focused on Connor, which caused the others to focus on him. He didn't change his bored expression on the waste of time game. Suddenly, something flew at his head. He looked up too late. Colorful fairy dust splattered all over him.

Lorcan laughed and then went serious. "Develop your instinct. Your computer games will not heighten your instincts. Things are about to turn ugly in your world. You need to prepare for the battle."

Natalie and Joel had firsthand experience with the fairy dust splatter game, so they kept their heads down and fought to contain their composure. They knew Connor wouldn't join in laughing at his ridiculous look. Madison, Skylar, and Pru looked and turned away, stifling laughs.

Connor's negative attitude annoyed Lorcan, but he ignored it. "Everyone, Breccan is returning to his homestead. The rest of us are going to the bookstore. Pru has volunteered to drive us there."

Walking outside, Lorcan transformed into Jericho as Natalie and the others bubbled with excitement while heading to Pru's car. Natalie glanced around for Connor, who lagged behind. She saw his expression and knew he didn't want to be a part of the group. It wasn't a surprise, but it disappointed her that he didn't give it a chance. Before she could call his name, Connor stormed off.

Chapter 19
Crossroads Barracks

It only took Pru a few minutes to pull her car into the Tallest of Tales' grassy parking lot. Nothing appeared to be unusual about them getting out of the car and heading into the old bookstore, except for the large black cat that trotted just ahead of them.

In soft light and warm air, Wilfred stood invisible behind a huge mound of books stacked on the old wooden front counter. The bell at the door jingled, announcing their arrival. He stepped around the counter and nodded at each one as they entered the store. His wide smile made it obvious he expected them.

"Lorcan, Natalie, all of you, so glad you made it to our humble shop." Wilfred bowed to Lorcan.

"You know Lorcan?" a shocked Natalie asked Wilfred. Cautiously, she glanced around the few open spaces to see if others were in the shop. It appeared they were the only customers.

"Not long. Things have developed over the last few months, but one of the most important developments is this group. We've been waiting for this day."

Wilfred turned to face the back of the store. He yelled, "Jonathan, they're here!"

Within minutes, Jonathan strolled through the center aisle and looked the group over.

"I thought there were six mages."

"One of us bailed," Joel said, reeling from the heat that had to be set on 80, and yet both Wilfred and Jonathan wore black trench coats.

"Ah," both said, looking at Lorcan.

"We'll talk with you later about the missing mage," Wilfred said.

"Now, follow me," Jonathan announced while Wilfred returned to the front desk.

Overstuffed, overflowing floor-to-ceiling rows of wooden bookshelves lined both sides of the center aisle. More books, piled high at the start of each bookshelf, waited to be shelved. Wasting no space, bookshelves also lined the windowless walls. Bargain bins were in the center of the store, creating a divided and narrow path on each side.

The store seemed like an intriguing, musty-smelling hoarder's maze, yet both store owners knew the exact location of any requested book. Usually, the endless sound of hammering reverberated throughout the store. There were never enough bookshelves.

Meandering to the back of the store, they took a sharp left and traveled down a long row of bookshelves that were neatly lined with identical-looking red books. Unlike the used books in the rest of the store, these books were in pristine condition.

Natalie had never noticed them before, but then again, she couldn't remember this part of the bookstore ever being open. Had they added on to the building?

At last, they came to the last shelf of books and stood before it. Jonathan reached out and, with fingers flying, he tapped a series of books. The bookshelf began to move and disappear into a wall pocket.

Fully open, Jonathan bowed and waved them into the tunnel. After they gathered inside and the door closed behind them, Jonathan stepped in front to lead the way. "Isn't this exciting? You are now entering a whole new world and beginning a whole new adventure."

Well, it didn't look like a whole new, exciting world; it looked more like a sinister, ancient, narrow stone hallway leading to a dark and dingy, musty-smelling dungeon of long ago. The tunnel, lit by fire crystal sconces, cast an ominous red light on the gradually descending cobblestone path.

Natalie wanted to reach into a sconce and take one of the illuminating crystals. She slowed and dropped back, waiting for her opportunity to grab one. The others excitedly chattered while they focused on the path. She stopped. On her tippy toes and one hand on the wall to steady herself, she took her other hand and reached into the top of a sconce. Heat swirled up to her hand at the same time Jonathan turned around to look at the group. He stopped. Natalie quickly dropped her hand by her side.

"Don't try for a keepsake. Those are dragon fire crystals. They burn."

"Good to know," Joel replied, "because it was tempting to take one home."

"Ditto," Natalie said, with relief in her voice.

Jonathan laughed. "Better to heed the warning than a severely burned hand, all for naught."

Continuing the long downward trek, Joel stayed by Pru, helping her along the narrow path. What seemed like a lengthy hike ended at an old archway with a thick wooden door. Excitement mounted along with a strong desire for fresh air. Jonathan lifted the heavy black metal handle and swung the door open.

Stunned, the new mages gawked at what lay before them. There stood what appeared to be an entire underground community, stretching well beyond their vision. Four long rows of three-story buildings, forming an x, faced into a large circular courtyard. At the circular courtyard were four pillars of white, red, blue, and green. The front building of each row matched the color of the pillar closest to that building. A sky of white, puffy clouds hung low over the tops of the three-story buildings as warm sunlight beamed down on them. The sunny scene seemed a little too perfect, but it disguised the overhead ceiling.

"Come on, come on," Jonathan exclaimed, motioning them to step out into the front entrance. "You can't learn anything all bunched up in the doorway."

Stepping out, apprehension immediately gripped them as they stood before the plain white gatehouse and its hideous guard.

Hidden in long, flowing layers of black garments, the gatekeeper ominously floated close to them. Terrified, they didn't dare move even though a powerful stench assailed their noses. They held their breaths while the gatekeeper paused at one and then moved to another. They avoided looking at the face covered by a black hood and veil.

The inspection took minutes, but it seemed like an eternity. Without a word, the gatekeeper turned and drifted back to the gatehouse.

After being cleared to enter, Lorcan transformed into his Ruiri gnome form and stepped to the front of the group, collectively gasping for air.

Smiling at the normal first reaction, Lorcan stated, "Hexel, our gatekeeper, is a mystery. However, we think she is a creature similar to a fury. We will probably never know, as her touch is deadly. What we do know is she is the best gatekeeper to keep us safe in the Crossroads Barracks."

Pausing, Lorcan gave them a couple of minutes to recover from the sensory overload before he continued.

"Four roads representing Air, Earth, Fire, and Water lead back to the courtyard. Paths are along each side of the buildings. At the back of the Fire elemental building is a classroom for all of you to attend mage classes. There are specialty shops and restaurants. Everything here is available if you have the money. The shops only deal in gold, silver, and copper. There are coin shops in the mageless world selling precious metals that can be used here. Even something as small as a Mercury silver dime will work. While copper is cheap above, it has greater value down here, so save your old copper pennies. Do you have questions?"

Still recovering from the close encounter with Hexel, the mages shook their heads no. Lorcan glanced at each one to see that they were okay before he continued providing information.

"As you explore the Barracks, you will see buildings all along the perimeter walls. Except for the leadership buildings, those buildings are private and used as apartments. In the near future, we will assign you to an apartment within one of those buildings. You will receive two keys. One key for entry to the building and the common area, and another key for your apartment. You can use your apartment to hold your treasure, as a retreat, or whatever you want for magic, except for black magic. No magical creatures are allowed here except by special permission and only for a short time. Ruiries, Hexel, and a few unique small critters are the exception."

Lorcan took a deep breath and continued. "Anyway, as you can see, the first building of each row has a different color. White for Aerial, Red for Thaumaturge, Blue for Alchemist, and Green for the Shadowlink. Classes will be in the afternoon on Tuesdays, Wednesdays, and Thursdays, with the exception that your introductory class today is on a Saturday. Weekday classes are training in your particular element. Let me clarify. Training will be your dominant element. Some of you have lesser ability in another element. After you master your first element, you will train in another element. Your mentor will give you a Saturday schedule of your traditional mage classes. Questions?"

"Aren't we going to look suspicious traipsing through the bookstore all the time?" Joel asked, still recovering from the decaying smell of Hexel.

"Excellent question, Joel. It's one of the reasons you need your old homesteads. Each homestead has a tunnel leading to the homestead of Natalie's property. Enter the homestead either by the tunnel from your homestead or by becoming best friends with Natalie. Her old homestead has a rail tunnel with a cart that transports you to a platform. From there, you will take the stairs to the door at the back of the bookstore. You won't need Jonathan's fancy hand movements to open the door. There's a handprint by the door. Simply place your hand on it. When you came through today, each of you had an enchantment placed on you that allows access to the Barracks. You can come and go as you please, except you'd better be attending your classes."

"Any more questions?"

"Lorcan," Natalie began, clearly puzzled, "all of this is just for us?"

"Another good question. No. This place has existed for decades, but it is a tightly guarded secret. Even Draon wasn't aware of the Crossroads Barracks. It hasn't been that long since I've known about it. What will surprise you is that there are people you deal with in real life down here. You certainly can be friends with them here, but you cannot change your relationship in the mageless world or speak of this place. That includes if you learn of a mage and that mage has not been introduced to the Barracks by Wilfred or Jonathan. For that person, this place doesn't exist. The fewer people that know about this place, the safer it is for the current members."

Looking at Pru, Lorcan stated, "Pru, you cannot give information to Lainey. None. You need to make sure she doesn't follow you or figure out the underground tunnel system. The candles will work to ensure she doesn't know, but you need to work at Lainey not discovering any new information."

Lorcan took his time to look at each mage. "That goes for all of you. No discussion with family or friends. Even if one of your parents is a mage and doesn't know it, it isn't up to you to inform that person. Things are about to become very complicated and dangerous. We need to be a complete secret. That means let no one outside this group and underground community know that you are a mage."

Natalie frowned, recalling how much Lainey already knew. "Lorcan, Lainey already knows the signs, Pru's magical abilities, and things my mother told Pru. Lainey also knows some of us are mages. Couldn't she let something slip out?"

"That is a serious possibility, especially when this new program starts at school. Wilfred and I will meet with Lainey at Pru's house. One of Lorcan's potions will erase Lainey's memory concerning magic. Are you going to be okay being a part of it, Pru?"

"Under the current circumstances, it will be better for her. Right now, she feels left out and abandoned."

"Thanks, Pru. It really is for the best," Jonathan said.

Still annoyed at Connor's behavior, Lorcan stated, "Oxley will promptly handle Connor. I expect he will soon attend classes."

"Do our mentors have a scary side?" Joel asked.

"Only if you are out of line," Lorcan said.

"Good to know," Joel said, wondering how Oxley planned on getting Connor to the Barracks.

"Any more questions?" Lorcan waited. "Seeing no more questions, it's time for you to go to your elemental training classes."

Entering the Earth building, Natalie looked around in surprise. A massive room of white walls and white marble floor brought the word stark to mind. If it hadn't been for a pile of rocks, a tower of white sand, and a chair on the other side of the room, it would be empty.

Intrigued, Natalie walked toward the pile of rocks and listened to the echoes of her steps. She leaned down and studied the various sizes of rocks. Hearing footsteps, Natalie refocused her attention on the man approaching her.

"Natalie," a dark-haired, dark-eyed man said her name as he walked up to her, "I'm your instructor, Alexander Martin. Since you're a Shadowlink, we're going to start out with the earth element. Don't lose hope if you don't succeed right away. Sometimes it takes weeks to learn to access the element. Do you have any questions?"

"Are you a Shadowlink?"

"No, you're the only Shadowlink here. However, I've trained many others in the other elements, so I have plenty of teaching experience. Any more questions?"

"No, sir."

"Great. Your first lesson is to have a rock come to you. The second part will be to send the rock to me. The smallest rocks are on top. Take your time and concentrate. It's all about concentration and seeing it in your mind. We will take breaks every 15 minutes to prevent you from exhausting yourself. Again, don't worry if nothing happens today, all week, or even an entire month."

"Thanks, that takes a lot of pressure off me."

Natalie walked over to the pile of rocks. The teacher walked to the back of the room and sat down in the only chair in the room. She looked at the rocks and then looked at the distance between her and the instructor.

"Whoa, that's a long way to send a rock."

Standing there trying to figure out the best way to achieve the goal, Natalie remembered Gary and the rubber band attack. Her mind replayed Gary and his chair slamming against the wall without any training. Maybe, she thought, she had a chance if she replayed him pelting her with rubber bands.

Closing her eyes, she took several deep breaths. She visualized Gary's rubber band hitting her painfully on the shoulder. She concentrated on the pain and her anger. Then she concentrated on his arrogant smile of victory. Her temper flared.

Visualizing the pile of rocks, she imagined picking some up. She heard a shifting sound but kept her mind on the rocks. Bringing her hands up as if juggling balls, she continued that motion until she pulled her left arm back and then swung out hard and fast.

A horrendous scream erupted from the teacher as he looked up from his phone, saw the incoming rocks, and ran behind his chair. Opening her eyes, the scene shocked Natalie. Instinctively, she flung her arms out, fingers straight, and yelled, "Stop!" Rocks that hadn't already reached the teacher hung in the air. Seconds later, a loud boom echoed throughout the room as the rocks crashed to the floor.

Visibly upset and angry, the teacher stormed up to a horrified Natalie.

"You've been practicing. You should have warned me!"

"I haven't been practicing! I know nothing about my powers."

"You lie," he pointed his finger in her face and accused her. "You're a boldface liar; that's what you are!"

Natalie, sensitive to people lying or someone accusing her of being a liar, became incensed.

"I am not a liar! I have not been training!" Natalie yelled back at him while backing away from his hand in her face.

"I'm familiar when someone has been training and when someone hasn't been training, so girlie, you can stop the act. You're a liar!" His eyes blazed in anger.

"You need to take that back! I'm telling you, I have never trained!" Incensed, Natalie yelled at the teacher. She had never done that in her entire life.

"It's the truth! You're a liar," the teacher spat at her. "You need to apologize now!"

"I won't apologize because it's the truth! Face the reality of being a liar!" the teacher screamed as he crossed his arms and stared hard at her.

Natalie, trembling in rage, looked over at the pile of sand and then directed her furious eyes back at the teacher. Before he could react, she snapped her fingers and pointed at him. The sand swirled up and engulfed him. Surrounded by a swirling tornado of sand, he yelled out one spell after another to counter her control, but nothing worked. Natalie crossed her arms and fumed while watching him.

"Natalie!" Lorcan yelled as he ran into the room as fast as his short legs would carry him. "What are you doing!?"

"He's calling me a liar!"

"Stop! Now!" Lorcan demanded.

"I can't."

"You can. Let your anger go. You know it isn't true."

"But he believes it."

"Natalie, now."

Anger raged within, but she obeyed Lorcan. She closed her eyes and asked the sand to return to the pile. Nothing happened. She angrily repeated the request in her mind several times, but nothing happened. Natalie couldn't let go of her rage.

Taking deep breaths while walking in short circles, she calmed down enough that the sand lost strength and piled up around the teacher. Awkwardly climbing over the sand pile surrounding him, he steered clear of Natalie and wobbled over to Lorcan.

"I won't work with her." Visibly shaking, the teacher turned and hurried out of the room.

Natalie watched him go. She felt he got what he deserved. How dare he call her a liar! The more she thought about it, the angrier she became.

Fuming, she looked out and saw the rocks spread across the room. She closed her eyes and asked the rocks to return to the pile. She heard the clunk, clunk, clunk sound of rocks piling up. When she opened her eyes, it was done.

Natalie looked over at Lorcan, expecting his approval. Instead, his wide-open eyes and distraught expression alarmed her. He started pacing and mumbling to himself.

"Are you casting a spell?"

"What? No, sorry. I knew something was different when the oracular stone threw out those fireworks. It has never acted that way. This isn't your fault. No, this is Draon's fault. He knows something, and he isn't telling us. I'm going to have a word with him. Unfortunately, you can't train today. The outcome would be the same in all elements. Come with me."

Sweet smells of sugar and cinnamon lingered in the air as Lorcan and Natalie neared Mademoiselle's Marvelous Calories Shop. Natalie relaxed when she read the sign and saw all the colorful, oversized lollipops plastered on the outside walls. Looking through the front window, endless pastries, candies, and drinks filled the large glass display cases.

"Lorcan, you know I don't have any precious metals with me."

"My treat. I feel awful. I should have been there. I knew the oracular stone had never reacted like that, but I ignored it. Alexander will never speak with me again."

"His fault. He shouldn't have called me a liar."

"I think he learned his lesson," Lorcan said as he recalled Alexander tightly wrapped in a sandstorm.

After Natalie had stuffed herself with two incredible raspberry-filled pastries and downed a cherry cola, she calmed down. "What's going to happen with my training?"

"New teacher."

"I hope the new teacher understands I haven't had any training."

"For no training, you had an impressive control of your power."

"That's called anger."

"Remind me not to get you mad."

Natalie didn't answer but smirked at the comment.

They still had time before the others finished with their training. Lorcan took her past the streets and to the perimeter. They looked at the various tan-colored buildings, all abutting one another. When they reached Building 208 in the back near the street with the Earth elemental training facility, Lorcan pulled a key from his pocket.

"Are you serious, Lorcan!?" Natalie said in surprise as she watched Lorcan open the door. It opened to a large room with a large wooden table and ten chairs. They walked through that room into a smaller room with a small white table and four chairs. Most likely, if they wanted to share meals, this is where they would eat. It had a kitchen and a bathroom. They looped back to the staircase by the large room.

"There are two apartments above the ground floor. You get to select which apartment you want to call home," Lorcan said as they started up the stairs.

"I'll probably regret it because of everything having to be lugged up or down two flights of stairs, but I want the top apartment."

Lorcan laughed. "Learn magic, and lugging things won't be an issue."

"True."

Lorcan produced another key from his pocket and handed it to Natalie. She placed the key in the lock and opened the door to an empty, stark white apartment. She didn't care. It belonged to her.

After she checked out the spacious two-bedroom apartment, they returned to the courtyard. The other mages stood there waiting for them. Excitement filled the air as they explained their tasks for the day. Each one talked over the other one. A jumble of excited voices. Natalie whispered good night to Hexel as they opened the door to the tunnel. All the way back, their happy voices echoed and bounced off the tunnel walls. Even as Pru dropped them off at Natalie's old homestead, no one noticed she wasn't saying anything.

She didn't attend training on Tuesday. That day, the others learned what had happened on Saturday. Coming over on Wednesday to enter the bookstore from Natalie's old homestead, all of them gave her a hard time about her incredible skills. While riding in the cart, they tried to cheer her up, hoping her earth training would start soon.

Natalie didn't go into the bookstore. No point. If she couldn't go to the Barracks, she didn't want to go inside. Entertaining herself, she rode the cart back and forth in the dim tunnel lit by the red dragon fire crystals. On the last trip out, Natalie glimpsed a hunched-back figure reaching into the crystals.

"They burn! Watch out!" Natalie stood up and yelled. Startled, whatever it was, it seemed to disappear into a darkened corner. She made one more trip to see if she could locate the person.

"Are you okay?" Natalie called out while bumping up to the bookstore steps. "Can I help you?" No reply. In the red, shadowy light, she could barely see anything. Disappointed and returning to her old homestead, she got out and went inside.

She rested comfortably on a pile of four pillows on the gemstone floor. Without knocking, Lorcan walked in carrying a huge, ornate book. She sat up as he dropped it down by her feet.

"I would suggest you take your Grimoire to your apartment and read it there. Your apartment enchantments will protect it."

"Wow, thanks! Pru had mentioned this book. Do I add to this book, or do I start my own?"

"Your mother started a new family Shadowlink Grimoire. You will continue your mother's Grimoire. In it, you will see events that have happened to you have also been recorded in there. While you wait for your teacher, read your book."

Natalie took several minutes to study the book cover. Then, she turned it over and looked at the back of the book. She looked up, puzzled.

"Strange, I thought it would have a roving eye, monster teeth, flaring nostrils, or some other outlandish feature on the cover. It's just a plain book. How terribly disappointing."

Lorcan laughed so hard that she started laughing, too.

"Just some fancy scrollwork with a huge emerald in the center of the golden book is all you get."

A few more chuckles, and then Natalie grew serious. "Do you think it's okay for me to go to the Barracks?"

"Sure. None of the teachers there will train you in any element, that's for sure. But they also respect you. I doubt anyone there is going to give you trouble."

"Thanks, I'll head over right now. Maybe I'll see that person in the tunnel again."

"Someone was in the tunnel?"

"I saw him with his hand in the dragon fire crystals. I yelled for him to stop, and just like that, he disappeared."

"I'm surprised you saw one of them. They maintain the dragon fire crystals in the tunnels. Don't trust them; don't go near them."

"What are they? He seemed deformed."

"Deformity caused by his actions. Character flaw; serious character flaw. Now, that's all I'm going to say. Get over to the Barracks before it gets too late to go."

Natalie picked the Grimoire up. Geez, the book had to weigh at least ten pounds. Feeling better about having something to do, she went down into the cavern below and hopped into the rail cart for the ride over to the bookstore. Climbing a few steps up, Natalie opened the door and crossed over to the door that would take her to the Barracks. She wondered why she had to go up to turn around and go down. It must have something to do with enchantments and spells.

Natalie said good morning to Hexel, disregarded the stores, and made her way to the far end of the Barracks. She unlocked the door and then hiked the two flights of stairs to her apartment. She didn't care that it was empty. It belonged to her. Plopping down on the front room floor, she leaned against a wall and opened the Grimoire.

A large childhood picture of her mother immediately caught her attention. Sadness overtook Natalie as she studied the picture. Her mother's eyes, with a mischievous twinkle, were full of hope and adventure as she started her mage training. Sadly, now it was her turn, but without her mother.

She changed her focus to her mother's first spells. Turning a few pages, she found simple spells written over full-page illustrations. Natalie wondered if Lorcan knew what he had given her. Was it safe to try the spells in the house? She'd need some things to do a deflecting spell, but she could try the illuminating and the lock spells right now.

Reading "inlumino" for the illuminating spell, she closed her eyes and practiced trying to turn the light on. Nothing. After several attempts, Natalie wondered if it would help if she had a wand. Lorcan didn't need a wand. Well, she didn't have one, so it was a moot point.

She repeated the word over and over, sometimes in a normal tone, and other times loudly. Sometimes, she said "inlumino" with her eyes closed, and sometimes she furiously stared at the light, but nothing happened.

Strange. She could hurl rocks and create sandstorms, but she couldn't even turn the light on.

It took almost two hours before she had success. It took another hour of repeatedly saying "nulla lumen" with various emphases before she could turn the light on and off. Feeling proud of herself, she got up and put the Grimoire in a kitchen cabinet.

She stretched, releasing a huge yawn. A short look around at the stark white walls had her sitting on the floor. Yawning again, she dropped to her back and closed her eyes.

Startled awake, Natalie looked at her phone, saw the time, and jumped up. She raced down the steps and hurried towards the front entrance.

While the others were quietly going through the gateway, Natalie said good night to Hexel. What a stark difference from the first day. Silence filled the air on the journey through the tunnel and the rail cart ride to the old homestead. The others were no longer excited as they struggled to achieve their goals.

As they departed the homestead, Natalie looked at their glum expressions and thought how strange that I'm a powder keg that everyone wants to avoid, and they are novices everyone is cheering on for success."

Chapter 20
Stormfield Elves

Excited and nervous, chattering filled the air as the six mages hurried past Hexel and headed towards the classroom at the back of the Fire elemental building for Basic Spells, their first mage class. Joel thumped Connor on the back.

"What's that about?" Connor frowned at Joel.

"I was horribly outnumbered. Four girls to me. I appreciate having another male in the group."

"Don't thank me. Thank Oxley."

"So, how'd Oxley make it happen?"

"It's hard to wrap my head around what happened. I always took Oxley as fat and lazy, but there's another side to our mentors when they're enraged."

"Did he flip out because you didn't want to be one of us?"

"One minute, he was talking about my loner attitude, and the next thing, he morphed into something I never want to see again. I assure you, I much prefer this group to dealing with a livid Oxley."

"One day, we need to sit down, and you tell us what happened."

Joel opened the door and saw Mr. Xanders sitting at the teacher's desk.

"Mr. Xanders," Joel exclaimed, "why didn't you give us some hints?"

"First, because of Jonathan and Wilfred, I knew Natalie was a mage, but I wasn't sure about you and Lainey. Second, the school is ground zero. I warned you weeks ago not to trust anyone."

Mr. Xanders looked over at Connor. "Glad to see you, Connor."

"Thanks," Connor said, meaning it.

215

Mr. Xanders had joined three tables together to form one long row facing him. Joel sat down, and Connor followed. Skylar walked behind them and took a seat. Madison entered from the other side, followed by Pru and Natalie.

"Your undivided attention up here because the first activity of class is going to consume most of our time today."

Mr. Xanders waited until they settled, and he had their full attention.

"Six Stormfield elves will enter the room shortly to take measurements of your dominant hand to create a custom wand for you. Wands for use in the mageless world are no longer made of wood or obvious."

Madison frowned and interrupted Mr. Xanders. "But we aren't going to look like real mages."

"Like many things, wands have advanced. You'll have a wand that connects to you."

"Is it going to look manly?" Connor asked. Joel snorted; Madison rolled her eyes.

"It'll be fine. No more questions or comments. I'm running out of time to forewarn you about them. First, if an elf offers you candy, food, or a drink, don't take it. There are serious consequences from eating or drinking something given by an elf. Second, be polite because they tend to have nasty tempers. Third, do no more than what is asked of you."

Mr. Xanders had barely finished giving the third rule when in waltzed six breathtakingly beautiful full-size elves. First, each of them gracefully strolled over to Mr. Xanders and shook his hand. Then, heading over to the students, each elf claimed a mage. As they did, the room darkened, and the ceiling took on a starry night appearance. Basking in hundreds of twinkling stars and a glowing full moon, everyone relaxed in the enchanted atmosphere.

Taking both hands of their student, the elves raised their hands up and intensely studied them. Lingering over each finger, thumb, palm, and back of the hand, it was as if there were vital clues to discover.

The elves gazed off for what seemed like an eternity into the full moon radiating from the night scene. They gave the illusion they were conversing with the stars and moon to design the perfect wand for each student.

Natalie struggled not to laugh. *Seriously, who believes these exaggerated performances?* Unfortunately, glancing over to Pru and then down the row, Natalie realized the elves had mesmerized the others.

"Good grief," Natalie uttered, "this is more drama than I see in a year. They don't see it?"

Natalie looked over at Mr. Xanders. He appeared enthralled with the show, just like the rest of them.

She wasn't buying this whole show. Something wasn't right. She became restless. Leaving her left hand with the elf, she pulled her right hand away and dropped it below the table. The elf pulled her right hand back up and slammed it on the table. The sound made the others look dreamily over at her.

Before Natalie could question their expressions, the elf moved within inches of her face, trying to captivate her with his beauty. She leaned forward and glared at him. Backing up, the elf picked up her right hand. With both hands in his hands, he gazed off at the stars and the moon.

Natalie burst out laughing. Instantly, she grabbed her stomach and doubled over in intense pain. She tried to catch her breath and wondered who had kicked her.

The elf pulled at her hands. She gave him a withering look that told him he had better back off. He stepped back and studied her. Meanwhile, the other elves gave him piercing looks that told him he had better handle his mage.

Still trying to catch her breath, Natalie glanced around the room, looking for something to stop this charade. Nothing stood out except the night sky.

As the rest continued to be mesmerized by their elves and oblivious to her pain, she gazed up at the twinkling stars and the mellow moon. Unaware of her elf approaching, Natalie closed her eyes and envisioned clouds moving in for an approaching hurricane.

Blustery winds swirled around them, rapidly increasing in strength. Within the rumbling thunder, Natalie heard her elf screaming unfamiliar words. She blocked him out and continued concentrating on building the storm. Lightning flashed, the wind howled, and ice-cold rain pelted them, penetrating their clothes.

Time marched on, accompanied by howling winds and battering rains, finally providing Natalie with relief. The pain diminished. Her anger and the storm remained.

"Natalie!"

She heard a deep male voice yell her name. The storm continued to rage.

"Natalie, stop!"

She heard her name louder and forced her eyes to open. Draon stood angrily before her. Furious winds whipped his crow-feathered cloak around him, but the winds were no match for the fury in his eyes. Even confused about what was happening, Natalie sensed trouble and froze. The hurricane abruptly ended.

Draon had her attention, but she couldn't clear her mind. Struggling, she started pinching her right arm over and over in the same spot until the pain forced her back to reality. Finally, the ebbing anger gave way to being conscious of staring up at Draon, who stood within inches of the soaked table. His blazing eyes studied her.

She glanced around. *Where did the others go?* Puzzled, she looked around again. This time, Natalie saw immense destruction. Most of the ceiling hung down, and the walls had cracks, holes, and black marks. *How could I have missed it?* Shocked, she hoped everyone escaped in time.

"What happened?" Draon demanded, never taking his eyes off her.

"My fault. I laughed at the ridiculously hokey act. My elf got angry and slammed me with indescribable pain. In anger and agony, I looked for a way to stop it."

"And that meant taking out the entire room and everyone in it?"

"I don't know what happened. One minute, I wanted to stop the pain, and the next minute, I became the storm itself." Natalie, soaked and cold, started to shiver.

"How long have you been practicing?"

"That's the weird thing, I haven't. The elemental teacher accused me of the same thing. Honestly, I haven't been practicing. I wouldn't even know where to start because I'm not even good with simple spells. The other day, Lorcan gave me the family Grimoire. It has some simple spells at the beginning of the book. After hours of practicing, I only succeeded in turning the lights on and off."

"Here you were using elemental power that always flows within you. Spells are entirely different. Even so, I am concerned about the amount of power you used on the storm. How do you feel?"

"Are you asking if I'm tired from creating the storm? The answer is no. I can still feel the remnants of the kick to the stomach, but that is mostly gone. If you're asking me how I feel drenched, the answer is I'm freezing."

"You realize this is the second disaster you have caused within a week?"

"Yes, of course, and by now, everyone knows I've created another disaster. No one wants to teach me, and soon they won't want me showing up, for fear I'll destroy the whole place." Natalie bit her lip to avoid crying.

"You have a teacher, and no one believes you are going to destroy the Barracks." Draon's thoughts didn't match his words.

"I hope so." She hugged herself, trying to get warm.

Draon spoke a few words, but they were not clearly audible. Natalie's clothes and his clothes became dry.

"Thank you! Seriously, I didn't come to class expecting to cause trouble. I thought we were going to have an easy class of getting our ring wands sized and ordered."

"That is what should have happened. However, elves do not tolerate someone not appreciating their beauty or what they consider their superior intellect. You insulted them by ignoring your elf and laughing at their elaborate scheme."

"Why am I the only one who thought the whole thing was a sham?"

"Because everyone they touched went under their spell except for you. It is a good thing. The elves were draining the powers of those under their spell. You almost destroyed the entire room with the violent storm, but you stopped them."

"Wow." Natalie looked around the room at the damage she had caused. "I should have known by their dazed expressions. I guess no wands for us."

"The elves had what they needed shortly after they touched your hands. Crafty and devious, they were after payment. A high price."

"They don't appear to be smart if they thought there wouldn't be consequences at some point."

"Unless I retested your group, it had a chance of being successful. Also, the more time between today and questioning why the mages were now average would hide what they did."

"And we just started, so we haven't had any success with our powers. Nothing to measure our abilities."

"True with the other mages. However, you have already provided us with a couple of examples."

"Scary examples. Maybe the ring will help channel my powers, but I don't think I want to wear anything they create."

"It will be perfectly fine to wear. Believe me, they are already paying a hefty price for trying to steal power. Bad choices always have consequences. Maybe not immediately, but eventually, karma balances things out. Here, Hexel is the karma."

"How do I fix this mess?" Natalie didn't want to think about Hexel or karma paying her back for not controlling her temper.

"I will fix it." Draon shifted his attention to the room. "You need to find your fellow students."

Natalie got up. At the door, she turned and apologized. "I'm sorry. Really, I am. I used to think of myself as an easygoing person, but when I'm angry or upset, these powers seem to take over with little effort on my part."

"That is true. When you are angry, your entire essence is connected with your raw elemental powers. It is dangerous without training. It will not be easy, but once you feel the connection, you will start to have control. To do that, I will be your elemental teacher."

Shocked, Natalie wasn't sure how to respond to that statement. Recalling how he had acted when he told her she was a Shadowlink, she knew he didn't like her. Yet, he had stopped the destruction and had brought her out of the storm.

She shuddered, thinking her rage would have continued until she burned herself out. *Don't go there.* She refocused to avoid thinking of the harm her anger could have caused her. Instead, she hoped her interactions with Draon would now be different.

"Thank you." She turned and walked out.

As she approached the group sitting outside the Flaky Kuchen, Joel yelled out, "That was quite a tantrum, Anderson!"

Natalie laughed. Sitting down next to Pru, Pru gave her a hug.

"What's that for?"

"Seriously, Anderson," Joel exclaimed, "we were being drained like a bathtub! We didn't realize what was happening. Moving more like drunken zombies, we numbly followed the elves out of the room. Draon saw us mindlessly staggering around the common area and had the elemental teachers seat us and stuff us with donuts and soda. Apparently, an overload of sugar is an antidote. It works in my book."

Natalie smiled and glanced around the area. "What happened to Mr. Xanders?"

Still trying to replay what happened in training, Connor focused on Natalie's question. "The element teachers sugar-loaded him, as well. They thought it would be better if the teacher didn't look like the elves tricked him, like the novice students. They took him away as soon as he started feeling better."

"Where are the elves?" Natalie looked around to see if she could spot them.

"Remember," Joel answered, "we weren't exactly sharp as tacks when we first came out. However, in our bumbling mode, we all remember Draon focusing on Hexel. Next thing we know, Hexel's floating towards the elves. We don't know what happened, but it couldn't be good. After summoning Hexel to deal with the elves, Draon dragged us over here, got the element teachers to deal with us, and then went looking for you."

"How did you know?" Skylar asked.

"How did I know it was a sham? Nothing special. Whatever they did, it didn't work on me. When my elf cursed me with horrendous pain, as if he kicked me in the stomach, I got mad. Apparently, when I'm angry, my instincts take over."

"Definitely a good thing," Madison said.

Skylar nodded her head in agreement. "Just know, we all want to stay on your good side. We also want you to be right here with us. Our own powerhouse."

"Thanks," Natalie said, proud that she had stopped a disaster but not so proud that she had created one.

"Looks like our first day of training is a total bust," Joel said as he finished his seventh donut.

"I don't know," Skylar said, glancing over at Joel, "you seem to have made out okay with the snacks."

"True. They were incredibly delicious, and sadly, they have been devoured. However, when there is money in my pocket, I know my first stop."

They all laughed, knowing he spoke the truth.

"Why don't we visit some shops here that have nothing to do with food?" Pru asked.

Starting out with the Aerial Road, they stopped in front of the Mystical Pets Treat Store. Joel opened the door to an ear-piercing sound of squawking birds.

"Well, that doorbell announces someone is entering the store," Connor said, holding his hands over his ears.

A short, elderly woman dressed in a long, flowing white dress with a navy-blue robe shuffled out of the back room. "How may I help you?"

"We're just looking," Pru said with a smile. "They dismissed our class for the day. It's giving us a chance to get familiar with the Barracks."

"I heard about your bad luck. Tsk. Thank goodness you're all safe. Never trust elves. Self-centered, devious pig farts."

They all looked at one another and burst out laughing.

The elderly woman ignored their laughter. "If you need help, let me know. I'll be in the back."

After she left, they walked around the shop, examining all the shelves and bins filled with toys and treats for their birds. The back wall of the store had an immense display of black cat clocks. The big green eyes moved back and forth along with the swing of the long tails. Once in a while, the eyes stopped moving and seemed to focus on them.

"They must represent our Ruiries," Pru said, watching an entire wall of cat clocks with the eyes and tails moving back and forth.

"I suppose, but do you have the feeling those cat clocks are watching us?" Skylar asked, creeping out over the sudden pause of the eyes in their direction.

"Yup," Natalie answered, "we should be used to it now, as that's a favorite pastime of the scarecrows."

"Yeah," Madison agreed, "let's get out of here. We can't afford anything, anyway."

Without money, they hadn't planned on visiting another shop, but the window display at the next store had each of them laughing.

"Is that shimmery emerald with thin white and gold stripes on those pants?" Connor asked in disbelief.

"I believe it goes with the red, green, gold, and blue plaid shirt that is displayed next to it," Skylar laughed.

"Only a Ruiri would wear that combination," Joel said, shaking his head.

"Wow! Now we know where the Ruiries get their clothes. I wonder if there's a tailor in there that helps them match up their wild outfits," Natalie said, opening the door.

"Seriously," Connor complained, "are we really going in here?"

Walking into the store, they spotted hundreds of shoe boxes stacked from floor to ceiling against the south wall. They looked at the pictures of the shoes on the outside of each box. They were unaware that the owner, a Ruiri, wildly dressed in a splattering of all colors, had walked up behind them.

"Look," Madison said, "all the shoes are the same design and are brown. The only thing different is the size."

"Excuse me," the offended shopkeeper said as they reacted in surprise, "but all the shoes are brown, so the shoes don't distract from our outfits. It is the outfit that matters, not a pair of shoes. Now, may I help you, or are you in here to insult?"

"Sorry," Natalie replied, trying not to stare at his outrageous outfit. "We each have a Ruiri mentoring us, so we were interested in where they go to purchase their clothes. We really didn't mean to be rude. It's been a rough day because of those elves."

"I should have known," the shopkeeper said, relaxing and studying them over his half-moon eyeglasses. "You're the students the elves tried to steal your powers. The nerve! Right here in the Crossroads Barracks, trying to steal your powers."

"Well, they didn't get away with it," Pru stated as the others nodded their heads in agreement.

"Which one of you is Natalie?"

Shocked that he knew her name, Natalie replied, "I am."

"You're getting quite the reputation," the shopkeeper stated as he moved closer. The others stepped back as he started walking around her. It seemed as if he was taking measurements.

"Not intentionally," Natalie replied, feeling awkward with his intense attention. She glanced down and saw that his chunky necklace had purple gemstones going around the center bead. When he moved towards her back, she glanced across the room to distract herself. Over in that direction, she saw several hat stands with tall brown hats. Before she put too much thought into the hats, the shopkeeper stopped and faced her. "Maybe not intentionally, but everyone in the Crossroads knows who you are."

"Definitely a force to be reckoned with," Madison agreed.

"Yes, indeed," the shopkeeper said, giving the entire group one last look before heading to the back of the store.

"Can we go now?" Connor asked.

"We're done," Joel stated as they all headed for the door.

Once they were outside, Natalie wanted to see if anyone else had noticed the hats. "Did you see the hats? The brown hats are like the ones we read in stories about gnomes."

"Well," Pru reasoned, "I guess there is some truth to those old fairy tales."

"Did you also notice his chunky necklace had purple gemstones circling the center bead?"

"Not really," Joel said, "we guys aren't into jewelry…if you can call those ugly necklaces jewelry."

"Joel, Lorcan has green gemstones circling his center bead. This guy has purple gemstones circling his center bead. Did you ever look at the necklace your mentor wears?"

"Can't say that I have," Joel said.

"It sounds like you're saying Joel's mentor will have red gemstones circling the center bead as Joel is a fire mage," Pru said.

"Exactly!" Natalie exclaimed.

"Mmm, I'm with Joel. I have never looked, but next time I see Oxley, I'll check it out," Connor said.

The rest of the time, they lingered at the windows of the shops with magical objects. For the window display of Daisy's Bodacious Nails, the boys had to force the girls to keep moving. With Dweomer Board Games, the girls had to drag the boys from the window display. All of them moved on when it came to furniture, clothes, and food. By the time they visited every magical store, they were ready to go home. Lorcan met them at the gatehouse, holding a tray of six jars of bubbling, muddy-colored liquid.

"What's this?" Connor asked, staring at the unpleasant concoction.

"Take one. This will protect you from magical creatures having the ability to steal your powers. You, too, Natalie. This time, you weren't under the elves' influence, but maybe next time, it will be different. We want you protected, too."

The jars were warm, and the ugly concoction and bubbling made it quite alarming that they had to drink this stuff. However, that wasn't the worst part.

Connor removed the lid. "No way! This smells worse than Hexel!"

"Shh," Natalie whispered, "you'll hurt Hexel's feelings."

"Who cares! What do you think this stuff is going to do to our insides?"

"No point in arguing," Lorcan stated, "because no one leaves here without drinking the potion."

Each student held a warm jar in their hands, studying the bubbling mud as the horrific stench assaulted their noses. This was an impossible task—no choice, but impossible.

"On the count of three, I'm drinking mine," Natalie said, raising the jar near her mouth. The others, shocked, looked at her in surprise, but she wanted to get it over with so she could leave. Looking back down at the bubbling stink potion in their hands, the others weren't so sure they could drink it and keep it down.

"One, two, three," Natalie held her breath, pinched her nose closed, put the jar to her mouth, and consumed the rancid-tasting potion in two big gulps. Pru and Skylar followed her. Intense heat engulfed them. Dropping and shattering the jars, sweat poured off their beet-red faces as they bent over and repeatedly gagged.

Freaked out by their reactions to the potion, Madison, Joel, and Connor backed away and turned away. Too horrific to watch their friends moan, gag, sweat, and burn, they put their hands over their ears and huddled together.

Somehow, Natalie, Pru, and Skylar managed to hang in there and survive the ordeal. Within a few minutes, drained of all energy, the three were almost back to normal.

As soon as they could talk, Pru pleaded, "Lorcan, can we leave? I'm afraid that if we have to witness the others drinking the potion, we may have a problem keeping ours down." Natalie and Skylar lightly shook their heads in agreement.

"Sure, you're free to wait in the tunnel for your friends." Lorcan waved them off. Natalie waved weakly at

Hexel before shuffling out behind Pru and Skylar, who were not moving any faster.

On the other side of the door, Natalie, Pru, and Skylar waited for the others. No talking. They were trying to recover from the rancid potion. When the others joined them, they slowly made their way through the tunnel, to the bookstore, and down to the rail cart. They were all happy to see the end of the day.

Chapter 21
Colorful Beach Balls

Natalie tossed and turned, waking up for the tenth time. Bleary-eyed, she squinted at the alarm clock. The orange glowing numbers said three. She moaned and fell back on her pillows.

By five o'clock, she gave up and dragged herself out of bed. Coal stayed on his pillow and chirped at her.

"Sorry, I woke you." Natalie turned the alarm clock off to avoid it going off at 8 a.m.

Coal stood up, fluttered his wings, and chirped.

"Coal, go back to sleep. I'll put your food out before I leave." She grabbed her clothes and headed for the shower.

By six o'clock, she had prepared Coal's breakfast and had completed the outside chores. Too nervous to eat, she headed to the old homestead, where she posted a note on the tunnel door, letting the others know she had gone ahead.

She fell asleep during the railroad cart ride to the bookstore. When the cart bumped the stop rail, she woke with a jolt.

"Figures, now I can sleep." Natalie yawned, climbed the stairs, headed to the bookstore's secret door, and stepped down into the tunnel.

Early morning, and by herself, the red fire crystals cast eerie dancing red shadows against the dungeon-like rock walls. Her eyes darted back and forth. Her ears strained for sounds other than her echoing footsteps. Anxious, Natalie scurried down the tunnel, hoping she wouldn't encounter the hunched back crystal keeper. When the Barracks door came into view, she sighed in relief.

Hexel floated towards Natalie. She paused and held her breath. Hexel moved closer and slowly circled her.

"Hexel, it's okay. Draon is teaching me today, so my nerves are shot." She stopped to take a breath. Ugh, a smell like a pile of dirty gym socks assaulted her nostrils. Repulsed, she opened her mouth and took a deep breath before continuing.

"Hexel, too little sleep and a fear of disappointing him are messing with me. Don't tell him that, okay?" She froze and hoped Hexel would let her pass before she had to breathe.

Hexel took her time. Natalie struggled to hold her breath. *Hexel, please leave. Go back to your guardhouse.* She opened her mouth to gasp for air, but at the same time, Hexel floated away.

Natalie took a breath of air as she jogged towards the Earth elemental building. She didn't notice the moon fade away or the sun peak through the clouds and beam down on the deserted streets. She focused on the smells of freshly brewed coffee and the sweet pastries of the opening restaurants.

Stopping outside the Earth element building, she enjoyed the wonderful aroma of breakfast foods and coffee. As she breathed in deeply, her thoughts turned to Draon as her teacher. *Could he teach me? He's ancient, so he might not have the patience to train me. What if he's cold towards me? Can I control my temper? If not, would he, too, say he couldn't teach me? Worse yet, what if I'm not teachable?*

Natalie's mood changed. She tried to clear the negative thoughts out of her head by breathing deeply and letting them out. She took another deep breath and let it out. Out with the negative thoughts, in with the positive thoughts.

Who am I kidding? I'm a walking disaster. Two for two on my powers taking over and scaring everyone.

She tried again to think positively, but the negative thoughts kept surfacing. She opened the door and froze in fear. *No, he can't be here. I need time to prepare myself. I'm not ready.*

She tried to read him as she walked towards him. Nothing. He didn't smile, causing her anxiety to skyrocket as he indifferently watched her approach.

She wondered if she should turn around and leave, as it felt like a nightmare coming true. *I'll not only screw up, but I'll disappoint him to the point he's going to tell me that I'm not worth his time and energy.* Natalie bit her lower lip in hopes she wouldn't cry.

Her face must have reflected her thoughts because Draon spoke in a gentle voice. "I do not know why Alexander used rocks and sand. He invited trouble."

Natalie glanced to see what she would be using— beach balls—colorful beach balls. She relaxed. Maybe this would work out.

"Natalie, two things. No use of temper. You can do this if you concentrate. Focus on the object and what you want to do with it. You already do this when you're angry. Now, do it without anger."

"Mr. Martin said it might take me up to a month to get it. Does that sound right?"

"No, you already have the ability. You need to learn to connect to the source. I expect we will have results today."

"Um, that's a lot of pressure."

"Natalie, you have already thrown rocks, retrieved rocks, created a tornado, and a hurricane. Do you really believe you cannot do it?"

"I'm scared I'm going to disappoint you, and you won't like me again." A tear escaped and ran down her cheek.

Solemnly studying Natalie, it took Draon a couple of minutes to respond.

"First, you will never disappoint me. I may get frustrated because there is an obvious difference in years, experience, and environment. Being out in the mageless world is new to me. We will adapt. Second, in trying to avoid being hurt again, I took it out on you. I hurt you. It was wrong. Please forgive me."

Natalie shook her head yes as tears trickled down her face.

Uncomfortable, Draon faltered on how to handle Natalie. "Please stop crying. I will make it up to you. How about flying lessons?"

Flying lessons! That got her attention. She hadn't even considered that possibility in these modern times. *Where would I fly? Would I fly on real brooms like Madison and Skylar make?* Natalie visualized herself on an enchanted broom. Then, she thought about the others.

"What about the others, and where would we fly? I surely don't want to be shot down from the sky."

"You want to include the others? Flying would be here. If you want to include the others, maybe we can make a competition out of it." Draon's expression changed as he built some scenarios in his mind. This could be entertaining.

"That sounds fun." Natalie wiped her face with her hands. She wiped her hands on her pants.

Draon stood quietly, giving Natalie a couple of minutes to regain her composure. "Are you feeling better?"

"I think so. Yes, definitely. It would be incredible to fly. That would be even better than learning how to drive a car."

"Good. Positive energy helps with training. You ready to start?"

"Yes." Natalie looked at the beach balls and the chair at the other end of the room. She would need to send a ball

all the way across the room to Draon. Without anger, it wouldn't be easy.

"The object is to get the ball into my hands," Draon stated as he headed over to the chair at the back wall.

Holding a ball in her hands, Natalie concentrated on lifting and flying it across the room to Draon. Nothing happened. Searching in her mind and then her body, trying to feel the flow of energy, she felt nothing. Natalie bit her lower lip in frustration. *How can I search for something when I don't even know what it is or what it feels like?* She had no clue. *Some help would be nice.*

Obviously, that would not happen, so Natalie asked the ball to fly over there. She pleaded with the ball to fly over there. She tried to visualize the ball floating over there. Over two hours and nothing happened. Getting frustrated, the ball suddenly lifted from her hands.

"No," Draon shouted.

The ball fell back into her hands. Another half hour passed as she concentrated on the ball and focused on Draon. Suddenly, she felt a connection. The ball took off and headed straight for Draon's head. Draon hit it away.

"Good. Now focus on getting it to my hands and not my head."

Wearily, Natalie concentrated, but she couldn't hold her focus. The ball went to the left of Draon. The next ball went to the right of Draon. Under his chair. Over his head. Faster and faster, she threw them out, and more and more, they were way off the mark. Draon casually returned them, one by one, right to her feet. Twenty beach balls were on the ground in front of her.

No break and struggling to get the ball to Draon's hands, she lost it. Twenty balls went flying at the same time toward Draon. He stood up, concentrated, and sent all twenty balls flying back at Natalie. Opening her eyes, she looked in horror at the ball missiles coming straight for her. She reached out with both hands and yelled, "Stop!" The balls froze in mid-air, suspended for a few minutes, and then dropped to the ground.

"Let's take a break," Draon announced.

"Thank you!"

They returned to the same routine. Natalie couldn't feel any control, even though the balls landed somewhere near Draon. It didn't count. The ball had to be in his hands.

After an hour, Natalie's temper exploded. She flung her hands out and sent all twenty beach balls zooming for Draon.

Draon stood up, concentrated with no effort, and returned them at equal force back to Natalie. Yelling "stop" had only half of the balls stop and drop. The others zoomed straight for her.

Natalie hit as many as she could away from her, but some hit her arms and legs. Red marks appeared on her body.

With all twenty beach balls at her feet, Natalie closed her eyes and took deep breaths, trying to calm down. Her breath slowed, but anger boiled inside her. She knew her anger would get a ball into Draon's hands, but it wouldn't count. *I want this day to end!*

Natalie opened her eyes and pointed at a ball. It flew into her hands. Draon cleared his throat. She frowned, slammed the ball down into the pile, causing the balls to scatter. She didn't care. She grabbed the nearest ball, almost popping it with her grip.

Sweat ran down her face as she focused on Draon. Nothing changed. Again and again, each ball went off course. Draon effortlessly returned each ball to Natalie. Annoyingly, this routine continually repeated itself. A never-ending loop of failure. Whether it was pure exhaustion or the fact that Draon made it look so simple, Natalie became short-tempered. Flushed and drenched in sweat, she could feel herself reaching a breaking point. She was losing control. Taking deep breaths, she tried to recover.

Nope, the next ball slammed the back wall behind Draon. He casually returned it. Natalie lost it. Instantly, twenty beach balls zoomed straight for Draon.

He jumped up, cast a protection spell, and let the balls smash against the shield. Sounds of rapid explosions echoed in the room as each ball smashed against the shield.

The big finale finished Natalie. She flopped down on the floor, laid back, and closed her eyes.

Draon walked over to her and looked down. "Are we done for the day?"

"I have nothing to give at the moment. Give me some time to recover. You say I can do it without my temper taking control. I want to believe you. Truly I do because I also want to believe in me." Natalie never opened her eyes while speaking with Draon.

"You also have Lorcan, who believes in you. In all the centuries I have known him, I have never seen him more loyal to the one he mentors. The other day, when he was upset with me and defending you, he became livid. Trust me; you never want a Ruiri to become livid and morph into his alter ego. He did it because of his protective nature for you. He believes in you."

Natalie nodded her head but said nothing. She recalled Lorcan being upset when she put the elemental teacher in the sand tornado. *He wasn't upset with me; he was upset with Draon.* A slight smile crossed her lips as she thought of Lorcan defending her to Draon. She wondered what he looked like in his alter ego. Natalie let her mind wander.

"Obviously, I need to get more beach balls," Draon said in a sarcastic tone.

Natalie wanted to glare at him, but exhaustion won out.

"I will be back in a few minutes."

As she listened to the sounds of Draon's retreating footsteps, she cleared her mind of all thoughts. It really wasn't hard to do, as the last burst of anger had drained her emotionally, mentally, and physically. Exhausted, Natalie fell asleep. She wasn't sure how long she slept. The next thing she knew, Draon stood over her.

"Natalie, when you are ready, I will be in place."

Draon's footsteps echoed as he walked back to the chair. Natalie tried to clear her weary mind. She wondered if the others had reached the point of exhaustion where they ended up flat out on the floor. Surely their teachers weren't pushing them to that point. She couldn't imagine Pru sprawled out on the floor. That thought had her smiling. *Joel, yes.* Now that she had spent time with him, she saw his quirky character. *Okay, no more stalling.*

With her eyes closed, she tried to make a connection with her mind. No success. Focusing on her heart as a possible source, nothing happened. She had fleetingly felt it once, but all the other times, the balls had responded to her frustration or her anger.

Still feeling tired, her mind wandered. She constantly had to bring her attention back to the task. *I should sit up or stand up. No, I'm comfortable. Besides, I don't have the energy.*

Natalie blindly reached over and picked up a beach ball. Placing it on her stomach, she strained to get it to lift. Asking the ball to float repeatedly, she failed to get it to move. Focusing and concentrating. Time dragged, but she was determined.

After another hour of struggling to get the ball to move, it rose and floated above her. Natalie felt a slight vibration coursing through her body. Visualizing Draon, she asked the ball to go to his hands.

"Perfect!" Draon exclaimed. "You did it!"

Natalie's eyes popped open. She rolled over, sat up, and then stood up. "Did I?"

"Success! You're done for the day!" Draon exclaimed.

Drenched in sweat, hair dripping wet, and exhausted, she didn't care. Natalie burst with pride at her achievement. Even better, she could still feel the vibration coursing through her body.

Chapter 22
The Third and Final Sign

Because of the old homestead enchantments that strangely affect familiars, Coal had never been there. Today was the exception, and he flew around the Room of Mirrors.

What strange powers this room held as Coal became aware and fascinated with the bird that kept waiting in the mirror for him. Flying up to the mirror, he would peck at it while the other bird did the same. Coal saw other birds flying around in the other mirrors, but this one always waited for him. Around and around, Coal would fly and come back to the bird waiting for him in the mirror.

Lorcan repeatedly shooed the annoying bird out of the room and away from the mirror. He understood the homestead's enchantments were affecting Coal. Still, he couldn't understand how the bird could not see that it was his reflection.

Concerned for Natalie's father, Lorcan didn't have the time or the desire to deal with the silly bird. Finally reaching his limit, he had the fairies and pixies distract Coal. Now that he could focus on the dire situation, Lorcan turned to Natalie. "Natalie, your father has to stay with us."

"You know my father wants nothing to do with magic." Distracted, Natalie watched Coal follow the fairies and pixies out of the room.

"Natalie, focus."

Natalie turned from watching Coal leave to seeing Lorcan standing sternly with his hands on his hips.

"Lorcan, I should have explained I already tried to get Dad to come here. The broken grand clocks endlessly chimed this morning. Nothing we did stopped the chiming. I knew it indicated the third sign, so I asked Dad to come with me. He said no."

"He doesn't have a choice because this isn't ordinary magic. We don't know what will happen in the third and final sign. Good and bad are out of balance. Your father isn't safe in your house, particularly since Samoon won't be coming to help. No one will be coming to help."

"What about the others? Are the others taking their parents into their homesteads?" Natalie knew the answer was no because the signs had never affected them.

"Yes, they are, but not the way I want your father to be here."

"What does that mean?" Natalie's eyes widened in surprise.

"I won't go into details, but the other families won't be aware they are in the old homesteads. They won't remember any part of it. Your father knows you're a mage, so he has a choice. If he willingly comes over here, it will be different for him. Otherwise, no."

Natalie hurried out of the homestead and ran through the path to the house. Heavily breathing, she found her father in the kitchen, loading his breakfast dishes into the dishwasher.

"Dad, you can't go to work today…at least, not on time. We can't trust what is going to happen and how far it will reach out to mages and their family members. So, you have two choices. You come willingly, or Lorcan forces you. We're out of time, so make your choice right now."

Natalie watched her dad shut the dishwasher and hesitate to face her. As if reading his mind, she cried out, "Come on, Dad. We need to be together. I can't stay in the house. You can't stay here or be on the road during the lunar eclipse. Now! We only have a few minutes."

"Fine. I'll be late and make up the time by staying later."

Natalie sighed in exasperation. "Dad, all you do is work. You've already worked enough extra hours to take an entire year off. This is important. I need you with me!"

"Okay, I heard you the first time." Karl grabbed his briefcase.

Natalie took his hand and pulled him through the path to the old homestead. Upon entering, Lorcan stopped pacing and let out a sigh of relief that Karl had made the choice to be with them.

It wasn't the first time Karl had seen Lorcan in his Ruiri form, so he wasn't shocked. However, the approaching pixies and fairies were a different matter. Before he could say a word, they yanked his briefcase from his hand, grabbed him, and pulled him to the center of the room. Directly under the massive chandelier, they happily circled him. As they continued to circle him, he relaxed. Some sat on his shoulders, and a couple sat on his head. Some continued to circle him.

Natalie stood frozen in shock, watching the fluttering chaos surrounding her father. It didn't make sense. He would never easily adapt to fairies and pixies, much less this endless fussing over him. She took a couple of steps forward and stopped.

"Lorcan?"

"What?"

"Is it me, or can you feel that weird vibration?"

Lorcan stopped his pacing and pulled his wand out. Directing it at the fairies and pixies, he yelled, "Stop!"

The vibration stopped. Puzzled, Natalie watched her dad shake his head as if to clear it. As he did, some pixies and fairies flew to Lorcan and started squeaking in high-pitched voices. Looking back at Natalie's father and then at Lorcan, they continued their high-pitched message. Lorcan relaxed and put his wand away.

"They've never been near a mageless. Being excited, they got carried away and started humming. Honestly, I don't think they were even aware they were putting your father into a trance."

"They were putting my father in a trance!?"

"Not on purpose. It wouldn't have hurt him other than he might have looked more like a tree with birds all over him…except it would be fairies and pixies." Lorcan laughed, visualizing all of them sitting on her father. Glancing over at Natalie and seeing she didn't find it funny, he became serious.

"I don't want to embarrass my father. He's out of his comfort zone. The last thing I want is for him to be uncomfortable and embarrassed."

"I agree," Lorcan said in an apologetic tone, "but if he sees any of what is about to happen, he may wish he were in a trance. I'm going to change the rules and have the winged ones take him downstairs. Normally, they are forbidden from being down there, but he will be safe in the protected room. No windows."

"He won't go down there. Dad will want to be with me."

"He will think you are there with him. He'll be okay, I promise. It's best for us to focus on what is about to happen outside. Do you trust me?"

"Of course, I trust you, but we're talking about my father."

"He'll be safer with them than he is with us. They need to go now."

Natalie looked over at her dad. Her eyes widened, and her mouth dropped open in shock when she saw her twin leading her father towards the door that would take him downstairs. Even more strange, he didn't seem interested in his briefcase.

"It's Sunshine Lily, your favorite fairy, projecting an illusion of you."

Lorcan turned to face the mirrors on the south wall. The lights dimmed. Shimmering silver light shone from within the four largest mirrors, which grew brighter one by one. Natalie watched as a Ruiri appeared in each mirror.

"The wind is increasing, along with the first signs of red," Oxley stated. Natalie could see Connor pacing behind him.

"Same here," the rest all responded. Movement and glimpses of the other mages behind their Ruiries confirmed they were all on edge as the lunar eclipse started.

"We just need to make it through the full lunar eclipse. We're talking less than two hours from the start of the full lunar eclipse to going back to a partial lunar eclipse. The enchantments and spells on the old homesteads will easily hold for the full moon and the partial lunar eclipse."

"Personally," Breccan responded, "I'm not so sure. We haven't seen anything like this in 150 years. It was bad enough last time without good and bad being out of balance. Now, we have mages all gathered here. I think it's going to get ugly."

The others murmured in agreement. Natalie stared at their serious expressions. Seeing how concerned they were about what was approaching, her pulse quickened at what might happen.

"We'll get through it. Our mages are powerful."

"Lorcan, I agree they are powerful, but they aren't trained," Oxley reminded him.

"We can keep the connection open in case one of us needs help," Lorcan said.

"Sounds good. Hopefully, this is soon behind us," Breccan responded.

At the left front window, Coal rested on Natalie's right shoulder as she peeked through a small opening in the curtains. In fascination, she watched as the sky turned dark red, and the ragged scarecrows held on even while being assaulted by strong winds. Violently twisting and turning, their hands remained tied together. Suddenly, a burst of wind turned the scarecrows just enough that Natalie could see their faces. She gasped. Their eyes glowed green. Stepping back, Natalie yelled, "Lorcan!"

He ran to the windows and saw the green glow.

"Come with me now. Shoo, Coal." Lorcan waved his arms at Coal before pulling Natalie towards the center of the Room of Mirrors.

Wasting no time, they plunked down under the chandelier. Lorcan reached for her hands.

"We need to awaken the Three-Headed Tree Stump."

"What?"

"We need to awaken the Three-Headed Tree Stump now! Natalie, concentrate on the stump! It needs to protect the scarecrows and the homestead! Don't ask questions, do it!"

Astounded, she couldn't believe she had to communicate with that horrifying stump. However, the wailing winds had her on edge.

Still gripping her hands, Lorcan closed his eyes and tried to have his powers meet Natalie's powers. She stared at Lorcan's hands and demanded that her power connect.

With crackling noises, high arcs of electricity danced in front of them. The arcs converged and formed a large energy ball that floated to the front door, where it escaped. Lorcan motioned for Natalie to stand. Still holding hands, they walked to the front window.

Through the small opening in the curtains, they could see their elemental power surround and then attach itself to the Three-Headed Tree Stump. Lorcan tightened his grip on her hands as she watched in horror the stump's awakening.

Three sets of eyes opened wide and glowed white. Three sets of mouths stretched wide open. Green, glowing slime began to gush from all three mouths. Groaning and moaning were increasing in volume. The slime streamed towards the scarecrows and encircled one scarecrow after another as if to create a barrier and seal them in place. She smelled something rancid. It reminded her of the mandatory potion they had to drink.

That's when she saw it. A gray, unformed mist trying to find its way through the shield. It hovered everywhere, looking for a weak link.

The green of the scarecrows' eyes grew more intense as the green light spread out. The mist couldn't come into contact with it. As the slime continued to spread, the green light continued to consume more space.

Natalie looked away. There was so much slime that she felt like she was going to be sick. She noticed that Lorcan continued to stare out the window.

"It's not pretty, but it protects the homestead by covering the yard, climbing the homestead, and coating the scarecrows." Lorcan kept a tight grip on her hands.

"We're being encased in nauseating slime."

"It's what protects us along with the scarecrows."

"It's too much."

The rancid smell, the moaning and groaning as slime poured out of the three mouths, and just the visual playing in Natalie's head had her gagging. Lorcan looked over at her sick expression.

"Not much longer, Natalie. Hold it together. We're winning. It can't penetrate if we can keep the connection to the stump."

"Easy for you to say. I'm fighting hard not to barf…seriously, barf."

"Tell me again what happened when you sent all twenty beach balls at supersonic speed toward Draon," Lorcan said, trying to take her mind off the smell and the slime.

"Seriously, I've told you that story ten times already."

"But I get a laugh out of hearing Draon jump up and put up a shield of protection. Those beach balls had to be traveling at the speed of light for him not to be able to stop them."

"Well, what was it? Five hours of trying to connect? Losing my temper and my patience so many times, I lost count?"

Lorcan laughed, recalling the first time she told the story.

"Lorcan?"

"What?"

"When this is over, is the slime going to vanish? Will the slime disappear the moment we're safe?"

"It will leave, but I will not tell you how. You wouldn't be able to handle it."

"Great. Don't you have any magical abilities to make it smell better here? How about blocking all the groans and moans, too?"

"Nope. All my power is being used for the stump. We have less than an hour to go. Hang in there. You're doing great. No word from the others, so they must be doing okay, too."

"Does everyone have a tree stump?"

"No, but every property has something equally disgusting." Lorcan visualized the two statutes that Madison and Skylar had at the front of their homestead.

"Do you think the candles at Pru's house will be okay?" Natalie couldn't believe she worried about those two wise guys.

"They'll be fine. Whatever evil this is, it doesn't want animated objects. It wants mages."

"They seem so real to the point I feel guilty if weeks go by before I can visit and bring them candy."

"I can change them back to what Draon created…boring on steroids."

"No, I like them."

Without warning, Natalie slumped from exhaustion. Fighting to keep her eyes open, she weakly whispered, "Lorcan, I'm blacking out."

"Hang on, Natalie. Think of Draon. He's going to be so proud you stopped the attack."

"I can't read Draon. He initially hated me, and I'm not sure he feels any different now." She struggled to stay awake.

"He never hated you. Your mother was like a daughter to him. She was the first person he truly loved, and it almost destroyed him when she died. He never wanted to put himself in that situation again. When he saw you, he saw your mother."

"So he's the man in the picture with my mother. I knew I had seen those eyes before." Natalie's body shook from the demand on her powers.

"Where did you see the picture?"

Just a few more minutes. Lorcan watched Natalie's eyes open and shut. She fought to stay awake, but there were long pauses between the questions and the answers. He didn't tell her; he could only give the stump ten percent of the power. The rest came from her.

Draon had forbidden help from Samoon. Lorcan had argued they weren't experienced, but Draon had been adamant that the mages needed to learn how to fight their own battles.

Lorcan's body jerked. His hands tightened around Natalie's hands.

She wanted to sleep and struggled to remember the question Lorcan had asked her. *What was it? My mother's eyes. No, Draon's eyes. Oh, the picture of them together.*

"Mom's secret room. I saw the mirror, too. It frightened me enough that I ran from the room. Now I know it was Draon on the other side of the mirror."

"How did you open the portal?" He fidgeted, waiting impatiently for the answer.

"The portal?" Natalie was confused. Were they talking about the mirror or something else? She didn't know anymore. Her mind wandered. She stood before the mirror, watching a gray mist completely cover it. A shadow formed. Wait, it didn't form. It remained unformed and misty. As it reached for her, she felt a horrendous pain in her back. Someone had shot her with an arrow! She screamed.

Suddenly awake and seeing the strange expression on Lorcan's face, Natalie shouted, "Lorcan," and tightened her grip. His crazed expression didn't change. Alarmed, Natalie summoned all her remaining energy and directed it right into Lorcan to save him. His back arched, his eyes lit up, and then he fell forward.

Natalie began to shake. She had felt the evil presence. They had won this time, but what about next time? The final sign was done; the real challenge begins.

Epilogue
A Peek Inside the Homestead

Hot, barefoot, and thirsty, Lorcan yanked the old refrigerator door open. Stunned, his eyes widened as he stepped back to get a better look. Glass pitchers filled with purple, red, green, yellow, orange, and blue punch filled every shelf.

While deciding if he wanted the lemon or the blueberry-flavored punch, twelve fairies swarmed around him. High-pitched whining assaulted his ears. He swatted the air, but they continued their chaotic movement and noise.

Lorcan wanted to stick his head in the refrigerator and wait for them to leave. No such luck, and besides, there wasn't any room in there. His eyes blazed in annoyance as he grabbed the blueberry-colored punch and slammed the refrigerator door. The refrigerator shook as the pitchers clanged against each other. The fairies flew back, lowered their voices, but continued to whine.

"Those are not inside voices. I'm not listening." Lorcan turned his back on them and poured a tall glass of ice-cold punch. He sniffed it.

"I hope it tastes as good as it smells." Lorcan took a tiny sip. A smile replaced his annoyance with their unruly noise. He took a big gulp, turned, and gave the fairies a thumbs-up sign.

They squealed in delight before calming down. Sunshine Firebow Lily, in a sparkly yellow dress, fluttered in front of Lorcan's face.

Lorcan listened to her pleading, high-pitched voice. He nodded; he understood the request.

"We all miss Nessa. I had hoped her daughter, Natalie, would enter the homestead by now, but her vivid imagination sees our home as a house of horrors."

Leafy Beefy Daylily squeaked her displeasure.

"Before long, she will have no choice but to join us. Meanwhile, Sunshine says you're bored, and you want to play Crystal Bingo."

A barrage of high-pitched voices sounding like fingernails raking across a chalkboard descended on Lorcan's ears. Fingers in his ears, he winced in pain.

"Instead of shaking the walls of the house with your gibberish noise, go get the cards and meet me in the Room of Mirrors." Lorcan headed in that direction.

A large round table appeared. Lorcan opened the largest mirror on the side wall and removed a blue woven bag containing crystal beads. He also grabbed a small brown bag that held white plastic chips. Grabbing a handful of chips, he placed them in front of the twelve bingo cards. He sat down, opened the blue bag, and poured a mound of various colored crystal beads in front of his small stack of cards.

"Take a crystal bead of your choice to put in the free space. You know the rules. You only get the crystal if you win a game." Lorcan waited while the fairies, bubbling with excitement, picked their crystal.

"Ruby."

Periwinkle Twinkle Blue Star, and Sooty Boots Kalina cheered.

"Okay, no need to show us you have the ruby symbol." At this rate, Lorcan's ears would ring for a week. He turned over the next card.

"Emerald."

More screaming this time from Rosie Poppertop and Wren Scolding Dahlia.

Lorcan gave up and muttered a spell. Humongous brown noise-canceling earbuds stuck out of his ears. He sighed in relief.

"Sapphire." Lorcan said and observed the reactions of those who had played in that match. *Better to see than to hear.*

Lorcan called fifteen different gemstones before Rosie Poppertop screamed bingo! Her red dress bounced up and down as she jumped on the table, cluing Lorcan that they had a winner. He removed an earbud as Rosie squealed out the winning pattern. She flew over and picked up a fuchsia crystal bead for the free spot in the next game.

Blueberry Bluest Bluebell won the next crystal bingo. Her bright blue dress was a blur as she twirled around and squeaked out the winning pattern. She flew over and picked up an aquamarine bead for the free spot on her card.

Pinky Fidgety Hollyhock won. Then, Cherrytoes Rose won. Rosie Poppertop won again. After Rosie, Lavendar Moonflower won. High fives started after Blueberry Bluest Bluebell won. Frowns appeared on the faces of those who had not won.

Lorcan had called twelve crystals when he needed a break. He knew better, but his raspy voice wanted the sugary punch.

Returning to the table with his glass full, he sat down, took a gulp, and called the next crystal. "Turquoise."

Stormy Tempered Iris screamed bingo. Startled, Lorcan jumped. The other fairies faced her and squealed in protest.

"Shh. Stormy, please read back your winning pattern."

Tension filled the air. Lorcan hesitated to take a drink as Stormy called back the crystals.

"Stormy, we didn't call Topaz."

Too late. The fairies that hadn't won swarmed her. Pulling hair and kicking as fairy dust filled the air. Lorcan sighed. *I wonder how Nessa kept them calm. It doesn't matter as we're done.* Sliding the crystals over, he scooped them into the blue bag. He gathered chips. No one noticed him putting the bags back into the mirror.

"If you won a crystal, claim it now. The table disappears in 10 seconds. 10, 9, 8, 7, 6…" Lorcan watched the winners grab their crystals and fly upstairs.

Frowning, he watched the mayhem. Six against one wasn't fair, even though Stormy impressed him with her fighting frenzy.

Lorcan pulled out his wand and muttered an amplification spell. Three taps on the wall sounded like punches through the wall. They turned, fluttered in place, and stared wide-eyed at the wand pointed at them.

High-pitched screams filled the air as six fairies flew to their upstairs bedroom. Stormy fluttered where they left her.

"Did you learn anything?" Lorcan stared at the battered fairy.

She nodded her head yes.

"I understand your desire to add crystals to your crystal suncatcher. I also understand how frustrating it can be to be just one away from winning crystal bingo, only to have it never called. However, winning by cheating means you are not a winner, but you are a cheater. You've cheated out the real winner. Do you understand?"

Stormy nodded her head yes. Her sad eyes, downturned lips, and slumped shoulders told him she regretted her actions.

"Come to the kitchen with me. I'm in the mood for Peanut Brittle. You can help me make it."

As tantalizing caramelizing sugars filled the air, fairies and pixies zoomed into the kitchen. Fluttering near Stormy, waiting for the treat, it was as if nothing ever happened.

Thank you for selecting my self-published book to read. You're entering a world of novice teenage mages, mischievous fairies, and Hexel, the formidable guardian of the underground Crossroads Barracks.

For more Shadowlink short stories - Facebook

Stefanie Schatzman, Author

Made in United States
Orlando, FL
16 October 2025